Share in the celebration of Mother's Day with this
charming collection from three talented Arabesque
authors. In these wonderful short stories you will
experience warmhearted romances in which all it
takes to start a family or mend a broken heart is
A MOTHER'S TOUCH

BOOK YOUR PLACE ON OUR WEBSITE
AND MAKE THE ARABESQUE
ROMANCE CONNECTION!

We've created a customized website just for our very special Arabesque readers, where you can get the inside scoop on everything that's going on with Arabesque romance novels.

When you come online, you'll have the exciting opportunity to:

- View covers of upcoming books
- Learn about our future publishing schedule (listed by publication month and author)
- Find out when your favorite authors will be visiting a city near you.
- Search for and order backlist books from our line catalog
- Check out author bios and background information
- Send e-mail to your favorite authors
- Join us in weekly chats with authors, readers and other guests
- Get writing guidelines
- AND MUCH MORE!

Visit our website at
http://www.arabesquebooks.com

A MOTHER'S TOUCH

CANDICE POARCH
RAYNETTA MAÑEES
VIVECA CARLYSLE

ARABESQUE

BET BOOKS

BET Publications, LLC
www.msbet.com
www.arabesquebooks.com

ARABESQUE BOOKS are published by

BET Publications, LLC
c/o BET BOOKS
One BET Plaza
1900 W Place NE
Washington, D.C. 20018-1211

First Printing: May, 1999
10 9 8 7 6 5 4 3 2 1

Printed in the United States of America

CONTENTS

More Than Friends by Candice Poarch   7

All The Way Home by Raynetta Mañees   129

Brianna's Garden by Viveca Carlysle   215

MORE THAN FRIENDS

CANDICE POARCH

CHAPTER 1

"For an intelligent woman, you just said the dumbest thing I've heard. No telling whose sperm you'd get." Exasperated, Yvonne Cook glared at her friend. "Haven't you followed the news?"

"My biological clock is ticking," Ariene Woods replied, straining her neck as she felt around for loose strands of her raven hair. She wanted to get the braid just right for church tomorrow.

"At thirty?"

"I'm not getting any younger, you know." Ariene dreamed of a boy, with tiny, soft hands that would some day be large and capable. Brownish–black hair and velvet brown eyes. He would be six–one, just like his dad—not a mere five-four like she was. Or a little girl she'd dress in pretty pink rompers and lacy dresses for church.

"Ariene!"

Ariene jerked, looking toward Yvonne. "I'm right here beside you. You don't have to yell."

"Are you listening to me?" Yvonne asked, perturbed.

"Of course I'm listening."

"I said, don't you remember the headlines a few years ago when that doctor used his own sperm at his fertility clinic? He had hundreds of offspring. Do you want to take that chance? Think of how you'd feel, worrying if your child was marrying a half–sibling."

"This clinic orders the sperm from California."

"Do you want your baby to be a beach bum?"

Ariene laughed.

"Besides, you live in a one bedroom apartment."

"I've finally saved enough for a down payment on a town house or a duplex. Rick's been talking about selling the one that joins his. He and his brother don't want the worry of tenants any longer."

"Ariene, it's not easy being a single parent. You can't walk away from a baby when the going gets tough."

"Nothing I do is ever easy."

Her friend's criticisms came from worry about more than renegade fertility clinics. Reared in a single parent household, Yvonne knew how difficult life was for single mothers. In contrast, Ariene felt her clothing boutique— Chic from Africa—provided enough to support a child. Still she paused.

"What's the alternative? I'm not dating anyone—and haven't dated seriously for more than two years." What a dismal thought.

"With your features, getting responses from the classifieds shouldn't be a problem. Let's see. Perfectly dark and oval face, with smooth complexion, striking black eyes, small nose, and generous mouth. That would do for the ads, don't you think?"

"I'm serious, Yvonne." Ariene sighed.

"Okay, okay. There's Tim." Yvonne rose to pour tea,

wearing jeans with a full blouse made of an African red, blue, and white tie–dyed print.

Ariene had dated Tim once. Once was enough. "He's nice, but too macho."

"Picky, picky. Let's see." Yvonne pursed her lips as she returned to her seat. "There's Junior, who brings his mother by my bookstore twice a month. He often asks about you."

"Absolutely not," Ariene said, shaking her head in denial. "He'd never leave his mother's house. Even though that seems ideal, I'd prefer my baby to have a more independent nature by the time he's forty." Being a free–spirited woman, she couldn't wish for less for her child. And since her own mom leaned on her husband far too much to satisfy Ariene's sense of independence, the child already had one strike against him or her.

"Can't you think of anyone with the qualities you want?"

"Actually, no." A vial of sperm from the fertility clinic suited her perfectly. College students were the primary donors.

"On the one hand, too macho, on the other, too meek. You know what your problem is?" Yvonne waved an admonishing finger in the air. "You're just so darn hard to please. You have to be more reasonable."

"My perfect match is somewhere in here." Finished with her braid, Ariene picked up a packet from the clinic and flipped through profiles.

"There's no dissuading you, is there? All right, then— Junior's all right." Interrupting Ariene's response before she could even rebut, Yvonne continued. "Now, don't misinterpret kindness for weakness. A congenial façade, along with a complete personality change on your part might help." She regarded Ariene shrewdly. "You can catch more flies with honey, you know."

"I'm not looking for Pooh Bear. No, dear friend, what he sees is what he gets."

"Which translates to no husband, no baby." Yvonne sipped delicately from the china cup, glancing at each sheet as Ariene discarded it.

"Sperm bank." Having made her decision, Ariene stood, rewrapped and tucked the ends of her red, yellow, and black wrap dress before she picked up her comb and mirror to store in the bathroom.

"There has to be one man who has the qualities you like." Yvonne's voice followed her. "Someone with a calm, compassionate personality to counter yours. Otherwise, that baby will end up being a hellion, if the man's anything like you."

"I resent that," Ariene called from the bedroom. The chime of the doorbell cut off the rest of her reply. Passing the kitchen to answer it, she slowed long enough to say, "Who do you suggest?" and continued through the living room, giving the antique white coffee and end tables and the overstuffed sofa a quick glance to make certain everything was in place. Then, as she glided across the Algerian carpeting covering hardwood floors, she remembered her toes were bare. "Do you think my fairy godmother is going to send me the handsome, perfect prince?" She waved her hands dramatically and opened the door.

On the threshold stood her best friend since nursery school. Rick Cordell was sienna, broad–shouldered, and barely over six feet. His hair, cut short, was as neat as always. For several years, he'd managed training programs in several countries in Africa.

"Oh Rick," she gasped in delight.

"Should I have called first?" came his deep and smooth response.

"Not on your life. Well, what are you waiting for? Give me a hug."

He opened his arms and she stepped into his embrace, expelling a sigh as he pressed her against his hard chest. She breathed in the wonderfully masculine, familiar scent of him, secure that they'd remained friends through the years.

"God, I've missed you," she said before she could stop herself, her voice holding an unintentionally desperate edge.

"I couldn't tell by your sparse letters," he replied as she let him go and backed into the room, pulling him with her.

"Oh, you know how I hate to write." Ariene waved a hand as she led him into the apartment. The Nigerian masks and Egyptian papyrus adorning her walls were gifts from him. "I mean, well, and you've always been number one with me."

He raised an eyebrow.

That's what she liked about him. He was comfortable, and she could let her hair down. In high school he'd lived through her first puppy love heartbreak with her, had rescued her when an overzealous date left her stranded at the movies. The date sported a suspicious black eye the next week in school.

For a very long time, Rick had shared her innermost secrets. She trusted him as she trusted no other—man or woman. She didn't have the long-lasting history she shared with Rick even with Yvonne. Still, she never felt comfortable enough to mention her body's call to nurture. A man wouldn't understand.

Knowing she wouldn't mention it even now, she led him to the kitchen.

"You remember Yvonne, don't you?"

"How are you, Yvonne?" He extended a hand. Yvonne barely touched his fingertips.

"We're having tea. Would you like a cup?"

"Coffee, if you have it."

"I still have the container you left the last time. Isn't it going to keep you up tonight?" she asked, searching in the freezer for his favorite blend.

"I need the caffeine kick. Got a late night at the office ahead of me." He eased onto a delicate bistro chair, dwarfing it. He looked out of place sitting at the lattice–topped bistro table with glass inset. It looked as if he were playing tea party with a child. Unfortunately, Ariene's kitchen wouldn't hold larger furniture.

She observed the dark circles under his eyes, circles that didn't detract from his good looks. "What you need is more sleep." Ariene also noticed the strange way Yvonne continued to watch him.

"Should I fix enough for you, Yvonne?"

When she didn't respond, Ariene said, "Earth to Yvonne."

"What?" Yvonne snapped, still in a trance.

Ariene rolled her eyes, turned the water on to wash out the coffeepot. "Nothing," she said finally.

Rick laughed, and Yvonne continued to watch him, clicking her rose–lacquered fingernails on the table.

"When did you arrive?" Ariene measured coffee beans into the grinder, trying not to snap at her friend over the irritating noise.

"This morning."

"I'm surprised you aren't still sleeping off jet lag." She often wondered why an eligible man like Rick had never married. Her attempts at matchmaking had come to a screeching halt when he threatened to end their friendship if she didn't cease. She never tried again. Their relationship was too important to her.

"I wanted to go over some contracts before I leave for California on Monday." He swiped a hand over his face. She wanted to comfort him, to make the weariness leave.

Then he moved his leg, and the snug fit of his jeans around his muscled thighs drew Ariene's attention. Jeans and a T-shirt should have looked plain, but on him they looked anything but. If he'd only try harder, he'd easily find someone.

Yvonne continued to stare at Rick. Ariene was accustomed to his attractiveness, but his good looks weren't the pretty boy, car–stopping variety. Virile strength, fortitude, and trust coated him as much as open good looks. It wasn't as if they were meeting for the first time, and it wasn't like Yvonne to act so idiotic. Her hypnotic state produced stilted conversation. Rick merely looked amused.

Exasperated, Ariene snapped, "Yvonne, what's wrong with you? You've been staring at Rick since he arrived."

Yvonne's hand hit the table, causing the cups to rattle. "He's perfect."

"For what?"

Engrossed in her own world, Yvonne smiled slyly, and her eyes lit up. "He's perfect. The answer to your problem."

Catching the gist, Ariene waved a hand frantically. "Yvonne, no . . ."

"Sure. Rick would make the perfect father for your baby," Yvonne blurted.

"Yvonne!" Too shocked for further comment, Ariene just stood there, cautiously glancing at Rick. In the silence of a few seconds Ariene viewed her surroundings in slow motion. She heard the slight tick of the kitchen clock, a baby's cry next door, the banging of music in another apartment, the muted sounds of the traffic flow from the busy street below. A horn blew. Tires screeched.

Rick stared at her intently. His facial muscles tightened almost imperceptibly, and his slate–gray eyes hardened. "You're pregnant?" His tone reminded her that underneath that carefree, relaxed façade of her childhood friend remained a layer of steel she'd often witnessed. He thought of her as a sister, and his reaction to pregnancy out of wedlock was as dramatic as it would be with one of his siblings.

"Not yet," Yvonne, the blabbermouth, answered, clearly pleased with herself, before Ariene could stammer a reply. "She's feeling her age, and wants a baby. Now."

"Yvonne—" If only the floor would open up to swallow her.

"You're handsome," she ticked off on one finger.

"Yvonne—"

"You're smart. You have your own business. You're considerate, a single man who loves his freedom . . ."—Ariene thought she could be describing a cocker spaniel—"*Independent* and not too *macho*. All the traits she likes. And you're going back to Uganda, so she can lead her single life with the baby."

"Yvonne, that's enough!" Ariene shouted, trying to put her notes in order and to buy time for a snappy comeback. None was forthcoming.

"Well, what do you say?" Yvonne asked Rick, as if she expected him to immediately jump at the prized opportunity.

Rick looked from Yvonne to Ariene. Ariene could see him relaxing again.

"Well," the chair scraped as Yvonne stood. "It's time for me to leave. Don't get up on my account. I'll see myself out," she said while grabbing up her purse.

"Perhaps you should have left five minutes ago," Ariene said, throwing daggers at Yvonne with her eyes, which the woman ignored. If Yvonne had, she wouldn't be in this embarrassing situation.

The closing of the door sounded as if a bomb had gone off. At the same time the coffee machine buzzed. Shakily, Ariene rose to get Rick a cup. She avoided looking at him as she gingerly set the filled cup and saucer on the table.

Some response to the woman's dramatic performance was required, Ariene thought, embarrassed. "Yvonne gets silly at times. I can't believe she said that." She sank into her seat.

Rick spooned sugar into his coffee. The silverware barely made a *ting* sound when he gently placed it on the saucer. "Is there someone special you haven't told me about?" His eyes were hooded but alert.

She blew out a breath. "No, but the fertility clinic I'll be using sent me the specs of some good candidates."

"Umm." He leaned back in his chair, assessing her, which only further unnerved her. "Doesn't that procedure strike you as impersonal? You won't even meet the father. Have you thought about the questions your child will ask once he starts school and wonders why other children have fathers and other relatives, and he doesn't? Children can be cruel. Then, there're your parents."

If there was one thing Ariene knew about men, it was that they always thought of what they deemed a *logical* solution to a problem. Logic and emotions didn't always mix. "There are many single mothers now," she said quietly. In seconds, he'd expressed all the fears she'd tried to resolve before deciding to take the step. She had so much love to offer. Maybe she was naive in thinking that her love for her child would conquer all.

Her mother wouldn't understand why she couldn't find a ready husband, but she'd accept Ariene's decision— eventually. Ariene often fought with her father, and she knew her decision would cause a barrier between them. The battles grew worrisome, but she had to make her own decisions.

"True, but at least most of the single mothers know who the father is, even if he doesn't live with them. He's not just frozen sperm in a vial."

"Rick. You don't understand how difficult this decision

was for me." She lifted a hand, hoping he could at least understand her dilemma, if not appreciate it. Her reasoning was emotional, and she could feel her calm slipping. He'd always understood in the past.

"It tears me up to see mothers cooing over their babies. I can't stand to walk into a department store and look at the cute baby clothing anymore, yet I can't avoid the children's section. It's as if I'm drawn by an invisible magnet." She had to stop a moment to keep from becoming maudlin. "I love children, always have." Her voice caught. "I want one of my own." She felt stupid, knowing Rick didn't have a clue as to why tears gathered in her eyes. A man wouldn't. Suddenly, she felt a hand on hers, a long finger caught one tear as it spilled over her lashes.

He scooted his chair closer to hers and wrapped an arm around her shoulders. Then she remembered why they'd remained friends from nursery school until now. "I understand, honey," he said softly. "I really do. But that doesn't change the facts. A fertility clinic is perfect for a couple who want children and don't have another choice. They go through the process together, and it's very special for them. You'll be alone."

She would have turned away from him, but he captured her chin to face him.

"Have you talked this over with your family?" His breath felt cold on her face where it mixed with her tears.

She inhaled the subtle, familiar aroma of his cologne, mixed with his male essence. "You know they wouldn't approve." She sighed and grabbed a napkin from the holder.

"Every parent wants the best for his child. To your parents, the best is a husband."

"Well, things have changed since my parents married. Men are a little harder to come by now." He didn't stop her when she turned away from him this time. She felt a little steadier—barely.

"Finding the right woman can be just as difficult." The soft, soothing resonance of his voice comforted her, if not his words.

"Give me a break. Look at the statistics."

"Statistics are questionable. I said the *right* woman. Not just *any* woman," he emphasized.

"That's what you get for being so picky." She sniffed.

"I guess you're right. But, you're still young."

"I want to enjoy my baby before I get too old to run after her . . . or him. It's time. A woman can tell when it's right for her."

His face softened as he lifted a hand and caressed her cheek. "Remember you used to tell me you were going to find the perfect man with big feet, and two years later your first of three children would appear?"

"Don't remind me." Mixed with the butterflies in her stomach from the caress, embarrassment spread through her. She'd said that a week after high school graduation, when she and some girlfriends had gotten tipsy with bottles of gin and soda they'd brought from the liquor store. They'd driven to a secluded area by the Chesapeake and started a fire on the beach. In late June, it was already hot, but the wind had picked up that night. They'd giggled and drunk for almost an hour before Rick and her friends' boyfriends drove up. The other girls had left, leaving Rick and her alone.

They'd stayed there for hours. She'd told him all her wildest dreams, and that silly saying about men and feet, deep into her first buzz that night. She still couldn't remember all of what had been said or occurred. Shyly, she looked up at Rick before diverting her eyes downward.

"Size thirteen. Big enough?" he teased, now.

"Don't be silly." She blushed because she had won-

dered—fleetingly—how it would be with him. Would his
kind, considerate nature carry over into lovemaking? Her
thoughts were becoming as ridiculous as the conversation.
She'd never wanted that kind of relationship with him, yet
the tingling from his touch stayed with her. "There's more
to a relationship than size."

"We aren't talking about relationships, are we?" His soft
whisper brought goosebumps to her arms.

He lifted her hand off the table and held it in his larger
one, stroking it with slow, comforting motions that were
having the opposite effect on her. *This was Rick, for goodness
sake.* "I'm not around enough to get on your nerves. But
if you want a baby," he said, pausing, "have it with me.
This way, if you need help for any reason, I'll be available
for you and the baby."

She scooted away to distance herself from him. Pulling
her hand away, she wiped it across her eyes. This was her
best friend. "You . . . you'd do that for me?" A strong-
minded businesswoman and not a sentimental fool, she
nonetheless felt weepy all over again.

He nodded.

"Why?" she whispered.

"What are friends for, if not for answering a dream or
two?" Those words were so easily spoken. So many people
said them. When the going got tough, though, the words
usually proved meaningless. She knew Rick could always
be counted on to carry through, though.

Still, fathering her baby stretched beyond friendship.
"I'd feel I was using you. Friends don't use friends."

"But friends offer their help. I'm offering mine," he
said, then deliberately paused. "The baby needs a father he
can identify with, talk to about certain things. I've already
pointed out why. I'll take no as an insult."

Suddenly, she didn't want to argue the issue again. Rick
seemed overbearing. She felt as though her prized control

was vanishing in the less than an hour he'd been there. "I've already come to terms with going it alone," she responded.

"Which isn't the best course, if you have an alternative. We get along, don't we? And since I'm thousands of miles away, that won't change, will it?"

"Instead, I'll have your mother breathing down my neck. Rick, she really hates me. She never got over our childhood spats." She shuddered at the notion of Ella Cordell showing up or calling at any time. She'd cried and made a pest of herself at each of her childrens' weddings.

"She'll come around eventually. She always does. In the meantime, Dad will handle her."

"He hasn't so far."

"The baby needs a family, sweetheart—grandparents, aunts, uncles, cousins. Would you really want him to feel alone? Shouldn't he be part of a family circle? He'll need the security of other loved ones in his life."

As an only child, Ariene realized he'd scored another point. For a lack of a suitable comeback, she said, "What if he's a she?"

"Gender doesn't matter. I'd welcome our daughter. What if the donor lied, or he has something the tests didn't pick up?"

"Even with you, we'd do the exchange through a clinic."

"Absolutely not." That layer of steel reared its head again. "We're going the traditional route."

Ariene's heart skipped a beat. Sitting close to her, he exuded a sex appeal that was impossible for her to ignore. Before, she'd never quite viewed him as a man in the sense of a boyfriend, lover, or husband. Rick was just a friend who'd been hanging around as far back as she could remember.

No. He was much *more* than just a friend. When she wanted to open a store, he'd flown her to Nigeria and

Ghana, set her up with tailors, fabric dyers, and all the other craftsmen she needed to start her business. To curtail expenses, she'd even stayed in his spare bedroom.

Owning a successful international training company himself, and having a nose for locations, he'd suggested the location for her shop in a middle–income neighborhood in Waldorf, Maryland. Her business had flourished.

She owed the success of her business to Rick's entrepreneurial skills. Location was essential to the flow of customers in her store. Now, he was willing to go out on the limb for her—again. She felt too needy.

"I can't use you that way," she finally said.

"You wouldn't be using me." He stroked the side of her face with the back of his strong, sensitive fingers.

Ariene tensed as her erratic senses took flight again. She straightened her shoulders. She was a strong, sensible woman, not one for flights of fancy.

"We'll share the baby as we've shared our friendship for the last twenty–six years. Women aren't the only ones with nesting instincts."

"I don't know."

"I think we'd make a great baby together." His voice had dropped an octave.

"What if you meet someone and want to marry one day?" Her heart pounded as she discarded her last thoughts. Why was she feeling these new emotions for Rick?

"I won't be the first man to remarry. We'll cross that bridge if we come to it."

"I don't know," she wavered. Her dreams were within her grasp, yet . . . "I couldn't."

"You don't have to make a decision tonight." He leaned back, giving her room to breathe. Ariene sucked in a breath as her world spun.

"How long are you going to be here?"

"A few months. That should give us enough time to plan a small wedding."

"A wedding?" she squeaked. Everything was moving too fast.

"You want to tell your mom and dad you're having a baby without a husband? And how do you think my parents are going to react, my getting you pregnant and not marrying you? Both our parents are from North Carolina. Half of my family will be down here telling me I was raised better. The other half would be buying ammo for your daddy's shotgun! Do you really want to embarrass our families that way?"

"But—"

"And the benefits."

"I don't want anything more from you."

"I have company health insurance. I'd want you and the baby covered. *Now*, you don't need anything. That doesn't mean that one day you won't. You'd be protected—and without me underfoot." Everything he said, as far-fetched as the whole concept was, sounded reasonable. "Soon, I'll be back in Uganda. You'd be pregnant and alone—exactly the way you want it. This isn't completely one-sided, you know. My mom will get off my back if I'm married. Well-meaning friends will stop throwing women at me."

Ariene remembered that at one time she had been one of those *well-meaning friends*. She dropped onto the seat and put her hands on her face. This was exactly what she wanted. Why did it sound so . . . "This is happening too fast. I need time to think."

"Think about it this week. If you decide this is what you want, we can tell our parents next weekend that we'll be getting married in three weeks." He got up and strolled to the door. His purposeful gait was always that of a man going somewhere, her mom always said. "Perhaps you'll get pregnant on our honeymoon."

"Honeymoon? What honeymoon? This wouldn't be a real marriage." In a daze, she looked after him.

"It has to look real. Call me." He kissed her at the corner of her mouth, barely touching her soft lips.

The power of suggestion is a powerful tool, Ariene thought as her heart thumped.

Looking into her confused face, Rick took his fill of the woman he hoped would be his bride. The bright, flowing red, black, and yellow sarong highlighted her copper-toned skin, just as the beautiful thick braid cleverly sculpted on her head complimented her classic facial structure. She had a special radiance and unconscious grace that made her look so real and so alive. She was a perfect height, he thought. At five-foot-five, she fit just under his chin.

He never, ever, wanted to see her as hurt as she'd been three years ago when he took her to Africa. She'd just come off a disastrous relationship with a man who abused her instead of cherishing her.

It still angered Rick that she'd put up with Todd's physical abuse for months before she severed the relationship. There had been nothing Rick could say to Ariene to make her see that Todd was destroying her. Todd was probably why she was willing to go to a fertility clinic instead of waiting for a partner who would love her for the loving, giving woman that she was.

Rick would spoil her in all the ways a woman should be spoiled, and forever erase the damage Todd inflicted from her mind.

Now, he had to send Veronica a telegram. She'd just broken off their engagement for the third time this year. This time he'll tell her that it was the end for them. He had to check his calendar to see exactly where she was.

His relationship with Veronica wasn't a love match. Her

uncle—who trained mostly in Asia—wanted to merge his company with Rick's, but he wanted it kept in the family by marrying his niece to Rick—this in twentieth century America.

Rick and his partners had decided not to merge, after all. Their company was doing fine on its own.

Rick steered his car toward the office, where he'd left his planner. He'd send that telegram off tonight.

CHAPTER 2

After the good news, the last place Rick wanted to go was to his office, but he needed to go over the package his partner had put together for him for next week's training in San Diego.

Entering the offices of Training International, Rick saw a light coming from one of the doors. Curt Kennedy peered out his office.

"Hey, buddy. Good to see you," he said as he walked toward Rick.

"Good to be back. How's it going?" Rick shook hands with Curt.

"Just finishing up the last of it. I shipped the materials off on Monday. Everything's waiting for you there."

"Good. If the training goes well, we'll get more business from them. We certainly need it, with the lease doubling next year."

"Yeah, it may be time to look for another location."

Curt reached across the desk for a folder and handed it to Rick. "You can go over this on the plane tomorrow."

"I'll do that." Rick turned. "I have some work to do here before I leave." He went into his own office to search through his planner for Veronica's schedule.

Eight years ago, before the ink was dry from their college diplomas, he, Curt, and Paulette Davis had started Training International. They trained in various areas, from starting a business and communications, to sessions on American and European business practices, to internet use. Gradually their business increased, and three years ago it had started to pay off enormously. Paulette had suggested they move to a more rural area, but Rick liked being near a major city. They had a few months yet to search for locations.

When Rick arrived home at midnight, he parked outside instead of using the two-car garage on the basement level of the duplex. He'd lucked out with the oversized housing. The finished rec room in the basement and the three bedrooms upstairs were all roomy. It was the perfect starter house for the three of them, at least for as long as it took him to convince Ariene to keep him. The trick was getting her to move in here.

Entering the living room, he realized he needed furniture. The ratty set he had now had been discarded by one of his sisters two years ago. He could more than afford furniture. He just wasn't ever home long enough for it to matter. That would all change if Ariene decided to marry him. The ringing telephone diverted his thoughts. He held his breath, hoping it was she.

It was his younger sister, Christine.

"Hi, big brother. I thought you'd never get home."

"Hi, yourself," he said. Since she'd been out of town

during his last visit, he hadn't seen her in more than a year.

"Mom told me you were back. Will this be another in and out trip for you?"

"Longer this time, I think." Rick sighed, glancing at his briefcase which held the financial reports.

"Rick, are you plotting your next corporate strategy again?" Christine asked impatiently.

"Maybe," he said good-naturedly. Rick's short attention span had been a family joke since high school, when he first decided he wanted his own business.

"It's always been difficult talking to you over the phone."

"Then I'll have to visit you, won't I?"

"Can you make it tomorrow? I'm going on a trip in two days. I'd like to use your big suitcase. You, know the one I like?"

"Sure, I'll come before I leave for California. You're barely giving me time to unpack, you know."

"Bad timing for you?"

"It's okay."

She paused a moment, then started in on the one subject that annoyed him the most. "Since you're in town for a while, I could introduce you to this wonderful lady who started working in our firm two months ago. She's an international lawyer, and just the type of woman who would appeal to you."

"No, Christine."

"Now Rick—" she started in her lawyer's convincing tones.

"We've discussed this a million times. No. If you continue, I'm not coming by."

Silence. Then, "You can be so difficult."

"Where are you off to this time?" he asked, changing the subject, just as he always did.

"To New York for a case, and on to Martha's Vineyard

for a few days after, so I have to carry a wardrobe for work and pleasure.''

They talked a few more minutes. By the end of the week, he hoped to tell her he was an engaged man. It would put an end to all these annoyances.

By Friday morning Ariene had lost several nights of sleep while tossing and turning, wavering between the donor's profile and Rick's proposal. Yesterday, she'd visited the clinic for another consultation. The procedure could take from three to six months, pulling at her pocketbook each visit. She had to choose a donor from the bank, talk to them about the profile of the donor, the features, education. That was simple, actually—she wanted a child like Rick.

Another shocker was that the fertility clinic could cost thousands of dollars before she even became pregnant. The whole process was daunting.

Sipping on her coffee, she looked at the 800 number she had to dial. She wasn't looking forward to it. Anyway, she'd have to wait until her lunch break because of the three hour difference. She really didn't want to talk about frozen sperm.

She looked around the boutique she was so proud of. Nigerian masks and colorful butterfly prints decorated her walls. Beautiful garments from Ghana and Nigeria hung gracefully on hangers, many draped with select pieces of jewelry. Her sales increased because of the special attention given to her displays and the personal touch she extended to her customers.

Her African contacts enabled her to charge less than most establishments which carried similar clothing, and that made her shop even more popular. She owed this all to Rick.

She sighed, knowing he'd hit on many points that had made the decision even to go to a fertility clinic a difficult one.

She didn't want to embarrass her parents by having a baby out of wedlock.

As much as she loved her parents, the idea of being in a confined relationship with a partner who didn't suit her was unpalatable. Her mother, the perfect homemaker, didn't even know what she and her husband were worth financially—she left all these details in the hands of her domineering husband. As Ariene grew older, she realized that her mother was happy under those conditions. She didn't want to worry about bank balances, taxes, and the other problems of day-to-day living.

Ariene, on the other hand, wouldn't be able to get a night's sleep if she didn't know about her own finances.

On the flip side, her mother had kept a spotless house, baked cakes for church functions and school while Ariene grew up, and was head usher in the church on second Sundays. She was content to let her husband make all the major decisions.

While Ariene wanted strength in a husband, she wanted equal control within the marriage. Finding a plum of a man who wasn't already married was a challenge she had yet to win, and she wondered if, at this point, she'd *ever* win. In the meantime, she wasn't willing to let all of her desires in life pass her by.

She scribbled on a sheet of paper. Several days ago, she'd made two columns of the pros and cons of marrying Rick. Her head was swimming with the pros: conventional family, lifetime friendship, psychological studies that showed children performed better in school and were happier in two parent households, a better sense of family, her parent's acceptance. The cons list remained daunting and depressing: lack of romantic love, losing control even though he'd be away, the impersonal and long drawn out fertility process, family strife, embarrassment, possible disillusionment.

She thought of being in Rick's warm, caring arms, and then of lying on a cold, sterile table with her feet in stirrups. There was no comparison. Stressed out over the dilemma, Ariene couldn't think of this another moment. She got up to rearrange garments on the display again. Work always soothed her.

She was so engrossed in what she was doing that she hadn't realized fifteen minutes had passed until, looking up from hanging a blue and yellow caftan, she heard urgent banging on the door.

Yvonne waved frantically on the other side. After her hasty apology for putting Ariene on the hook, Ariene had told Yvonne of Rick's proposal. After warning Ariene to accept, Yvonne had made herself scarce lately, for which Ariene was grateful. Her friend seemed to sense that Ariene needed to think without pressure.

She unlocked the door to admit Yvonne.

"Hi," she greeted as she barged in.

Ariene grunted.

Yvonne plunked her purse and bag on the countertop. "When is Rick due back?" She helped herself to a cup of coffee.

"Late tonight," Ariene replied as she carefully draped a necklace around the neckline of the caftan.

"Before you brush Rick off, I want you to read this article." Yvonne handed her the newspaper.

In the Metro section the heading "Sperm Mix–up in Fertility Clinic" glared at Ariene. The article dealt with the clinic inducing pregnancy in a woman, using the wrong sperm. Luckily, the couple's relationship was so strong that the husband accepted the child as his own, but he'd had to do much soul—searching and grief to come to those terms. It helped that he loved his wife immensely.

The article was just the final straw of a harrowing week, Ariene thought.

Then Ariene glanced at a photograph on the page showing a beautiful, chubby baby with cute, pudgy cheeks and laughed at her dilemma. Soon the laughter changed into tears.

Yvonne rushed over and hugged her. "Oh, Ariene, don't do this to yourself. Just marry Rick, and be done with it."

Blaming the emotional outburst on a lack of sleep, with effort she pulled herself together. She had a business to run, and she wasn't going to present red, teary eyes to her customers.

"Girl, go open up your store. It's almost ten," Ariene said, wiping her eyes.

"Are you going to be all right?"

Ariene plucked a tissue, blew her nose, and waved Yvonne out of the store. "I'm okay, really I am. I just haven't slept well lately. Go on."

"I know I'm losing my mind, but I'll marry you," Ariene said early Saturday morning to a sleepy Rick at the other end of the phone.

The ensuing silence that followed almost had her changing her mind.

"I'll be there in an hour," he said and slammed the phone in her ear.

Ariene looked at the receiver and wondered if he'd show up at all.

*   *   *

Snatching back her hand, Ariene glared at the diamond Rick held out to her. She seemed to resist its weight on her finger as much as she'd resisted marriage.

"Rick, you shouldn't have spent money on an engagement ring. This won't be a traditional marriage, after all."

"Depends on which century you're referencing," he quipped. His humor fell flat, and he sighed. "Relax, honey. It's expected, if we want our families to believe it's real."

Rejecting the padded, striped, rattan chair she'd indicated across from her, he sat beside her on her rose print sofa and took her left hand in his, talking to her in a soothing voice as he slid the ring onto her finger. "Besides, I bought the stone at a discount in Uganda." Perhaps he should have reconsidered giving her the ring this early in their relationship.

"I talked to Reverend Reign this morning. Saturday three weeks from now will work for him." He let her go, his eyes hooded as he waited for her reaction. "Think you can throw a wedding together in three weeks?"

"You're getting the ring back once everything is over." It was too much to hope that she'd let the ring issue drop. Her sigh made Rick wish he could rush in and take all her problems away.

"Everything's changed so much." She examined the ring as she spoke to him. "I thought we'd just go to the courthouse and make this a simple affair." Her lashes lifted, and Rich was mesmerized by their dark beauty.

He also had to stifle his impatience, knowing that if he rushed her she'd call it off. "First, I can afford the ring. Second, Reverend Reign baptized both of us. He'd be disappointed—not to mention everyone else, family and friends—to not be included."

"A divorce is even worse. It's not just you and me anymore, and it's dishonest."

"It could be years before we divorce. I've gone this long without meeting someone. I don't expect to find true love around the next corner, do you?"

"Well, no," she responded, uncertainty reflecting in her speech and manner.

He chose not to dwell on that. "See? It will all work out to everyone's advantage. Our parents will have the grandchild they crave." He touched her soft cheek. "You and I will have the baby we want."

She softened a little, losing the doe-eyed, shell-shocked look she'd had since his arrival.

Wearing a sky-blue pantsuit dotted with soft, orange designs, Ariene got up to pace. Her hair, barely touching her shoulders, was worn loose today, the ends tucked under. It swirled as she swiveled and turned.

"You always did have a way of railroading me into doing whatever you wanted," she finally said as she stopped abruptly in front of him, her hands on her hips. It had the advantage of showing off her rounded figure. Rick crossed his legs, trying to divert his attention from the view. Where was this attraction coming from?

"I'm not forcing you." He leaned back in the seat as he watched her.

She merely grunted and continued her pacing, an indication that she needed to work off nervous energy. It was either pacing or a frantic cleaning spree. She couldn't actually start emptying closets while he was there, but having gone through this before, he knew it was in his best interests to conclude this before he found himself moving furniture.

"Good. It's all settled, then."

She looked surprised at his statement. "Rick. . . . For a temporary marriage, this is turning out to be very expensive and involved."

He walked up behind her, massaged her shoulders.

"Relax," he implored. "Don't worry so much. You can't plan everything that's going to happen for the next twenty years. Leave something for us to deal with next year," he said lightly. He kneaded the tense muscles and continued to talk to her, soothing her, until finally she unwound just a little.

"It's time to tell our parents the good news." There was no way around it if they were to marry in three weeks.

She blew out a breath. "Oh, God," she moaned. "They'll be so pleased."

He grinned and thought, *Me, too.* "Come on, let's get it over with." He steered her toward her bedroom. Watching the sway of her hips as she left the room, Rick took deep breaths to cool the fire burning in him. In three weeks those hips would fit snugly in his hands.

He went to the kitchen for a glass of water, hoping it would cool the bulge in his jeans.

Ariene was back in five minutes with a powdered nose, a touch of lipstick, and a small purse hanging from her shoulder. Having grown up in a household with sisters, he appreciated a woman who readied herself in mere minutes.

After the long, cold winter that seemed to extend into spring, the temperature had finally climbed to seventy degrees. It brought hordes of people outside—men washing and waxing their vehicles, women jogging to enjoy the brisk spring breeze, children swinging and climbing monkey bars in the small playground. Using the excuse of pleasant weather to stay outside, parents left chores for another day. As one mother steered her toddler down the slide, Rick took Ariene's hand in his. Soon, this would be their scene.

An hour later, they arrived at Ariene's parents' home, a small, three bedroom brick ranch house. Her father's azaleas and roses were in magnificent bloom, the grass freshly cut, the hedges neatly trimmed. Rick could feel

Ariene tense up as he turned off the ignition. In a world of her own, she watched the house.

Rick wished he could take all her worries away. If only she felt for him a fraction of the love that flowed in him for her. Leaving the safety of the Lincoln, her footsteps almost dragged.

"Come on, Ariene, you have to help me here. We're friends, remember? We trust each other."

She gave him a wan smile, reached up to touch his face. "You're my best friend," she whispered.

"Then don't look as if your best friend is going to strangle you." At that moment, he felt like doing exactly that.

Then she laughed the light airy laugh he loved so much, the tension seeming to drain out of her for the first time since he'd arrived at her apartment. "You're probably ready to do exactly that by now, I bet," she teased.

"It's crossed my mind." He was only half joking.

They walked to the door hand in hand and Ariene opened it, calling out to her parents as they entered. They still didn't lock their doors during the day.

"Well, look who's here," her mother said, a smile curving her attractive, full lips. "And you brought Rick with you. How are you, son?" Pleasantly plump and wearing a bright yellow housedress, Mrs. Woods grabbed Rick in an exuberant bear hug, and then her daughter. "I'm so glad to see you."

"You're looking as pretty as ever." Rick's charm brought a sparkle of embarrassment from the older woman.

"You always were a smooth one." She blushed. "Where is that daddy of yours, Ariene? Fred!" she hollered down the hallway. A moment later, Fred Woods sauntered in, wearing old workpants and a Baltimore Orioles shirt.

"Well, son, you've been a stranger to these parts. They still got you in Africa?" He gave Rick a hearty handshake before hugging his daughter.

"Yes, I just completed a project there." Casually Rick put an arm around Ariene's shoulder and felt her stiffen at the surprised contact.

"So, you're home to stay for a while? You're over there more than you're here, now." Her father eyed them, curiosity furrowing his brows.

"I'll be here for a few months."

"How many months?" Ariene asked, looking up at him.

"Three or four. We'll see."

"Have a seat," Mrs. Woods said. "No sense in everyone standing around."

Rick guided Ariene to the overstuffed, green paisley sofa, where they shuffled aside the little satin pillows her mother loved to make. Pictures of Dr. Martin Luther King and *The Last Supper* hung on the wall behind them.

"I just made my special lemonade you always loved, Rick. Let me get you a glass."

"Thank you."

She ambled into the kitchen while Mr. Woods made himself comfortable in the well-worn recliner, where Rick remembered he read the newspaper every evening after supper.

Mrs. Woods was back in no time, handing them frosted glasses. Rick took a sip. "I think I missed your lemonade most when I left here. I hope you gave Ariene your recipe." He placed his glass on the coaster on the coffee table filled with china birds, milk glass baskets, and other knickknacks, then took Ariene's hand in his.

"I tried. Lord knows she never enjoyed the kitchen." She tsk-tsked.

Resigned, Ariene shifted in her seat. Her mother watched them closely.

"I've asked Ariene to marry me, and she agreed," Rick announced suddenly. "We'd like your blessing."

Mrs. Woods screeched, fell back in the chair and threw up her arms.

"Thank you, Jesus! A June wedding will be perfect."

"Oh, we've set the date for three weeks," Rick quickly corrected.

"She's not in the family way, is she?" Mr. Woods asked, suspicion oozing from his direct stare.

A prospective groom didn't tell this North Carolina father of the bride—who kept two hunting rifles perched on the basement wall, even if they were collector's items— his precious daughter was pregnant before the "I do's." Thank goodness, in this case it wasn't true.

"Ah, no sir. We hope we'll be so blessed on our honeymoon." He patted Ariene's hand.

"Why the rush?" he asked suspiciously. Rick's parents had mentioned many times that Fred had been around the block a few times. He tried his best to make sure his daughter didn't follow in his footsteps. He hadn't settled down until he met up with Mrs. Woods.

"Oh, Dad. Will you stop it?"

"Fred, at least she's getting married, thank the Good Lord."

"If they're getting married, he needs to move back home. You can't take care of a wife and raise kids thousands of miles away, son." He pointed a finger at them, ready to dispense parental advice. "I was home to look after mine. I expect the same for my daughter." He leaned back and sucked on his teeth.

"There's just too much for younguns to get into today," he began again. "They need a strong family support group." Her dad was in his element, dispensing advice on how to do anything and everything, a sore point with Ariene. She was still uncertain how this would work. She hated to live in limbo. She needed plans. She needed to know exactly what would happen, and when.

Still, she bristled. "I—"

"We're looking into that possibility, sir," Rick cut in to diffuse a battle.

"A child needs a father at home with him. That's the trouble with the world, now. Not enough time spent on the little ones. I remember—"

"Dad—"

"I agree, which is why I've been looking for contracts near home," Rick cut in.

"You didn't say anything about that," Ariene interrupted.

He squeezed her hand again in a warning.

"Maybe you can hang the clothes on the line for me, Ariene, dear. We'll just have a nice little visit with Rick while you're gone," Mrs. Woods interrupted smoothly.

"I'm not a child, Mom. You don't need to send me out back when the company comes." She didn't move.

"Why don't you do as your mom asked, honey? I'll be fine." Rick put a hand behind her to urge her up.

"No," she said adamantly.

That purposeful look that often meant he was determined to get his way was back in his eyes. "Please, Ariene. We won't devour each other for dinner while you're gone. I've known your parents all my life."

Irritated at the lot of them, Ariene got up and marched off to the glassed-in back porch, where the washer and dryer were kept. Even though her mother owned a dryer, she didn't use it on sunny days. She still loved to hang clothing out in the fresh air. Ariene had no such qualms, but this was her mother's house.

Ariene abhorred being sent out back like a teenager, too naive to make decisions about her life or too young to hear the grownups talk. Her parents were of the old school, planning to grill the prospective groom on their expectations and his intentions. Her cousins—younger cousins—had often mentioned that their own parents had done the same. Ariene wasn't that young any longer.

The engagement announcement didn't go as smoothly at Rick's parents' home. Ella Cordell, Rick's mom, received the news with her usual lack of enthusiasm and emotional uproar. In shock, she finally said, "Well, I guess congratulations are in order." She gave Ariene a stern glare, and looked as though she was going to burst into tears when she looked at Rick, as if Ariene were going to murder her son in the middle of the night.

Mr. Cordell cleared his throat. "I'm happy for you, son. Welcome to the family, Ariene."

Mrs. Cordell let out a screech, jumped up, and ran into the back room.

Mr. Cordell sent a helpless look at his son that said *Here we go again.*

"Excuse me a moment, sweetheart." Rick kissed her lightly on the lips and went in search of his mom. She was stretched out across the bed crying, hugging the pillow. "Mom, you should be happy for me. You know I've always loved Ariene." He plucked a tissue from the box on the nightstand and handed it to her. Then he gathered her in his arms.

"What you want isn't always the best for you," she finally said as she sat up and blew into the tissue. "She's going to make your life miserable. Absolutely miserable. She doesn't love you the way you love her." She pointed a shaky finger at him. "She's too bossy. You're not going to have a minute's peace with that woman. You mark my words, Richard. Men never did use a lick of sense around a pretty woman. And she's got the wiles to just lead you into anything."

She burst into tears again and clutched Rick, squeezing

him even harder as if to imprint him in her memory forever, this soft, plump woman who'd always loved him. She needed grandchildren to fuss over.

"She's not as bad as all that," he said, trying to be tolerant of her distress. He leaned back to pluck another tissue and handed it to her. "Just be happy for me."

"How can I be happy when you're making the biggest mistake of your life? She beat you up at four, didn't she? And she always tried to run your life." She started wailing again. Rick hoped they couldn't hear her in the living room.

"That was decades ago. She's grown up, and so have I."

"But she's still bossy." Suddenly looking hopeful, she stopped the wailing. "Well, you still have time to change your mind, sweetheart." She patted his back. "Set the date a year from now. Or better yet, leave that part for later. I'll help you find someone else by then."

That was the last thing he needed. "We're getting married in three weeks."

"Three weeks!" Rick knew they heard that. She hit him on the shoulder. "Didn't you have enough sense to keep your breeches zipped around her? She trapped you is what she did."

"She's not pregnant, Mom."

"Thank God!" she bellowed. "Then you can wait."

"We don't want to wait. I have to go back to Africa."

"Is she going with you?"

"No. She has a business to run here."

"Thank goodness for that. At least you can get some peace. But, son, why marry her at all? All those nice young ladies out there, couldn't you choose one of them? Tell you what. They're having a singles party at the church next Saturday. You can come to that. Shirley Anne's husband died last year, and she doesn't have any children. She'd make a wonderful wife."

"I'm marrying Ariene. I'm not in love with Shirley Anne."

"You always had to be difficult. You're doing it to hurt me."

She finished dabbing her eyes and blew her nose, throwing the tissue into a tulip-shaped wastebasket. She had revived enough so that Rick knew she'd be all right.

He led her back to the living room.

"This has been the most difficult day of my life," Ariene said at around six that evening as they neared her apartment. I could hear your mother carrying on."

"She was surprised. She'll get over it." As his brothers had, Rick knew that she needed this time to adjust. His mother would eventually come around—especially when she was presented with a grandchild. This was the most important step in his life. He had to do it right.

"I don't know about that. She's very protective of you."

Rick reached over and took Ariene's hand in his. "Don't worry, she's not going to travel an hour just to make your life miserable."

"She can do it by phone." Nervously, she raked her fingers through her hair. "What did you and my parents talk about, and why did you insist that I leave? This isn't the fifteen or eighteen hundreds, when marriages were arranged in secret by the parents. You're taking over, Rick. I've lost control. It's . . . it's as if I don't know you anymore," she croaked.

In the close confines of the car, trembles that shouldn't be there raced through her. All of this was having a strange effect on her. Unconsciously, she twisted the ring on her finger. It reminded her of the binding commitment a marriage would enforce.

"I'm the same man you've known forever, Ariene."

"Our friendship will change. The divorce will just kill them."

"What do you want, Ariene? We're friends, have always been friends. I'm not coming into this expecting you to change, and I know you don't have those expectations for me. Who knows what it takes to make a marriage work anymore? We can just make the best of what we have, remembering that we're friends first—will always be friends. I've . . . I've always loved you like a friend."

"I feel the same about you."

"Then we'll take one year at a time. I'll still be in Uganda. You'll be here. The only change will be the intimacy and the baby."

"That's just it, Rick," she said, willing him to see her point of view. "Those are major changes. They'll change the whole relationship."

"They don't have to."

"Yes, they do." Once he made a decision, everything had seemed so simple to him. The situation wasn't so cut and dry for Ariene. "When we share intimacies, there are expectations that weren't there before. Certain freedoms are lost."

"I'm not dating. I don't have a problem with that. Do you?"

"Well, no, but married, I'm no longer free to do so, either."

His irritation at her excuses edged forward. "Then you can wait to have a baby when you find your dream lover."

Ariene had never heard that tone before. She started to tell him he was overstepping his bounds when she glanced at him out of the corner of her eye. His hand was clenched around the steering wheel. All this was hard on him, too, she realized suddenly. What right did she have to voice all her worries to him? After he'd offered so much, she shouldn't bombard him with her insecurities.

As unrealistic as this all seemed, she knew a dream mate might never arrive. He hadn't so far. All across America, thousands of women had waited forever for that illusive mate, in vain.

At thirty she still wasn't marrying for love. And her mother had been married at twenty.

"Ariene, give us a chance."

Ariene sighed. The alternative was worse. "All right."

Everything was going as planned. Mentally drained with having to convince Ariene at every turn, Rick still patted himself on the shoulder for finally alleviating some of her fears and at least moving their engagement along. He still, however, winced at his mom's overly dramatic reaction. He knew she had reservations about Ariene, but he'd underestimated the extent of her disapproval.

The answering machine was blinking as he entered his kitchen. He went to it immediately and listened to the messages. His mother's voice came over.

"Please, son. You're making the biggest mistake of your life. It isn't too late. You haven't marched down that aisle yet. Mavis's daughter is still single. She'll be at the singles party. Please come. It's from eight P.M. to two A.M. Lots of single women. I'm doing this because I love you. Call me please, son. Remember, I love you. Mom.

Rick grinned and climbed the stairs to his bedroom. The quicker he married Ariene and put an end to this, the better off they all would be. Ariene's down-to-earth personality would be a nice change from his mom's dramatic tendencies.

CHAPTER 3

Ariene looked at the stack of wedding invitations Edward
Noble had left with her that morning. Her mom had shown
up, at her apartment Monday morning, suitcase in hand,
to help with the wedding. The first order of business had
been getting the invitations ordered. Edward owned the
printing shop in the plaza, at the opposite end from her
store. He assured her mom he could get them done by
Wednesday afternoon.

Her mother had decided the reception would have to
be in the church hall, since Ariene hadn't given her much
time to plan. The envelopes were delivered on Tuesday,
and for the last two days Yvonne, her mother, Rick's sister,
and she had addressed envelopes until Ariene had cramps
in her fingers. Her mom had brought a long list of names
with her, and even though Rick's mother rebelled against
the marriage, it didn't keep her from providing an even
longer list of names. Rick had dozens of business associates
and friends of his own to add to the list. Every shop owner

at the plaza had stopped by, expecting invitations. Even she finally had to come up with a list.

"I'm going to drop these off at the post office and talk to the caterers this afternoon," Mrs. Woods said. "Lord have mercy. We have so much to do. Start looking at wedding gowns. It may need to be altered. Also, you need to get your part-timer to work more hours until after the honeymoon."

"We're taking the honeymoon later," Ariene assured her.

"Rick says differently." That said it all as far as her mother was concerned. "I'll be back in two days. I don't know how we're going to get through this without a mishap. There's just so much to do."

Mrs. Woods waved and pranced briskly away.

Ariene reminded herself these were the inconveniences one had to endure so that the gift of a precious baby would one day be hers. She wondered if going to the fertility clinic might have been the easier route, after all. The problem was, plans had progressed much too far to turn back now.

"You do need to think about a decent wedding gown," Yvonne said. "Going to the minister would have been one thing, but a huge affair like this is quite another."

"Don't I know it. Every time I talk to Rick, he claims to be so busy and says, 'Go ahead, let your mom have fun with all this. You're their only daughter.' "

She tapped her fingers on the table. "It's costing me a fortune. I don't want my parents paying for a fake wedding."

"It isn't a fake wedding. You and Rick are paying for most of it. He doesn't want your parents to feel left out. Look at how much fun your mother's having. She's in seventh heaven."

"Don't remind me. If I pay any more for this wedding, I'll be using my down payment for the town house."

"Who knows? You and Rick just might fall in love and decide to stay married."

"You're reading far too many fairy tales again. At least I'll have nine months to save up the money for another down payment."

She felt guilty that her parents had insisted on purchasing her wedding gown. They expected something nice, and her mother had offered to choose the gown for her. At least her parents would get the opportunity to plan one wedding.

Yvonne fingered through the nightgowns. "And don't forget you have to choose something for the wedding night."

"Wedding night?"

"Sure. You're in this to procreate, remember? You're going to need something to put him in the mood."

The woman perused her items with a frown. "Leave the nightgown to me. It will be my wedding gift to you. If it's left up to you, you'll end up with something covering you from head-to-toe."

"I have plenty of gowns to take care of the job."

"Uh uh." Yvonne waved a hand and looked at her watch. "Time to go home." She grabbed her purse. "See you later, girl. Don't worry yourself."

Ariene could imagine what Yvonne would purchase for her. Most of the sleepwear Ariene donned were oversize T-shirts. That wouldn't do. Ariene added serviceable lingerie to her list of things to do. She had to entice Rick for two months. During her research she had discovered that fresh sperm was more potent than the frozen kind used in artificial insemination. The clinical insemination process took three to six months. With Rick she should get pregnant much quicker.

Then the one idea she'd been trying to avoid crept into her mind. She would have to go to bed with Rick. Butterflies fluttered in her stomach at the thought. They were friends, not intimate lovers.

Would lovemaking destroy their relationship? She'd hate for intimacy to destroy that.

Lately she'd been staying awake nights wondering how it would feel to be in his arms as a woman, *not* as a friend. Surprisingly, a fine stirring started. Then sleep eluded her for a while as she thought about Rick, apprehensive. She couldn't deny that he was attractive. When did that happen? No longer was he the tall, gangly adolescent or the pimply teen. He was a man, a well-built man with whom she would make love in a little over two weeks.

As Mrs. Woods pinned the veil on her daughter's hair, tears of happiness and nostalgia gathered in her eyes. "You're such a beautiful woman, you know," the older woman whispered.

"Mom, every mother thinks her daughter's beautiful." Ariene smiled, and all was okay with her. Never mind that she'd moved out of her parent's home years ago—weddings were sentimental occasions.

"Perhaps that's true. But you are *truly* beautiful."

Ariene smiled and hugged her mother, who seemed unusually preoccupied today, though she had mentioned many times that she thought Ariene had made a good catch with Rick. Ariene put her preoccupied air down as a mother's right on her daughter's wedding day.

Her mom fingered the soft curls that outlined Ariene's face. The hair in back was caught in a spiral weave. "I've waited so long for this day." Mrs. Woods paused and straightened a pleat in the peplum of Ariene's dress. Never remembering the correct term, she still called it a skirt.

"I know that one of the reasons you waited so long for marriage was because of me."

"That's not true," Ariene immediately contradicted. "I've just never found the right man before."

"Of course it is," she responded as if Ariene hadn't contradicted her at all. "You hate the way your father and I live. You don't like the fact that I've always been content with my lot, and gave your father freedom to run things. You've measured all of your friends against your father."

"You do let him push you around, make all the decisions. I remember when you were planning a vacation one year. You really wanted to go to Atlanta to visit your sister. He wanted to go to Niagara Falls. You gave up too easily."

"We went to Atlanta for Thanksgiving. I understood that he needed to get away to relax. You can't always relax around family." Her brows puckered. So many times their discussions had led to fights in the past. Ariene hated to argue today, but she was so nervous. At least it took her mind off Rick.

Her mom seemed to weigh her words before continuing. "There's compromise in a marriage, honey. Otherwise it wouldn't work. Your father and I compliment each other, and he's never mistreated me." Mrs. Woods surveyed the veil. It was perfect. "I've never been good with math. He is. He, on the other hand could never cook a decent meal, or plan a wedding in three weeks or keep a spotless house. Each of us has our strengths and weaknesses. He makes me feel special. You'll see. Rick will make you feel equally special."

"Only because you've always been here to do those things for him." Ariene didn't want to argue with her mother today. Feeling like a fraud, she was much too nervous and expectant, more than she should have been, given the reason for the wedding. She thought of the beautiful flowers her mom had guided her in selecting, the menu she'd help plan. Alone, Ariene couldn't have done it all in three weeks.

"I love you, Mom. You do have your own special talents." Ariene hugged her again.

Her mom was lacking in one talent she was thankful for. She didn't possess the talent for reading her daughter, Ariene thought, and she was glad for that. She wanted her mother to enjoy the day, and the fruits of her labor. If she knew the truth, it would break her heart. It was a good thing she and Rick were going to try this out for a few years at least.

"Your dad loves you, too. It hurts him to argue with you so much."

"I know he does. It's just—"

"Having to have the last word, both of you. You're more alike than you realize." Her smile was both hopeful and sad.

Never! Ariene thought. She wasn't that overbearing.

Just before the organist struck the first chord for the wedding march, Rick faced the church entrance. Ariene stood with her father, her hand delicately clasping his arm. The white brocade, a traditional fabric of African dress, had a sheen to it. The low, scalloped neckline and fitted bodice clenched at the waist, and pleats from the peplum flowed downward. The slit just above the left knee gave him a tantalizing peekaboo glimpse of the white silk stockings that ended at the graceful white slipper. She was close enough now so that he could see the intricate embroidery at the neckline, bodice, and around the hem of the long sleeves and skirt. He'd learned so much about clothing when Ariene visited him in Africa.

The white veil covering her face hid her emotions as

she marched toward him in cadence to the music, but the silhouette behind the veil couldn't mask the breathtaking view of her high cheekbones, her wide eyes, her flawless complexion. Even if her graceful form had been lacking in beauty, her spirited gait and personality would compensate.

In a matter of minutes she'd be his. Rick couldn't stop the beginnings of a smile. How many times had he dreamed of this moment? His love approaching him, dressed in white.

The image was marred only a little by his mother's sniffles. He glanced at her, at the wad of tissues in her lap, and his father's disgusted expression. He'd really wanted his father as best man, but cautious of his mother's behavior he thought it best to leave his father with her. At least he could keep her in the seat when the preacher asked if there was any reason the couple shouldn't be married.

Ariene slowed her steps as she neared Rick, who was imposing in a black tux and Kente cummerbund. The sight of him took her breath away. In a sense, he was a stranger. A gorgeous stranger who seemed so different from the person she grew up with, who had maintained a relationship with her since she was just four years old. Now she was marrying him, and she needed to reacquaint herself with him all over again.

Just when Ariene thought of changing her mind about the whole farce he smiled at her, and once again he was the old familiar Rick she'd come to adore. Walking between the walls of people, she thought of him and gazed at him alone. How wide his strong shoulders were, how capable her Rick was.

One day she'd find a way to return the many favors he'd offered her.

* * *

"Finally." Rick's wedding night was weighing heavily on his mind. Although Ariene only expected enough to produce a baby, Rick wanted it to be the best experience of her life.

He looked up to see his mom still sniffling into her tissue, bearing down on him. Her eyes were puffy and red from her tear binge.

"I just don't know what I'm going to do." She fell into his arms. "It's too late to make changes now." Her wide-brimmed, summer hat fell to the side.

"Be happy for me, Mama." Rick straightened her hat on her tight curls. Luckily, his dad came and detached her from his shoulder. His sisters and brothers had taken their turn with her throughout the reception. "I'll be fine."

Ariene's mother approached them. "Ariene went in to change, Rick. You don't want to miss your plane."

His mom sent up a loud wail, then.

Mrs. Woods and his dad looked at each other, resigned to his mom's melodramatic performance. "Ella, calm yourself," Mrs. Wood said. "He's a grown man now. And you raised him right. The rest will take care of itself."

Rick gave her a last kiss, untangled himself from her, and went in search of his wife. He liked the sound of that. His wife.

Ariene pulled out the nightgown Yvonne had marked in huge letters FOR YOUR WEDDING NIGHT and looked at the wisp of fabric skeptically before slipping it over her head. Perusing herself in the mirror, she knew she wasn't going to greet Rick in it. The floor-length white gown was see-through just down to her nipples, and dipped to a V. Then the silk molded gracefully to every curve. She turned to glimpse the back, which was non-existent until the waist. It was perfect for a couple in love, but with Rick, it wouldn't do.

Ariene returned to her suitcase and searched. The gowns she'd packed weren't there. They were all replaced by revealing ones. It had to be Yvonne's doing. Now she remembered the woman saying that she needed to add something just before Ariene closed the suitcase. That must have been when the switch occurred. Since Yvonne had helped Ariene pack, she knew exactly where the gowns were located, and Yvonne had been the last person to put something into the suitcase before closing it for the flight.

At least it was the perfect excuse for a shopping spree. Not that she needed one, Ariene thought. Tonight, however, she had to make do with what she had.

A light tap on the door drew her attention. "Do you need any help in there?" Rick asked.

"No . . . no, thank you." What was she to do? Frantically, she searched some more and came up with a kimono. It was barely enough to cover the top portion of the revealing but beautiful gown. She eased into it, tied the belt, took a fortifying breath, and unlocked the door. Rick turned at hearing her.

At the sight of him, she stopped. He wore silk pajama bottoms. She'd seen his chest thousands of times before when he'd cut the grass, at pool parties, during yard work, and even when she'd showed up unexpectedly at his house. So why did she feel as if she'd never seen his naked chest tonight? She exhaled and advanced into the room, glancing at two glasses filled with champagne. Putting the cork back in the bottle, he placed it in the ice bucket, all while watching her.

The curly hair on his chest that disappeared into his silk pajama bottoms captured Ariene's attention. Her heart thumped, her fingers trembled, her senses were heightened.

Trying to gather a measure of control, she looked through the open balcony doors. The Bahamian twilight cast a romantic glow over their honeymoon suite, overlooking the Atlantic Ocean. She could hear the waves tumbling against the shore. A gentle tropical breeze stirred the air, but not nearly as much as Rick stirred her senses. In the background, Ariene realized, a low, tropical beat resonated. Rick must have turned on the radio.

Suddenly, she wasn't at all ready for this. The three weeks had been too rushed for her to really contemplate what she was getting herself into. Now, it was all done, and they were finally at the point of the results of the hasty marriage. And she was ill-prepared.

"I . . . I don't know if I can do this." She tightened the belt around her waist until it pinched, then loosened it.

Rick's deep laughter didn't lighten the mood. "You won't be doing anything alone. Remember, your friend is here to help you."

If that was supposed to reassure her, it failed miserably. "I know, it's just—"

He approached her, handed her a glass of champagne and guided her to the sofa.

"To us, and making a beautiful child in the image of you. To friends." He touched his glass to hers.

Tentatively, she took a sip. "Or you."

"Did I tell you how beautiful you were today?" Was there a slight tremble in his hand as he set his glass on the coffee table? It must have been the play of lights that distorted her image.

"I don't think you did."

"You were. And you are."

Ariene nervously glanced down at her kimono, then

she cleared her throat. "Thank you. You were very fine looking—in your tux." She glanced at him. "Still are."

He put his hand around her shoulder. She jumped.

"Relax," came his smooth voice, as smooth as the champagne and music, if not as soothing. His hand moved up and down her arm, sending hot tentacles of desire through her.

She drew away from him, stood, and walked across the room. "Rick, I'm really nervous about this. I think we should just . . . just get it over with."

"It's not an operation." His efforts at trying to make light of their situation fell flat. "Why don't we just relax tonight, and see what happens tomorrow?"

She shook her head no. "I wouldn't be able to sleep tonight. The waiting is torture."

He rose and approached her. "No more you than me." His reply was husky. "Try to relax and enjoy this. In a few months you'll be enjoying your pregnancy, each stage of our baby's development."

He took the glass out of her hand and set it on a table. Turning back to her, he held her tenderly, looking into her eyes. His own darkened, the teasing smile leaving his face. In its wake naked desire painted his features. Then he kissed her tentatively before he deepened the contact. "Think about the result and just enjoy the rest," he whispered against her lips. He caught the belt in his hand, kissing her neck at the same time.

Her mind went blank except for him.

"You don't have to—"

"Shhh . . ." he responded.

Nervously, her hand stole upward, touching the hair she'd been itching to touch since she saw his naked chest. He eased the robe off her shoulders and looked at her. This wasn't the look of a friend. It was the gaze of a lover.

Slowly he lowered his head until, through the sheer

gown, his teeth closed gently on a nipple. She moaned in response to the exquisite sensations. His hand stole up, caressing her thigh. All thought disintegrated, leaving nothing but sensations in its wake. And Rick.

Her world tilted when he lifted her and carried her to the bedroom, placing her on the center of the king–size bed. When he didn't remove her gown but merely slid his hand up her leg, she said, "Aren't you—"

"Shhh," he rasped, "lie back and enjoy."

Somewhere in the back of her mind she thought that she wasn't supposed to enjoy this, but she did as she dropped back and he kissed the arch of her foot, caressing her ankle.

Sensations weren't supposed to flow from that simple gesture, but they spiraled through her. He kissed his way up her leg, nudging the clinging gown up bit by bit.

She forgot this was her friend, and that they were only doing this to make a baby. She forgot it was an obligation.

Ariene grabbed at his head when his hand touched her intimately, no longer able to curtail a moan of pleasure. He kissed her stomach, her hands stroked his shoulders and his back, and then, with her gown bunched under her arms, he caressed her breasts, touching the tips, the heat of his tongue captivating her. Then he lifted her arms above her head, slowly gilding the gown up. Like a dance, his movements were slow, sensuous, rhythmic.

As soon as her arms were free, she was unable to resist touching him for another moment. Sliding her hands along his backside and thighs, she felt the sinewy strength in them. She reached down, slipped her hands under the waistband, and touched him intimately, curving her fingers around his thickness. He moaned and kissed her deeply, his hot tongue mingling with hers. And suddenly he shifted, shucked his pants, and in moments, he was touching her opening. He entered her. Feeling the fullness of him and his weight on her, she curved her legs around him.

Rick, her friend, had disappeared. In his place was her lover, her husband, the man who touched her core as none had before. It was as if she were losing a tiny part of herself. She was no longer entirely just Ariene Woods. She had bonded that part of herself with Rick forever.

Have mercy, was all Ariene could think to say. In her deepest imaginings, she'd never even considered he had it in him. She'd just basked in an early morning lovemaking marathon. Even now, the weight of his arm secured her next to him, his leg intimately entwined with hers. She stroked the arm that rested below her breasts. It tightened around her.

"Ummm," Rick said. "I guess it's time for us to get up and about."

Ariene didn't think she could move, much less stand on her rubbery legs.

Two hours later, Rick looked down on Ariene as the boat's speed accelerated and their feet left the deck. She let out a screech.

"We're parasailing, Ariene. You won't be catapulted into the air. You're going to barely feel the ascent."

"I'm going to murder you as soon as this is over," she shouted up. "This isn't how I'd planned to spend my restful vacation you talked me into. We're supposed to be lying on the beach under a shady tree."

"This is better. You wouldn't want a boring vacation. I promised you excitement."

"Remind me to tell your mother that *you* were the bad influence on *me.*"

He only laughed.

"Look around you, Ariene." With the wind hitting his face, Rick drew in a breath. The sparkling, blue-green Nassau water shimmered below them. The boat now looked only a fraction of its size. Looking farther out, he spotted another island, one lone house immersed in the trees and hedges. He caught the pink tops of oleander bushes the islands were dotted with. "Isn't the view breath-taking?"

He could barely hear her. "God, it really is."

"I knew you'd enjoy it."

Starved from their invigorating morning of parasailing and swimming, they drove up Bay Street to the Fish Market. Cooking aromas breezed from the open-air huts that were arranged in a circular pattern.

They entered the Catch of the Day, which had been recommended by one of Rick's friends, and sat on two of the tall stools surrounding the bar. They chose the area directly in front of a man who was cutting something up.

"What are you making?" Ariene asked. Wearing the sarong Rick had insisted on purchasing for her earlier that morning, she leaned over to get a better view.

"Conch for conch salad," he answered in his lilting Bahamian accent. He sent a sly grin in Rick's direction. "Lots of energy, this conch." He didn't miss a beat as he picked up another one and sliced it into small perfect cubes.

"It's raw," Rick added.

"How long you been married?"

"We're newlyweds," Rick answered.

"Conch is great for making babies. Can I get you conch salad today?" he asked with a friendly demeanor.

Rick grinned wickedly at Ariene. "I'll take a bowl, then," he answered the man.

Another waitress asked if Ariene would have the same.

"I'll have conch fritters with corn puffs." Ariene had never developed a taste for raw fish.

The waitress left them and she and Rick watched the man as he expertly chopped up tomatoes, onions, peppers, and added other fresh ingredients to the salad mixture. While watching his skillful maneuvers, they conversed with him as they waited for their order.

"Enjoying our beach?"

"We are. We went parasailing today. It was wonderful, man, just a little calmer than hanggliding."

"Admit it," he said to Ariene. "You enjoyed it." With the tip of his finger, he tilted her chin toward him. Such a simple gesture.

The waitress set the plate of conch fritters in front of Ariene and left, after asking if everything was to their satisfaction. Rick's eyes never left Ariene's.

"All right. I enjoyed it." Her voice husky, Ariene glanced away from Rick's direct stare.

The man at the bar laughed as he came back and set the bowl of conch salad in front of Rick. Rick gathered a forkful and put it to Ariene's lips. She opened her mouth, cautiously tasting.

She ate half the bowl.

After shifting her toes through the pink sand, swimming in the blue-green ocean in the April sunshine, browsing in quaint shops, steering a moped for the first time, and making endless love with Rick, Ariene was well rested when they returned to her boutique after the week long honeymoon. She didn't realize how much she needed to get away, how relaxed she would feel after just a week. But she still wasn't resigned to having a man in the bathroom, or making sure she was fully clothed in her bedroom, or waking up in his arms.

Rick drove her to Chic From Africa first. He would drop her off and then go to his office. First, however, he went in to greet her mother.

"Don't you two look wonderful," Mrs. Woods said. "You need to take more vacations, Ariene. You sparkle."

"How did everything go?" Ariene asked her mother, choosing not to comment on the sparkling. At a quick glance, everything looked in place. But then, her mother was always ordered and neat. "Thanks for keeping the shop for me."

"I knew you'd worry about the store. Everything went fine."

Ariene let out a sigh of relief. This store was her lifeline.

"I've gotten lots accomplished this week. I've packed your things, so you only have to move the boxes and furniture to Rick's. I even talked to your landlord. No sense making payments on two homes. When I asked about boxes, he asked if you will be leaving. I told him yes, and since a nice young lady who reminds me of you came by who wants your apartment, he's going to let you go without the usual notice."

"What!" Ariene shouted. "How could you do that!"

"That saves us a lot of work, honey. Thank you." Rick put an arm around her bunched shoulder.

"But, you—"

"Don't mention it. Fred's coming up tomorrow with the truck to help you move. I don't think it'll take long."

"Mom!"

"Good. I'll get a couple of friends to help with the lifting," Rick said.

"Wait a minute. I can't move yet."

"Well, why not? You're married. You can be so silly at times. Where else would you live but with your husband?"

"Isn't this great, sweetheart?" He released Ariene with a last warning squeeze and hugged her mom.

All Ariene's protests died in her throat. She hadn't begun to decipher her feelings for Rick and their arrangement. She couldn't possibly live with him every day. She needed time to examine this new arrangement. He'd continued to refer to them as friends. There seemed to be more involved than mere friendship.

"Well, I really have to go, now. Why don't you take the rest of the day off, Ariene? Tanya can handle the shop."

"Thanks, Mom, for taking care of everything for me." She had to get to her apartment manager immediately, and see if the woman had actually signed the contract. She couldn't make changes at this stage. "I think I'll take off, after all."

"We'll be back first thing in the morning to help you move. Rick, your brother, and dad are coming too. I thought I'd round up a few people while you were on your honeymoon, so you wouldn't have so much to do when you returned."

"Thank you, Mrs. Woods. You've been a godsend."

"You're so welcome, dear."

As soon as her mother's car left the parking lot, Ariene said, "Let's go." She grabbed Rick's hand and ran out of the store.

Yvonne stopped her on the sidewalk.

"Hi, Yvonne, I'll talk to you later. I have to go save my apartment. My mom released my lease."

"Umm, Ariene, I have more bad news. I think you need to know now," she said, hanging out the door.

"What is it?" Rick pulled Ariene up short.

"I hate to hit you with this right after your honeymoon, but you'll find out soon, anyway. Mr. McAdam's selling the plaza, and we all have to move out. You'll find the letter in the mail.''

"He can't do that!''

"It seems some big company's offering big bucks to buy him out, and wants to tear this down. It's gonna take months before they reopen. The leases are going to be a lot more, and I don't know if I'll be able to come back. Some large bookstore chain will probably get the contract instead of me.''

"Has the contract for the sale been signed yet?'' Rick asked while supporting Ariene.

"No, but we can't compete with a large conglomerate.''

"This can't be happening,'' Ariene said. A move would change everything. With no sure means of support, she couldn't have a baby. She clutched her stomach. Even now she could be pregnant.

"Everybody's in an uproar. Mr. McAdam's meeting with us tonight at the restaurant after closing. Try to make it, okay?''

"I wouldn't miss it,'' Ariene answered weakly.

"Both of us will be there,'' Rick said, supporting Ariene as he led her to the car. She desperately needed a seat.

She was homeless, soon to lose her shop. And after spending most of her savings on the wedding, she now didn't have the funds to open another boutique.

CHAPTER 4

Ariene couldn't save her apartment, and although Rick seemed fine with her moving in with him, she was reluctant to impose on him any more than necessary. They both needed their space—or *she* needed *her* space. She hadn't thought ahead to the questions people would ask once they realized she was still living in her apartment instead of his duplex. She'd been prepared to use the excuse of his frequent absences. Her mother had changed all that. Ariene had learned a valuable lesson—secrets made for tricky situations.

"Losing your apartment isn't the worst thing that could have happened," Rick said, across the table from Ariene. They'd dined at the Chavez's restaurant, and would stay for the meeting.

"For me it is. I need my space." Ariene sliced a bite of an enchilada.

"You'll have your space," came his terse reply.

"No, I won't. Even when you're thousands of miles away,

I'm still living in your home. I want my own home," she insisted.

"Where did you think you were going to live?" Rick asked between clenched teeth. He dropped the fork onto his plate. Then, with jerky movements, he grabbed up a glass of beer and sipped.

"It wasn't an issue before. You've spent a total of four weeks here in the last two years. I could easily have lived in my *own* place, or purchased a town house, which I had planned to do before I spent a fortune on this wedding."

"I offered to help out," he snapped. "You wouldn't let me, remember—always have to do it yourself."

"You were doing enough already. Besides, you paid for the honeymoon." Ariene laid down her own fork, her dinner ruined.

"All right. Now that we're living together, you can save for anything you want."

"I won't be dependent on any man. That includes you."

Rick snatched up his napkin, wiped his mouth, and looked away. He seemed to be counting to himself. "I'm not just any man, Ariene. I'm your husband, and your friend." His words were measured, a sure indication of rising annoyance.

But Ariene plowed ahead doggedly. "You weren't meant to take on this responsibility." She wished he'd understand her position without anger.

"Why did you think I married you?" he asked quietly.

Ariene glanced at the flickering candle on the table, wishing she could find some measure of peace. "Not to be my caretaker."

"I'm not Todd," he reminded her. "Don't get us confused." His posture was erect and combative.

After a short silence she asked, "Why did you bring him up?"

"Because this whole conversation is because of him."

Ariene exploded. "I hope you don't plan to mention Todd every time we have a disagreement! This has nothing to do with Todd."

"He's the reason you won't trust me."

"That isn't true. I trust you more than anyone." She lowered her voice when the waitress walked by. "I still need my independence."

"You're living with me—your husband. We are interdependent," he snapped, and leaned back in his chair.

"I just don't want to be a burden. And this problem with the plaza . . ." She tightened her hand into a fist on the table.

Rick relaxed and inhaled. He reached across the table and stroked her hand. "If you have to move your boutique, then you'll move," he said. "You sell top of the line clothing, and you can open anywhere."

"I sell at reasonable prices because the lease is affordable. If I get a lease that's too high, I can't sell at these reasonable rates. My prices will increase, and I'll lose business."

"Ariene, wait until after the meeting, honey. Don't buy trouble."

She sighed, turning her finger in his. "All right. I don't want to fight, Rick."

"Neither do I." Rick glanced at the waitress as she cleaned off tables. "The Chavez's are closing. It's almost time for the meeting." He signaled for the waitress and asked for the check.

"I can pay—"

"Do we have to fight about the bill, too?" He obviously was at the end of his patience.

"You've paid for everything since we got married."

He shoved the bill across the table. "Pay it if it'll make you happy." He rose from his chair. "I'll be right back."

He walked away, but Edward, the print shop owner, stopped him to talk.

Ariene dug into her purse for the money to cover the check and tip. After paying the bill she went into the ladies' room, dampened a towel, and patted it over her face.

Nothing seemed to be going right with her today.

Wildwood Plaza had finally taken the route that so many businesses had in this decade of mergers and uncertainty. The only people who could afford to relax today were retirees who'd saved well for their later years. Working Americans no longer had the security afforded them in the past. Her dad had worked at the same company for thirty-five years, and retired on a comfortable pension.

Ariene focused again on the plaza meeting. It was disintegrating by the minute.

"Why did we have to find out about the sale by accident, Mr. McAdam? Why didn't you tell us?" one of Ariene's fellow leasees asked. Ariene turned to face him. He sat at a rectangular table that abutted the wall. A sombrero and serape hung overhead on the smooth, cream-colored wall of the Mexican restaurant.

"I hung on as long as I could. I don't have a firm commitment yet. Things are still in the research and planning stage. I told you as early as I could." He leaned his arms on the podium and entwined his fingers. "If they decide to purchase this property, they've agreed to allow you to stay on a few months after it changes hands, to give you time to save up for the time the building will be unavailable. Or you can find a new location." Jerry took a white linen handkerchief out of his breast pocket and wiped it across the bald spot on top of his head.

"But we like this location. How much would our lease increase?" Yvonne asked. She sat between Ariene and Rick.

"How long will the renovation take?" asked Maria Chavez, who owned the restaurant with her husband.

"The plan is to tear down the building and rebuild a mall from scratch." A unified rumble emerged from the agitated group, as many exclaimed that they couldn't afford to close the doors for several months.

"How long will the shops be closed?" Ariene asked.

Then, one by one, questions fired off.

"Do they have to build on this spot?"

"Can they leave us intact while they build on back of here?"

"There's plenty of land here. When the building is completed, they can tear this down and turn it into parking space."

"Whoa! I can't promise you anything," Jerry said. "The decision will be out of my hands. The new owners will talk to you once they complete their research and make a decision."

"Does that mean a firm offer hasn't been made yet?" Ariene asked, hoping it wasn't too late for them.

"I said it wasn't. I didn't expect the word to spread so soon."

"But we wouldn't have known, and wouldn't have prepared ourselves," Ramon Chavez stated.

"Can we offer a bid for this property?" Rick asked.

A ray of hope sprang up in Ariene, then she realized they wouldn't have the funds for such a large undertaking. Even Rick couldn't bail her out of this one.

"We can't afford to buy this property!" a tenant said, repeating her very thoughts. "We make enough to live off of, but not that kind of money." Another collective moan rumbled through the crowd.

"Which is the nice thing about this group coming in. They can afford to bring in a grocery store and expand.

That will bring in more customers for you. With the increase in business, you can afford the new leases.''

"Will you give us the opportunity to purchase the property?" Ariene asked, wondering how they could possibly get a loan that large.

Jerry paused, looking tired and out of sorts. Then he sighed. The meeting had been going on for two hours. "If you can afford the property and the surrounding land. It's all one package. But I won't cut my price."

"Well, that's no solution," Edward Noble muttered from his seat on the far side of the restaurant. Ariene saw the worry etched on his face. He had three children to support, one of whom was starting college next fall.

"How much time will you give us?" Ariene asked, anxiety slicing up her spine.

"Three months. And I don't have any more time tonight. The meeting is adjourned." Jerry picked up his sparse notes and left through the side door before anyone could waylay him.

"Where did this bright idea about *us* buying this place come from?" Yvonne whispered to Ariene. "You know we don't have that kind of money." Her orange-lacquered nails clicked on the table top.

Ariene rose slowly from her heavy wooden chair, wishing she could stay and debate longer, but knowing it wouldn't do any good. "I need to think. We have to be able to come up with something."

"There are several options we can try. Finding backers is only one of them," Rick offered.

"And where are we going to get someone to purchase this place? Jerry hasn't been able to fill the other shops in months," Edward said.

"He may have known he was going to sell and that the people he'd contacted were going to oust everyone." Rick dug his hands in his pockets. "This location is surrounded by families, yet there isn't a specialty grocery store in the area."

"We can't afford to open a grocery store," Ramon said quietly. "Profit margin on groceries is even less than on a restaurant."

"We need to go home and sleep on this, and call a meeting in a week. If it's okay with the Chavez's, we can meet back here." Rick glanced at the couple.

They looked at each other and nodded. "All right by us. Our place is involved, too," Ramon supplied.

"Use the week to think of options and bring them to the table next week." Rick took Ariene's elbow. "Goodnight, everyone." He, Ariene, and Yvonne walked to the door, sliding past tables and speaking to other lessees on their way.

Rick held the door for Yvonne and Ariene. She hadn't realized he'd taken her hand as they walked toward the car in somber silence.

Yvonne finally broke the silence. "Ariene, what's on your mind? You don't say anything unless you have a plan."

"I don't know, Yvonne. But we have to be proactive. We can't sit around and just let things happen to us. All I know is that if we don't try, we're doomed."

"You and your positive thinking kick again. Well, tomorrow I'll be over to help you move."

"I could have done without the reminder that I'm homeless," she said, thinking of the work ahead.

"Bye," Yvonne called out and slid her key into her door.

Rick opened their car door for her and Ariene slid onto the soft, leather seat. He leaned over her, his hand on the window, looking much too good for her equilibrium. "You are not homeless. We're staying at your new home tonight." Shutting the door, he walked around to the driver's side.

The car was parked under the halogen light in the parking lot. Rick left the keys dangling in the ignition, put his arm along the back of the seat, and faced her. "Let's get something straight right now. You're not just some woman I'm helping out. You're my wife. And the baby you'll carry soon will be my baby."

"Not in the traditional sense," Ariene said, not wanting to rehash the argument.

"Traditional or not, that's the way it is. Let me be as happy about this baby as you are, Ariene."

Ariene glanced at him, the light throwing shadows on his tense face. He was so persuasive. "I can't get pregnant right now."

Rick inhaled slowly. "Things have a way of working out. By the time you're pregnant, you'll wonder why you worried at all." He slid a finger along her chin, leaned over and kissed her softly.

Ariene shook her head to clear her thoughts. His kisses always took her breath away. "I can't take that chance. Everything might not work out."

"We'll work on your problems together," he insisted. His fingers caressing her neck made her want to curl up and believe anything he said. "It's not as if I can't afford to support us. I'll be your husband for years. Get used to it."

"It's all so unfair to you," she whispered in the quiet interior of the rented Lincoln that was just as solid and stable as Rick.

"You didn't force me to marry you. Actually, it's the other way around."

Reaching for the key in the ignition, Rick faced front and turned on the motor. Ariene leaned her head against the headrest and closed her eyes. She still felt aroused from his touch, but concentrated on her problems instead. Whenever life poured on too much at one time, she compartmentalized. And tomorrow meant moving day. She'd concentrate on that instead of the dilemma of her store and Rick's words.

Everything was packed at her apartment and two trips in her dad's and Rick's dad's trucks would have everything moved from her small, one bedroom apartment in no time. She and Rick could go over tonight and move a carload, but what was the use? From lifelong experience, Ariene knew her mom would have enough people to handle the move quickly.

Rick turned on the radio but kept the tone low. Friday night soul with its mellow notes poured from the speakers as he pulled out into the traffic. Ariene turned her head and watched him maneuver the vehicle smoothly through the traffic.

Pinpoints of desire cascaded through her. Even her worries didn't stem the attraction. She reached out and put a hand on his thigh. He glanced at her, the side of his mouth kicking up. At the light, he took her hand in his and kissed her palm. Ariene could have melted to the floor. When the light flashed green, he placed her hand back on his thigh and drove on.

"Hold that thought." His voice held promise—a promise she eagerly awaited for him to deliver. She had to be losing her mind.

Ariene closed her eyes, and the outside world almost seemed a dream. Barry White's soothing voice wrapped around her, and Ariene relaxed deeper into the butter-soft seat, her arm resting comfortably on the armrest, but she found herself too distracted to doze off.

At the duplex, Ariene unpacked her suitcase and ran two extra large loads of clothing, washing hers and Rick's in the machines closeted away near the kitchen. Already, she loved his duplex. She didn't have to count quarters for laundry or drag the clothing to the basement, or drive to a laundromat, as she'd done for years.

"I'll take that to the bedroom for you," Rick told Ariene, who was starting up the stairs with a basket of laundry.

Instead of lingering downstairs, she followed him.

The master suite was located at the opposite end from the other two bedrooms, one of which Ariene had decided to use.

"Aren't you going in the wrong direction?" she asked. This fascination with Rick had to stop. She felt guilty for leading him on the way she had in the car. What had come over her?

"I only have one bed."

Ariene saw the beginning of temper, but doggedly trudged on. She reached for the basket. "I'll sleep downstairs, then."

He nudged her hand away. "We've slept together for the last week." He inhaled sharply. "Fine," Rick snapped, finally. "I'll sleep on the sofa. We're not rehashing this again tonight."

"I'm not putting you—"

He faced her, brimming with male impatience. "Not another word."

Dumping the basket on the bed, he trod to the walk-in closet with quick, long strides, pulled the door open with an angry jerk, and disappeared inside. In a minute he reappeared with a sheet and pillow. Without even a cursory glance in her direction, he left the room, and Ariene heard his swift steps descending the stairs.

Now, he was angry at her. Like most men, he'd probably stew until tomorrow. Ariene sat on his bed, feeling stupid and uncertain for making him sleep downstairs when she had this huge, king-size bed all to herself. She wondered how to approach him next.

Mechanically, she reached into the basket, pulled out her slip, and folded it. She had to clear the problem between them.

She folded clothing for several minutes, then she dropped the shirt she was folding onto the neat pile of clothing she'd stacked for him on the bed, and went to join him. The back door leading to the deck was open. Rick stood at the railing, looking out into the darkness. She put a hand on his shoulder and he tensed at her touch.

"Don't be angry, Rick. It's just . . . so much is happening right now."

He threw her an impatient glance. "I know that. I just want to make it easier for you."

"Just give me some time to work things out."

He turned and gathered her in his strong arms. She leaned her head against her chest and immediately felt warm and comforted. "I'll give you all the time you need," he said in his deep voice and stroked her back. She could just curl up like a kitten. "Why don't I fix you some tea? That always calms you."

"You start the water, and I'll start the coffeemaker for you."

She was being silly, she thought as they entered the house together. They were already sleeping together, and knowing his moral standards, he wouldn't have an affair outside of the marriage. Even better, would she want him to? Hell no, Ariene thought as she reached into the cabinet for the coffee.

She'd never envisioned she'd want intimacy with her very best friend—or that she'd have the best loving of her life with him. Within the last month, they'd become more than friends. She still couldn't categorize what they shared.

It wasn't lightning bolt love. But their arrangement was comfortable. Very—very comfortable.

After they talked of inconsequential things over coffee and tea, they took separate showers and prepared for bed. Ariene plumped the pillow against the headboard and leaned against it. She knew she wouldn't sleep for hours. She needed to talk to Rick, but didn't have the stamina for another confrontation. The business with the plaza kept stirring at the edge of her consciousness.

Telling the other shopkeepers to think about their situation for a week seemed fruitless. None of them would be able to raise funds to save the plaza. They were all everyday business owners making decent livings, but not enough to purchase the plaza.

Ariene ran her hand over her freshly scrubbed face. In the process she turned her head, and noticed the remote control for the television on the bedside table. She picked it up and pressed the On button. The screen flashed into view just in time to quote that the NYSE had dropped fifty points. One day the DOW was up, the next down.

Wouldn't it be great if they could sell shares of stock! *As if we'd have any buyers.* Her fellow owners could purchase some shares, as could she, but not enough to save the plaza. If she mentioned that at the next meeting, they'd throw salsa at her, and rightly so.

Ariene had neglected to think about what had been nagging her all afternoon—she could be pregnant this very moment. She rubbed a hand across her stomach and thought of the many women who got pregnant but didn't know how they'd support a child. Suddenly, she'd been thrown into the same category.

Rick was willing to help, but regardless of what he'd said that was unfair to him. When he'd taken her to Africa, at least she had paid her own way. Now, with the expenses of a child, her funds would quickly dwindle.

She was grateful she hadn't gone the fertility clinic route. Then she'd really be on her own. Still, she was luckier than many women—had she gone that route, her parents would have helped her. At thirty, she didn't want to be a burden to them, though. She'd always been self-reliant. To change would be unthinkable.

Ariene sipped on her bottled water. The soft knock at her door startled her, and water dripped down her chin.

"Come in," Ariene called out, wiping off the drops with her hand.

Wearing pajama bottoms and no shirt, Rick wandered over and sat on the edge of the bed, looking entirely too good. After a week of intimacy, she'd hoped their attraction would settle down to comfortable and predictable. Instead, her body sang, the hairs raised on her arms, and her heartbeat skidded into overdrive. She only hoped he couldn't hear the beats, they were so loud. She eased over to give him more room.

Last night, as she'd run her fingers through the curly hairs on his chest, she'd remembered when his first few strings of hair started to grow in only months before his seventeenth birthday. He'd come a long, long way since he was seventeen, laden with gangly youth.

Since he only wore briefs to bed, the bottoms he wore tonight were in deference to her. She wished he'd left them off.

"You want to talk about it?" he asked, regarding her closely.

"Us?" she asked.

"We'll get to that later. I'm talking about the plaza."

"Ummm," she said, plucking at the edge of the spread. "I've been wracking my brain, and haven't come up with any viable solution. I guess it's time I start looking for another location."

"You know, the same thing can happen in another three

or four years. The locations you're after are usually small plazas surrounded by housing developments. They're being bought in buyouts right and left, now. It's the present business trend."

"If I want to run my own shop, there isn't another alternative." She refused to be pessimistic. Ariene would find another location, and still another, if she had to.

"Perhaps there is," Rick mused. "Monday, I'll get the updated demographics of the area, and we can work from there."

"What do you have in mind?"

"Do you mind if I lean back?"

"No." She shifted her knees up and linked her hands around them. Rick stretched out with his hands behind his head, his chest open and wide for her unguarded inspection and fascination.

"This area is around fifty percent African-American. You probably have at least ten to twenty churches nearby, each with memberships ranging from a thousand and more. And incomes close to the highest in the country. You have a very large community with at least some post high school education. It's the perfect investment opportunity."

Ariene had just thought the same thing. "How are you going to get them to invest in it?"

"By working up a professional proposal. I know of an organic and specialty grocery chain that may be interested in opening a store in this area. One is certainly needed to promote the diversity in the population. The conglomerate who wants to buy this property must have considered this."

"It sounds wonderful." For the first time, hope sprang in Ariene.

"With this plan you'll be able to purchase the space for your shop. The whole program can run almost like a co-op housing arrangement, and you won't have to worry about anyone closing down or making you move."

She smiled down at him. How could she have thought he was a nerd all these years, Ariene wondered as she scanned the curly hairs starting at his chest and disappearing into the waistband of his pajama bottoms.

His gaze met hers and he slowly sat up, only to lean on her legs, pressing them apart so he could fit between them. Lightning shot through Ariene's body and she tensed in expectation of what was to come. "And we don't have to wait for our baby." His voice lowered, its smoky intensity causing goosebumps to break out on her arms.

"Th . . . these are just ideas," she stammered, and she cleared her throat, wanting him every bit as much as the intensity of his gaze broadcasted his need. "They're not even on paper yet, much less presented to the owners."

"It'll work," he said against her lips, and pressed her back.

Her hands came up to his shoulders. "It . . . it's still a good idea to wait." Her objection was weak at best.

He leaned closer and pressed her legs wider. Her juices flowed in readiness, and he'd only whispered so far.

His lips pressed against hers, and her hands moved of their own accord to bring him closer.

She was having too much fun making this baby with Rick. Where was her willpower? she wondered as her mouth opened beneath his to draw him inside.

CHAPTER 5

"How is married life treating you, old man?" Curt grunted with the effort of lifting his end of the sofa from Ariene's apartment.

"Just fine," Rick said as they turned it sideways to get it out the door. Straining, working with it, and twisting the sofa in several different ways, they accomplished the feat without damage.

"She must have gotten the biggest sofa in the store." Rick put his end on the floor. "Let's rest a minute."

"I'm all for that." Puffing and wiping his face, Curt sat on one end of the sofa and glanced at Rick. "What are you going to do about Veronica, man?"

"Nothing. Our engagements were never serious. You know that." Rick leaned against the doorjamb. "How many times have we broken up in the last year?"

"Who knows? What did she say when you told her?"

"I sent her a telegram." He straightened and approached the chair. "She's in Baluchistan. Getting a phone call through over there is just about impossible, even with satellite communications."

Curt shook his head and chuckled. "I can't believe you."

"Hey, she'd already broken it. I just confirmed." He bent to get a grip on the sofa. "Ready?"

This time they made it to the service elevator before putting it down.

"Veronica sure is a looker. How could you give her up?"

Rick punched the DOWN button. "Must be that thing called love," he joked.

Curt laughed. "I couldn't believe it. Thought you'd stay single forever." He resumed his position on the seat and tapped his fingers on the armrest. "Kinda sudden, wasn't it?"

Rick wondered when Curt would say what was really on his mind. "Yeah, I hadn't seen Ariene in almost a year. When I did, she just knocked me off my feet."

"That's good." He nodded, absently and cleared his throat. "Is it okay with you if I try for Veronica?"

Rick let out a throaty laugh so that was it. "Help yourself."

He held up his hand. "There's nothing wrong with Ariene. Just that she's spoken for."

Rick didn't know what it was about Ariene that drove him crazy. He was acting like a teenager with the hots for a woman he couldn't get enough of. He'd never felt like that about Ariene before. They were friends, for heaven's sake. Put her in a room with him, now, though, and his body tightened up immediately.

Anger tore through him every time she hit him with that independence crap. He married her to help her achieve her dream. He expected to make a real marriage out of the situation. There was no reason for her to act as if she were alone in this. He was a man, after all. He expected to provide for his wife and child. But no. She bitched and carried on about living arrangements, and who paid the bills.

All this could be traced to that fool Todd. He'd treated Ariene like trash under his feet, and so she now felt she had to have *space*, when space had never been a problem with their friendship before.

Rick strove for calm. It infuriated him that anyone would treat someone as sweet as Ariene callously. He'd see to it that she had nothing but the best from here on out.

For now, he almost had to walk on eggs to get her to agree with anything. He was a patient man, but she brought even his patience to the edge.

Two emotions dominated his life these days, anger and lust. He wondered which one would win out in the end.

The entire contents of Ariene's one bedroom apartment filled the excess area in Rick's home. Before they fell asleep last night, she and Rick had outlined where each piece of furniture would fit. After their lovemaking, it was hard to get him to concentrate on furniture, so, between yawns, she did most of the planning. With his arms wrapped around her and snuggled up against her side, he'd lifted his head to agree with whatever she'd said, finally commenting that he didn't really care where the furniture went, to put it anyplace she wanted to.

Ariene smiled in remembrance. As the men carried in each item she directed them to exactly where it would fit. No sense in moving furniture twice.

Yvonne, Christine, Carrie—Ariene's mom—and Ella rinsed dishes and stacked them on the spacious shelves. Fitting them in wasn't a problem, since all Rick's kitchen appliances fit on one shelf. His younger brothers and sisters had cleaned him out of both furniture and appliances while he'd been stationed in Africa the last few years.

"I didn't know so many dishes could fit in one kitchen," Yvonne said, bending over to put a pan under the cabinet.

Ariene laughed while washing out a plate. "I never knew I had that many."

"I've never seen most of these," Yvonne continued.

"That's because they were packed away in the closet. You know I didn't have much room in my kitchen."

"You and my big brother," Christine said. "I still can't believe you finally did it." She put glasses in the dishwater.

Ariene smiled.

"Humph." Ella Cordell pinched her lips together, pulled a heavy copper frying pan out of a box and inspected it. "My son will be broke in no time if he has to keep you in expensive things like this."

"Since I own it, he won't have to buy it for me." Ariene countered. She refrained from telling the older woman that it had been a gift from Rick three Christmases ago.

"Mom, Rick's happy. Be happy for him," Christine said, rubbing her mother's back.

"Humph." Ella moaned again, setting the pan on the counter near Ariene. She'd complained about one thing or another all morning.

The women talked uncomfortably as they finished the last of the dishes. Soon after, the men came in with pizzas.

"Honey, why don't we eat on the deck?" Rick offered. "It's nice out."

"Okay by me."

"Aren't you the thoughtful one?" Ella said, smiling at her favored son. "I guess you got to make do when you got nobody to cook for you."

"You're not starting trouble with my new wife, now are you, Mom? I want my two favorite ladies to get along. It'll make me a very happy man."

"Well," Ella sputtered. "I'll do my best."

"I'm so proud of you," he said, and gave her a hug.

"Oh, go on with you. You always knew your way around me."

Christine rolled her eyes. "Come on, Mom." She urged her mother outside.

Rick put an arm around Ariene, while everyone else followed the pizzas to the deck.

"She getting to you?" he asked while nuzzling her neck.

"And then some. It's only one day. There are small blessings."

"At least everything's done, and now you can relax."

"Yes, thank heaven." She turned in his arms and touched his face. Even in shorts and a sweaty T-shirt, he looked good. "Go on out. I'll be right there." He gave her another squeeze and joined the others.

Ariene inhaled and stood where she was, enjoying the solitude. Standing in the center of the kitchen, she glanced around, marveling that the move was done so quickly.

Her café table fit nicely under a kitchen window that overlooked a fenced-in backyard. It was a yard perfect for children. She'd put a sandbox and swing set out, and spend time there with her child each morning before going in to work. While her toddler played, she'd putter around in the flower garden, maybe even tickle the little tyke with a marigold and bask in happy laughter.

On weekends, Rick, the baby, and she—now, where did that thought come from? The three of them? She'd barely moved into his home, and already she was putting them all together.

Ariene could easily grow accustomed to the larger accommodations. She'd been thinking more and more about offering to buy the duplex attached to Rick's. His brother and he had purchased it for rental property years ago. Rick had said that his brother was mumbling about selling it. Ariene sighed. She couldn't buy anything until her business was on even footing. Besides, Rick didn't want to hear that their arrangement was temporary again.

Looking to the side, Ariene saw that her rattan furniture had been moved onto the glassed-in sunroom located in back of the house, and her sofa in the family room. It presented a gorgeous view of a backyard which desperately needed tending.

To Ariene's mother's happiness and Ella's consternation, Rick had been giving Ariene newlywed, puppy love looks and easy, familiar kisses all morning. Ariene found she actually liked his attention.

She'd had to put up with Ella since six this morning. She could stomach the woman through lunch—hopefully.

"I'm going into the office for a few hours. Do you want me to drop you off?" Rick asked Ariene after everyone left.

"I'll drive."

Rick gathered her around the waist and kissed her neck from behind. He let her go with a worried frown.

He'd had dreams of sweeping her off her feet from the moment they married and made love together.

The fact that Ariene still thought of them as a temporary arrangement ate into Rick like a worrisome tick. He wondered why she'd want a child like him if she didn't feel that special accord.

Why couldn't she see they fit like two peas in a pod, the way they connected—all he'd had to do was touch her and she'd burst into flames. Yet, she could still say she was sleeping in a separate room. He hoped that after last night that issue was settled.

But Rick also realized that he wanted to give her time to accept him as a husband before they had a child together. That shouldn't be difficult, since she wanted to wait until the dilemma with the plaza was solved before getting pregnant.

Rick pulled into his office building parking lot. If he could arrange things as he wanted, he and his partners could build space as part of the co-op. It wouldn't cost more than they were paying now. Opening the car door, he remembered his partner saying the lease was due for renewal soon. But first, he'd call New York. One of his friends owned a grocery chain with several partners. They might be ready to expand in the metro DC area.

Ariene reconciled her books for the first two hours before she went on the floor to help customers. Around five-thirty, business slowed.

"Married life's treating you good already, girl," came a voice from behind her. She'd know that husky voice anywhere.

"Sylvia!" Ariene swiveled to face her college roommate. "I'm so glad to see you." They hugged, then held each other at arm's length. "How long has it been?"

"Too long," Sylvia said, wearing a smart black pantsuit. "I wanted to come to the wedding, but I couldn't cancel my trip."

"That's okay. I'm so happy to see you now."

"Talking about a hasty wedding, girl. It wasn't a shotgun one, was it?"

"Of course not." She had hit close to the reason for the wedding.

"Well, I wasn't surprised a bit when I got the invitation. You two were as thick as thieves at State. I wondered when you'd see that you two had that special connection—and see what was clear to the people around you."

Ariene drew pensive. "I didn't realize you thought that. You never said anything to me about it."

"If I had, you'd have gone screaming in the opposite direction. You know how obstinate you are when an idea lodges itself in your head."

Sylvia was the second person to say that today, Ariene mused.

"I didn't come emptyhanded." She picked up a shopping bag and handed it to Ariene. Peering in it, Ariene saw a wrapped package.

"Open it when the two of you are together, okay?" Sylvia patted Ariene on the hand. "It will bring back fond memories."

"Can you join us for dinner tonight? Rick will be thrilled to see you."

Sylvia waved a hand. "I wish I could. But I have plans. Besides, you're newlyweds. You don't need me intruding." Sylvia glanced at her watch. "I really have to go. I wish you nothing but happiness in your marriage."

Unbidden, tears came to Ariene's eyes. "Thank you," she whispered.

Sylvia gave her a quick hug and left. Ariene thought about their conversation after she stored the bag in back and returned to decorate the mannequin. Slowly draping a scarf around its neck, she wondered how many of her friends thought she and Rick were the perfect couple. And she wondered what she felt about Rick, now that they'd been lovers for a week.

Though she saw stars and comets during their lovemaking, she still felt a calm, comforting connection. She liked being with him, as she always had, which was why she was certain that a baby with him would make for a wonderful relationship, even though she and he would have separate lives.

At six, Yvonne came over while Ariene did last minute cleaning before leaving.

"We haven't had a minute to ourselves since you

returned. How was that honeymoon?'' Yvonne asked, and plunked her purse on the countertop.

"More than it should have been. I always have fun with Rick. You know that."

"Now you know I'm not talking about the fun. I'm talking about how he is in bed."

"We aren't teenagers, Yvonne." Ariene rolled her eyes.

"Yeah, yeah. Come on. Tell all."

"Let me just say that Rick's great at everything he does."

"Uh oh." Yvonne clutched her chest and sank into a chair. "Packed more than you thought, huh?"

"You know, I think I looked at him as a man for the first time. I was accustomed to seeing him as my gangly, high school friend."

"Uh huh." She nodded her head in agreement.

Ariene wasn't ready to discuss her feelings, so she changed the subject. "I'm really worried about this sell."

"Join the club." Yvonne put her elbow on the countertop and shook her head. "I started looking at rental properties in the want ads. The prices are phenomenal!"

"I know."

"At least you're married now. That's some consolation."

"Actually, it's not. I hope I'm not pregnant yet. We've decided to wait on the baby until I get another place."

Yvonne raised an eyebrow. "We, or you?"

"Okay, *I've* decided. Rick wants to go ahead with the plans. I think he wants a real marriage. But I can't even think of having a baby until this is resolved."

"I thought the marriage was real."

"You know what I mean."

"If you'd just met Rick, you'd see him in a different light than you see him now. I think every time you see him you remember the boy from the past, instead of the man now."

"I see the man now. I really do." Ariene sighed and walked behind the counter. "What a mess."

"So the two of you will just stay married indefinitely?"

Ariene pulled out a stool and sat beside her friend. "I don't know. He's so eager to be a dad. I hate to disappoint him."

"Let him be one, then. He'll make a good husband, and a great father."

"I'd planned to marry the man who . . ." Ariene inhaled. "I don't know." She massaged her forehead.

Yvonne covered Ariene's hand with her own. "You know, love isn't always fireworks. Sometimes it comes on slowly."

"I know I love Rick—like a friend." She paused and then went on. "Sylvia was here today. I haven't told anyone but you that this wedding is a farce, and she went on and on about how she'd known Rick and I were in love since she was my roommate in college."

"Ummm."

"I didn't have the heart to tell her why we really married. Yvonne, I'm such a fake."

"Ariene, don't worry yourself about this. The situation with Rick and you will work out."

Ariene knew it would—but how? Would she lose the best friend she'd ever had? Would sex eventually destroy their friendship? How would she ever bear it if he were no longer in her life? That frightened her most of all.

"Ariene. Your feelings for Rick aren't mixed up with what happened with Todd, are they?"

Ariene shook her head. "No. Of course not." Rick had made the same suggestion. Maybe she was cautious because of what she'd put up with with Todd. The cheating—the horrible treatment—the shouting and the pushing. She couldn't go out with her friends without him thinking she was meeting some man and berating her for hours once she returned. The final straw had come when he thought she should use her hard-earned money to pay for his fix. She hadn't even known he used drugs. She hadn't realized what a strain she'd been under until she put Todd out of her apartment.

To say that her parents disapproved of her arrangement was an understatement. It was one of the reasons her father was so protective now.

Rick was different. He would never treat her with less than his highest regard.

As Ariene and Rick prepared for bed that night, Ariene remembered the gift from Sylvia. She ran downstairs to retrieve the shopping bag from the closet.

"You went shopping today?" Rick asked when she returned to the bedroom after his shower. He wore only briefs.

Ariene tried to nonchalantly sit on the side of the bed. But her eyes kept straying to powerful thigh and chest muscles, and the image of how good they felt underneath her fingertips, as he paraded about the room. The illusion of his skin pressing against her body took her breath away. With only half her attention, she took the beautifully wrapped package out of the bag, and remembered his question. "No," she answered minutes later. "It's a gift from Sylvia. She visited the shop today."

"Oh?" He sat beside her on the bed, and stretched out his long, powerful legs.

Ariene sucked in a breath, knowing calm wasn't coming her way anytime soon. "Do you want to open it?"

"You do it," he whispered in her ear, and slid an arm around her waist. The thin silk gown she wore offered no protection against the heat of his body leaning against her or his fingers touching her. She wanted more.

"You're coming on a little strong, aren't you?"

"Is it working?" He nuzzled her neck.

"Do you want to see this gift or not?" Ariene asked as her fingers fumbled with the ribbons.

"Let me help you with that." The hand around her waist caressed her abdomen while he used the free hand to help with the ribbon and paper.

With her mind diverted to Rick's naughty fingers, Ariene finally just ripped the remainder of the paper off to reveal a beautiful silver and white album. Opening it, she gasped. On the first page was a picture of Rick and her at eighteen with their heads together and looking straight into the camera lens. They looked thoroughly happy.

Sylvia had been a photography buff in college and often took impromptu pictures of her friends.

Rick turned the pages because Ariene's senses were totally engrossed on his hands at this point, and getting him into bed. He revealed page after page of photographs of the two of them through their college years in various poses. They resembled a couple who belonged together.

What Yvonne and Sylvia had said to her was clearly evident in the photos—that special kinship with Rick.

Rick snapped the book closed, and put it on the bedside table. He pressed her back onto the bed, and Ariene knew there wouldn't be any separate beds for them anytime soon.

CHAPTER 6

One by one, the shopkeepers poured into the restaurant wearing pensive, worried expressions on their faces. Whispered comments abounded while Ariene talked to Yvonne, they all believed that they'd either have to move or start saving and prepare to pay more per square foot. Ariene adjusted the belt on the pin-striped suit she'd worn all day. She didn't have time to return home to change. At ten she took the lead in opening the meeting.

"First, I'd like to thank you for coming out tonight," she said in a clear, crisp voice, scanning the expectant faces. "Rick and I have made some inquiries on what can be done to save the plaza. But before he speaks, I'd like to know if any of you have any ideas." She paused, allowing time for someone to stand, but no one did.

"We want to know what you've come up with," Ramon called out, standing on the sidelines, his wife seated beside him.

"Then I'll turn the floor over to Rick." Ariene left the

podium and sat at a large round table close by to gather the papers she'd had Edward print earlier.

Dressed in a Italian-cut beige suit with dark brown stripes, Rick took the podium. "Good evening, everyone," he said.

Mumbled greetings were returned.

Ariene rose quietly from her chair and walked around the room, skirting the edges of the crowd to pass out the informational package as he talked.

"Ariene and I debated the issue this week, and spent a lot of time trying to come up with a tactic that would best serve all of us. We felt that a co-operative arrangement, where each shop owner would own his or her own space, would work well. And we'd have bylaws to keep standards on a professional level." He dug his hands into his pockets and walked to the front of the podium.

"I contacted a grocery chain, Always Fresh Grocers, in New York, who are ready to expand into this area. They have a group who are ready to begin their feasibility study, if you all agree to this arrangement. If they like this location, they are willing to work with us in developing a business plan and bylaws. They also have an approach to a bank that will include all of us. For our part, we will have to find buyers for the empty spaces."

Ariene watched Rick weave his spell on the room. She had a side view of him, and he reminded her so much of their school years. It seemed that, in every group project, she and Rick had been thrown together. And regardless of the number of people in the project, she and he had spent nights and weekends planning together. He was always so serious and thorough.

And he looked so good, Ariene thought. Her heart beat too fast and too hard as she watched him move with smooth, masculine grace.

He shucked his jacket as questions erupted from the

audience. Ariene rose from her comfortable chair and walked over to him to take the coat before he could move forward. Placing it on back of a chair, she sat and faced him again, watching the play of his shoulders and chest muscles and his nice, tight behind as he pounced back and forth, all male power and exuberance.

Why couldn't she love him as a wife should? She shouldn't have married him without loving him whole-heartedly, but he had some hold on her. Every night she found herself willingly and eagerly in his bed, in his arms, with him inside her. She couldn't say no to him—not because he wouldn't let her, but because *she* wanted *him*.

Yvonne stood. "Your plan is going to leave some of us out. Some of us have mortgages, and a bank isn't going to approve a loan that size."

"Which is the logic behind working up a comprehensive business plan. From the research I've done so far, the mortgages shouldn't be more than what you're paying right now. Remember, rates are going lower. It might do some good for most of you to refinance, anyway. The package Ariene handed to you details the information we will need for the plan. All information, of course, will be completely confidential. Remember, this will be a co-operative effort."

Everyone nodded, with worried frowns.

Edward stood. "That's well and good, but large conglomerates like that take forever to make decisions. We only have three months."

"They understand the time constraints we're working under." Rick said. "Remember, I know these people, and how they've worked before."

When the flow of questions slowed, Rick said. "You may want to think in terms of contacting local churches or business associations. With the land included in this deal, we can triple the number of shop spaces, and the demographics will support additional businesses as long as they aren't competing. There isn't enough land within a five mile radius to build a plaza of this size, and people will come if they see something new."

Everyone nodded, some of the worry decreasing, but not leaving.

"When will we know their decision?"

"They want to meet with us next Friday night, perhaps make some suggestions. I need to know how you feel about this."

"It sounds good to me," Ramon said. His swift response had everyone laughing, and the laughter served to expel the tension locked in the audiences' chest.

Yvonne nodded her head.

They received unanimous approval for the plans. Everyone was teetering on the edge—afraid to be too optimistic, yet burgeoning hope sprang to the surface, nevertheless.

Ramon bounded to the front, clapped Rick on the back, and shook his hand. "Wonderful, wonderful. Maria and I will get this completed for you immediately."

"Good," Rick responded, then turned as someone else clapped him on the shoulder. It was fifteen minutes before he and Ariene could leave.

Rick escorted Ariene to the car, wishing she were as enthusiastic about their marriage and as easily won over as the shopkeepers. He glanced down at her energetic form, looking svelte and businesslike yet pretty in her green suit. He couldn't wait to unwrap each article of clothing.

It was a good thing he hadn't been this attracted to her in school. Her dad would really have had reason to keep a close eye on them.

Rick swiped a hand across his head, trying to control his response to her.

"Thank you, Rick. Everyone's so pleased."

When he stopped at a red light, he leaned over and

kissed her lightly on the lips, his body responding from even that slight touch. "You're welcome," he said and pulled back as a horn honked. Looking forward and accelerating, he said, "Do you think you can get some time away tomorrow?"

"What for?" Ariene asked in the quiet darkness of the car's interior.

"I've been thinking of getting a living room set." He shrugged his shoulders. "I don't know a thing about furniture."

"Why? You're not in the States long enough to make a major investment and then leave it sitting for most of the year. That reminds me—will you be leaving soon?"

"It'll be a while yet," he responded. "But I really want that living room set. I can't entertain clients at home because I don't have decent furniture."

"Sure, I'll help you. Do you have something in mind?"

"Something elegant and understated, I think. Furniture I'll be comfortable with for entertaining, but not afraid to use. Something warm," he mused. "We might as well get a nice dining room set while we're at it."

"Have you thought about a color scheme?"

"Whatever you like."

Ariene laughed. "You have to live with it, not me."

Rick's hand tightened on the steering wheel. *Here we go again.* "But you have excellent taste. I trust you. You decorated my office, and I loved it. I was thousands of miles away when you did it."

Ariene took her day planner out of her huge purse. "Can you get away at three tomorrow afternoon?"

"That will work."

"We'll shop the discount furniture stores that sell name brand quality furniture. You want something that will last," she said scribbling her thoughts. "And we need art for the walls. Do you prefer prints or paintings?"

Rick shrugged.

"You already have some nice pieces you've brought from Africa. Why don't we look at them tonight, so when we're browsing furniture, we'll keep that in mind." She made a notation in her planner.

"Sounds good to me."

"That Ashanti rug you have rolled up in the garage is just beautiful, and will go wonderfully on the living room floor. Such understated blues, reds, and yellows on a cream background. We'll spread it out tonight." Ariene continued to write.

"It's late. Are you sure you want to do that tonight?"

"Definitely. I need to imprint the colors in my mind. Once we decide on the design of the sofa, we'll bring swatches home to match against the rug. It'll make it easier to select them if I have something stored in my mind." She closed the planner and shoved it into her overstuffed purse.

"You're the expert." Ariene had perked up some. Maybe the shopping would take her mind off the shopping center. He'd make sure she was taken care of, but he couldn't tell her that. She was too independent to accept his help.

He wanted what he'd had at Nassau: quiet walks hand in hand; a leisurely awakening with her after the best sleep, with her snuggled in his arms; protecting her when she was troubled; touching her at his will and not having to be careful because he was *only* a friend.

At least she was in his home. That was a start.

"I don't want you overdoing it. If you feel tired, let me know."

"I'm a bundle of energy. This isn't work for me. This

is a mission of love. I love decorating," she said as he pulled into the driveway in front of the duplex.

Quick and decisive by nature, Ariene had Rick marching from furniture store to furniture store the next day, looking at couch designs. She had him sitting on the cushions, asking him if they were too soft, too hard, too high, or too low. He was soon sick of the whole thing. Then she planted her own lush backside in the seats, wiggling and making him hot. She had the nerve to squeeze the armrest, and he had to put his jacket in front of him to keep from embarrassing himself.

How could there be so many samples of fabric for one lousy couch? In every store they sifted from page to page of contemporary, floral, paisleys, and others he couldn't remember.

It reminded him of the days in Africa when she'd searched for dyers, buttons, fabrics, seamstresses, and the million of little details that had to be taken care of to start her business. His head had spun then, too.

The only redeeming factor was that he stood close to her and could touch her without suspicion.

At least she wasn't thinking of losing her business again. All he could think of was getting her hot, lush behind home to bed. How he'd execute that hadn't come to mind just yet, he thought as she dragged him through another door.

"Look at that couch, Rick. I like that style."

"We'll get it, then," he quickly agreed and eased out a pleased sigh.

"Don't be too hasty," she warned as she urged him into the seat.

"All I know is, I'm hungry." He eased into yet another

cushion. By now he couldn't remember how one felt from the other.

"Just a little longer, then we'll call it quits for tonight. I think I can get off tomorrow early, so we can continue to look."

Not again. "We don't have to look every evening."

"I know, but it takes three months for them to make the couch. The sooner we select, the better."

"One of those floor models will do." Rick's eyes glazed over at the row upon row of couches, chairs, and tables, and he sighed as yet another salesman barreled down on them.

"If you've waited this long for a nice set, we might as well get something you can live with for years. You can afford it, so stop complaining," she said as she sat on the couch to test the cushions, wrapped her hand around the armrest, and squeezed.

"Let's go." Rick grabbed her hand, tugged her up, and dragged her out of the store before the salesman could reach them—him and his good ideas.

"What is wrong with you?" She skipped steps beside him, her purse swinging in the air.

"Nothing. Just tired of shopping."

"Will you slow down? I have to run to keep up with you."

"We're almost to the car." Rick slowed, just barely.

"If shopping is that bad for you, I'll do it alone. This is ridiculous." Winded, she breathed in puffs beside the car while Rick opened the door. Ariene glanced around. Just a few scattered cars were parked in this deserted, dark area of the parking lot.

Rick opened the door, but instead of letting her in he plastered her against the car with his body. The bulge in his pants against her stomach was solid evidence of his need for haste to get out of the store.

"Shopping does this to you?" she asked when he released her lips and kissed her neck.

"You and your couches," came his choppy reply.

"Maybe I'll bring you shopping, after all."

He groaned, but they heard some voices and he eased up, letting her slide onto the seat. Closing the door, he slowly walked around to his side. *How in the world did shopping for couches get him this hot and bothered?* Ariene wondered.

CHAPTER 7

Ariene's period was two days late. She could always count on it, like the days on a calendar. After sharing a breakfast with Rick of pancakes covered with whipped cream and fresh strawberries—for which she'd had a real craving—and urging him out the door early Wednesday morning, Ariene drove, dodging rush hour traffic, to the twenty-four hour CVS. Jumping out of her car, she slammed the door and ran to the store, trotting down two aisles before finding the pregnancy kits. Thumbing through them, she selected one, quickly paid for it, and drove home with a mixture of hope and dread pumping through her—hope because she could be pregnant with the baby she desired more than anything, and dread because this couldn't have happened at a worse time.

Once in the bathroom she followed the directions, and waited apprehensively as two pink lines appeared. She was pregnant. Of course, her honeymoon had hit at just the *right* week.

Ariene put the appliance on the sink. She had to tell Rick. If the plaza salvation attempt failed, that would add an added burden to him.

Ariene rubbed her abdomen, unable to hold back a smile at the image of her baby, no bigger than her thumbnail, harbored inside her womb that very moment—her very own, precious bundle of joy. She couldn't be anything but ecstatic. Funny, she didn't look any different—didn't feel any different.

What a great dad Rick would make. The image of him holding their child—loving it—brought tears of joy to her eyes. He had so much love to give.

But it was only temporary. Rick would be back in Uganda soon. She'd miss snuggling up with him, kissing him, loving him, touching him. If someone in high school had told her that she and Rick would be lovers one day, that she'd bask in his touch, she'd have told them they were crazy. But here she was, with not enough strength to move away from his bed and his loving, all the while knowing she should. If she felt this strongly about him now, how was she going to let him go after the baby arrived?

Love came into Ariene's mind. She knew she loved Rick—like the friend he'd been since forever.

So why wouldn't they fit in every way? Rick gave so much. Ariene needed to give something back. She'd be happy to decorate his home and entertain for him. Actually, she loved entertaining.

She was meeting him early today, to drag him along furniture shopping. She'd tell him about the baby when he picked her up.

Ariene wondered at his reaction. Would he love this precious baby as much as she did? It didn't take very long for her to come up with the answer. She knew he would love their child. By nature, Rick was a loving and caring man. She wanted their baby to know him, and for him to be around enough for the baby to benefit from his many stellar qualities.

Ariene dressed in a sky-blue pantsuit with tiny orange designs. In a few months, the suit wouldn't fit any longer.

In the end, Ariene called Rick and asked him to pick her up at home instead of at work. She changed into jeans and a red loose top, and swept her hair up into a French roll.

He looked so tired when he came in she almost didn't have the heart to break the news to him, but she couldn't tell anyone before she told him, and she was bursting to tell her parents and Yvonne.

"You look beautiful," he said and kissed her. "What's the occasion?"

"Thank you." She took his briefcase and put it in the closet, giving herself time to come up with the perfect phrase.

He scrubbed a hand over his face and headed for the stairs. "I'll be ready in five minutes," he said, and put his foot on the bottom step.

Ariene approached him. "Before that, there's something I have to tell you." She entwined her fingers in an uncustomary nervous gesture.

"Don't tell me. You've picked out ten more stores to drag me to," he said, facing her as he slid an arm around her. Standing there, Ariene was reminded that they needed something in the bare foyer.

Ariene laughed, her humor breaking up the tension. "Actually, I think I'm pregnant. I bought one of those home pregnancy kits at the store."

He'd stopped in his tracks and Ariene glanced up at him. She squealed when he squeezed her in his arms. He drew her back immediately.

"Did I hurt you?" Concern creased his face.

"Of course not." She laughed at his silliness.

He squeezed her again, lifted her up, and swirled her around and around in his arms. She held onto him, caught up in and loving every minute of his exuberance. Then he kissed her, deep, demanding, hot.

Ariene held onto her husband, loving the feel, the touch, the smell of him. Slowly easing her to her feet, he never let his lips lose contact with hers, but his hands, his sinful hands, charted his road map on her body, pulling ardent moans and sighs from her lips.

Her arms roamed his shoulders, scoring, soothing, stroking. Then cool air touched her skin. So involved was she in the sensations Rick drove through her, she didn't realize he'd undone her clothing. She stood before him in her bra and panties.

His lips left hers. "Are you happy?" he whispered.

"Very," she whispered back, "Are you?"

"Very." He scooped her into his arms and carried her up the stairs. She finished unbuttoning his shirt and reached inside, sliding her hand over the contours of his hard chest, feeling the unsteady beat of his heart.

They made it to the bedroom, and he eased her onto the spread and glided his large hands up her legs.

"You're driving me wild," he croaked.

"Am I?" Her husky voice was unrecognizable even to her.

He leaned on his elbows, his eyes smoldering with passion. "I'll touch every spot that's driving me wild."

"Promise?" she asked, a saucy tilt to her head.

"Promise," he moaned, and then fulfilled the promise.

An hour later, with her head on Rick's shoulder, Ariene felt that shopping was the farthest thing from her mind.

She stroked the arm lying across her breast, basking in contentment.

"How do you feel?" Rick asked her, his warm breath brushing her hot skin.

"Marvelous," she responded, too languid to move.

He kissed her on top of her head. "You got your wish." He moved to lean against the headboard and positioned her to lean against him. Her head fit just under his chin.

Suddenly, Ariene didn't feel quite as complete as she thought she would. Although she was ecstatic about the baby, something was missing. She was reminded of a childhood adage: "Be careful what you wish for. You just might get it."

"Yes," she sighed. "I got my wish." She turned in his arms to face him, their breaths mingling. "What about you? What do you feel?"

"I'm happy for you, Ariene."

"What would make you happy?"

The smile left his face. "I am happy. I've got all I need or want in my arms."

Ariene stroked his face. Rick tightened his arms around her, easing his lips on hers. This time the kiss was gentle, the touching less harried.

"If we keep this up, we'll never eat. And you're eating for two, now."

"Ummm." Ariene snuggled closer. "I'll fix dinner."

"In a few min—" he cut off at the sound of the doorbell. Wrinkles appeared in his forehead as he frowned down at her. "You expecting someone?"

"No."

Rick eased out of bed, and Ariene watched the strong line of his body as he stepped into his jeans and grabbed a T-shirt. When he left the room, she rose from the wrinkled covers and went into the bathroom to shower. Stopping in front of the mirror, she ran a hand down her abdomen, knowing she wouldn't look any different but feeling different, nevertheless.

She took a long, leisurely shower, using her subtle, rose-scented gel, expecting Rick to join her at any moment. When he didn't, she exited and dried herself with a soft, fluffy towel and wiped the steam off the mirror.

Leaving the bathroom, she entered the bedroom and searched through the drawers for lacy panties and bra. She had barely pulled them on when Rick appeared at the door.

"Honey, are you ready to come downstairs?" he asked hesitantly.

"Yes, why? Who was at the door?"

"My mom."

"Oh." She didn't want the moment spoiled by Rick's mom.

"It won't be that bad," he said, but Ariene knew that wasn't the case.

"Yes, it will. Did your dad come with her?" He could stem her acerbic tongue.

"He's here."

"Thank goodness. I'll be right down." Rick turned and left, the carpet cushioning his steps. Ariene rushed to the closet and rooted for a caftan. She found a beige one with green and red stripes down one side. Donning it, she brushed out her hair and reluctantly descended the stairs to join them.

Mr. Cordell stood and kissed Ariene on the cheek. "How's my favorite daughter-in-law?" he said by way of greeting.

"Just wonderful. How is my favorite father-in-law?" Ariene returned.

"Couldn't be better," he said, and returned to the black leather couch, sitting close to his wife.

She and Rick really needed to find better furniture for

the living room, Ariene thought. Then maybe this set could go the route of Rick's other furniture. He still had a brother in college who could probably use it.

"Rick, dear. That's chicken and dumplings I brought for you," Ella said. "I know how much you love it, and you probably don't get it anymore."

"Thank you, Mom. Ariene and I will enjoy it. But she's a wonderful cook. Her mother taught her well." Ella tended to forget that Rick was in Africa most of the time, and had to fare for himself.

"I guess you can have it for dinner. I don't smell anything cooking."

"Ariene and I just got home from work, Mom."

His dad captured Ella's hand and gave it a warning squeeze, then stood. "We need to be heading back. It's a long drive." He tugged on her arm.

"But—" she sputtered, coming reluctantly to her feet.

"Come on, Ella." He took her elbow and urged her toward the door.

Rick and Ariene stood, as well, Ariene happy because the visit was short. "It's so nice of you to stop by," she said to them.

Rick's father patted her hand and exited the door.

"Well, we'll be checking up on you, Rick. Make sure you don't lose any weight," Ella said.

"I'm well fed, Mom, but thanks."

Rick's dad opened the car door for his wife and she dropped into the seat. Then he went around to his own door.

Ariene and Rick waved at them as they backed out into the road.

"I can't imagine dealing with your mother until this baby reaches eighteen." Ariene groaned at the thought.

"She'll get better once she has the baby to fuss over."

"She's going to think I got pregnant and you *had* to marry me."

Rick eased an arm around her. "Don't worry so much. I'm the one you have to worry about." He opened the door and they entered the kitchen, Ariene's mouth watering at the aroma from the chicken and dumplings. "At least you don't have to cook supper."

CHAPTER 8

Two months later, Ariene discovered that if she ate, she regurgitated, that if she didn't eat, it was worse. After throwing up the second time that morning, she ran cold water over a washcloth and wiped it across her face. The cold wetness against her clammy skin felt heavenly.

Hanging the cloth on the towel bar, she pressed her hand against the bulky shirt and perused her shape in the mirror. It was still too early to see a change. Her body responded to the differences, though. Her breasts were larger, tender, and more sensitive to Rick's touch. She enjoyed that part of pregnancy. In two months her tummy would start to enlarge with her growing baby.

She reached for the toothbrush and applied paste, thinking of the plaza. Everyone was nervously awaiting a call from the bank to see if their business plan was approved. Rick and she had worked harder than they ever had, burning the midnight oil, perfecting the plan to the very last

detail. They even had firm commitments for the empty
spaces, and those had been included.

Finished with brushing, Ariene rinsed her mouth and
headed downstairs. On her way to the kitchen, she
glimpsed the living room and stopped. The cream colored
sofa set arrived a few days ago, and Rick and she had hung
the African art on the walls. The room was comfortable
and elegant, just as Rick had requested.

Ariene's noisy stomach reminded her that she was on
her way to the kitchen. She was starving—again.

The phone rang, and she ambled to the counter to
answer it.

"Hello, honey, how're you feeling?" Rick's voice still
sent pleasurable warmth through her.

Ariene sank onto the stool. "Don't ask." She grabbed
an apple from the fruit bowl.

"I have got good news for you. Are you sitting?" he
asked.

"Yes . . ." She dropped the apple and clutched the
countertop. "What is it?"

"The bank approved the plan."

"Oh, my God." She stood, walking the cord to its length.
"I can't believe it!" she shouted.

"Believe it." He laughed at her excitement.

"Everyone will be so pleased. I can't wait to tell Yvonne."

"I'm calling the other owners, but I wanted to tell you
first, sweetheart." The endearment held a promise for
later.

"How can I ever thank you?"

"You don't have to. I'm getting office space in the back,
and I don't have to worry about increases in the lease."

"Yeah, but you didn't *have* to move. I do."

"I'll see if the other owners would like to have a celebration dinner later this week. Perhaps Saturday night after
the restaurant closes? Everyone can relax this time."

"That's a wonderful idea."

"I'll call the Chavez's after I hang up and get back to you with their answer."

"Sure." Ariene twisted the cord around her finger. "And Rick?"

"Yeah?"

"Thank you isn't enough."

"It's more than enough. We'll celebrate tonight, so wear something special."

"I'm treating you, Mr. Cordell."

He paused. "I'm looking forward to it, Mrs. Cordell."

Ariene eased the phone on the receiver, *Mrs. Cordell* still resounding in her mind. Though her last name had technically changed, she'd never gone through the process of getting her driver's license, credit cards, or check statements changed.

Temporary. Ariene didn't like the sound of that any longer, and wondered why. Did she really want to leave Rick once the baby came? She was really happy with him—happier than she'd ever been. Ah. She was being silly. She'd lived all these years alone. Her life would be full with the baby and her business when he left on his assignment, and he would return to visit their child.

Ariene sighed. None of these thoughts were very palatable at the moment. The pregnancy was responsible for all these silly feelings. They would go away when the baby arrived.

Ariene ate her apple while she cooked a ham and cheese omelet. She had a craving for eggs.

Crepe streamers were strung around the room, candles adding romantic luminance. When Rick and Ariene entered, Rick used a moment to take in the scene. Party hats were placed at each place setting, along with party whistles.

Several tables were pulled together to form one huge table, and a side buffet was laden with hors d'oeuvres and punch.

All the shop owners attended the Saturday night dinner. The happy crowd was the complete opposite of the somber group from the last few meetings. It was truly a celebrative experience. Even the people from Always Fresh Grocers made an appearance.

Ariene looked lovelier than he'd ever seen her. She wore a long gown made in Ghana. It fit beautifully, and was still tight enough to outline her shape.

He hadn't wanted a woman as much since his teenage years. Even after being married for nearly three months, they came together as if they couldn't get enough of each other.

Love really made a man crazy. Rick wondered if she realized she loved him, as well. Knowing Ariene, she'd deny it, kicking and screaming, to the very end. She didn't realize yet that fifty years from now they'd still be together. He'd wanted her too much, for too long, to ever let her go.

He realized he didn't create the fireworks of a more macho type, but he certainly hoped he was growing on her, little by little.

She was so beautiful. He observed her as she talked animatedly with Edward's wife, debating ads they could work up for advertising the plaza business in local churches.

"Ah, the man of the hour," Ramon said.

Rick glanced at the man, who stood next to his table, and who raised his hand now to get everyone's attention.

"We promised there will be no speeches tonight, so I left the podium and microphone in storage. But we did collect a little something for a gift for you." He clutched the envelope to his chest. "Come here, Ariene," he called out.

She left Maria and Yvonne to stand beside Ramon.

"You've worked so hard on this project. We know you need to get away with your beautiful wife. So this is just a tiny token of our undying gratitude. We can never thank you enough for your assistance."

Everyone stood and clapped as Rick accepted his gift and opened it. It was a coupon for a weekend at a famous bed and breakfast at the foot of the Blue Ridge Mountains. Rick stood.

After the cheering, he said, "Thank you. I couldn't have wished for any better gift than one that would let me enjoy a weekend with my lovely wife." Everyone cheered and laughed. "Thank you so much."

CHAPTER 9

In her ninth month of pregnancy Ariene looked, walked, moved, and sat like a beached whale, and she hadn't been able to tilt her head to see her feet in months. Even though her obstetrician assured her that only one baby was in her womb, Ariene was certain there had to be at least two.

She eyed the newspaper—ten feet away. It would stay right where it was until Rick made an appearance. Ariene closed the front door and poured her cup of tea, sighing—it would have been nice to read the paper while she sipped on it.

Just as she eased her bulk into the kitchen chair, the doorbell rang. She looked toward the stairs and took her time standing. After a sound night of sleep, Rick was singing some silly song while he dressed. She didn't know what a full night of sleep was anymore. The baby, pressing right on her bladder, kept her jumping up half the night, and leg cramps were the order of the day, not to mention bruised ribs from the fierce kicks. Ariene rubbed her distended abdomen with a loving stroke. This little bundle of joy was worth all the discomforts. In two more weeks was her due date.

Ariene opened the door. A beautiful woman wearing a smart, fitted gray business suit, looking like Ariene wanted to look, extended the paper to her. At the sight of Ariene a surprised look crossed her flawless, creamed-coffee face. Ariene took the paper.

"Thank you. It's not easy getting down there any longer."

The woman smiled and looked at the brass numbers by the door. "I must have copied the wrong address."

"Who were you looking for?" Ariene had met the neighbors, and could point her in the right direction.

"I'm looking for Rick Cordell's home."

"Rick lives here. Come in." Ariene stepped back so the woman could enter.

The singing had subsided to a whistle as Rick came bounding down the stairs.

"Rick, you have company," Ariene said.

On the last step, he stopped. "Veronica."

Veronica crossed her arms, her expression pinched as she looked from Ariene's extended belly to Rick. "You've got some explaining to do."

"Veronica, meet my wife, Ariene."

The woman uncrossed her arms to let them dangle at her side. "Your wife! How *dare* you marry another woman while you were engaged to me!"

"Engaged!" Ariene shouted. "You married me when you were engaged to her? How could you do that?" Ariene felt like smacking him on the arm for his callousness, which was totally unlike him.

Rick shrugged his shoulders as if it were nothing. "She broke the engagement. As far as I was concerned, it was over." He said it as if breaking an engagement was nothing, but Ariene knew he wasn't a callous man.

"Let's go out and talk, Veronica. I don't want to upset Ariene in her condition."

"You know I didn't mean it, Rick. How many times have we broken the engagement and then repaired it?"

"That's neither here nor there. It was over ten months ago. I sent you a telegram in Baluchistan, confirming it. Didn't you get it?"

"No, I didn't."

"I guess their telegraph system is no better than the phones." Rick strode to the kitchen and picked up his keys. "I'll be back within an hour, in plenty of time to take you to work. Call me on the portable phone if you need me." He had the nerve to kiss Ariene before he left with that woman!

The man she loved was engaged to another woman. Ariene lumbered to the kitchen and slid into the café chair. Plunking her elbows on the table, she looked out onto the backyard.

For a while now, she'd dreamed that she and Rick might even stay together and raise their baby.

Reassuring little kicks plummeted against her abdomen. Ariene rubbed the area like an Aladdin's lamp, the hope of a traditional family for her child dying.

Ariene stiffened her spine. She'd fight for him. They'd been living under one roof for nine months, now. He had to feel something for her. She could work on that.

How could she trap a friend who had been even more than a friend to her though? How many men would have come to her rescue? The least she could do was give him his freedom to live with the woman he loved.

But her baby deserved the best, too. Ariene stroked her abdomen. How could she have put her precious little baby in this dilemma? Why couldn't she have thought beyond her maternal craving?

Headstrong and *stubborn* were verbs her father often used when referring to her. They certainly proved true.

She loved Rick. He was no longer the pimply teenager who was her friend. He was a virile, strong, understanding man she'd grown up with. How could she have missed this part of him all her life?

Ariene rose to go upstairs. It was time to dress for work. A smile crossed her face at the thought of work. The renovation of her store was completed two weeks ago. The brightly illuminated space was light, airy, and inviting to her customers. Best of all, all the space had been sold, and Ariene had been able to save more money than ever. It was time she started searching for a home for her baby and herself.

She waddled into the baby's room she and Rick had spent weeks decorating so beautifully. Rick had painted the walls green, and they had put up wallpaper decorated with yellow, pink, blue, and green balloons on the bottom half of the room.

A mobile was attached over the white crib, and the white dresser and changing table awaited their baby's arrival. All this had been done with expectancy, fun ribbing, and laughter.

Her baby's father wouldn't live with them, but she'd do everything in her power to make his or her life as rewarding as she could. *Oh, Rick. Please spend some time with our child. At least let him know that you love him as much as I do.*

Ariene and Rick had shared the king-size bed for the last few months. With his fianceé back, they couldn't share a bed any longer. She'd move back to her own bedroom tonight. Right now, it was going to take all her effort to dress and get to work.

Ariene rubbed her back. She'd done too much work

yesterday, and she was paying for it today. It wasn't often that she got a burst of energy these days. She'd decided to take advantage of it. At least the house was sparkling. Rick had eventually dragged her to bed, but she'd finished by that time.

Angry, Rick stopped by the shop to talk to her, but so many customers were there that she couldn't spare the time. She should be grateful for his help, but along the edges of her senses she was angry. She'd asked him if he were involved with anyone, and he'd said no.

"I'll talk to you later," he whispered. "I have to go into the office. You shouldn't have left the house."

"I couldn't be late for work waiting for you to finish your *conversation* with your fianceé."

His lips tightened. "She's *not* my fianceé. I'll see you later." Just to be defiant, he kissed her again and charged out.

Suddenly, keeping him meant more than the biological functioning of fatherhood. It was having the most physically and emotionally secure home possible for her child. Having both a father and mother was necessary for that. Rick had stressed that point from the very beginning— the traitor.

On that point he'd been correct. He'd always said she doggedly charged straight ahead—sometimes without thought. Look at what charging ahead had gotten her this time. And it was all her fault. She was the one who went into this thinking that she could be both mother and father. She was the one who insisted that she could do this all alone.

A sharp pain ran through Ariene's back. She didn't have the time to sit it out. She had two weeks before the baby was due, so she couldn't be in labor. She could time her pregnancy almost to the day.

Ariene berated herself for working so hard yesterday. Sparing only a brief moment to rub her back, she ambled over to help a customer.

At six that evening, as Ariene made what seemed like her hundredth trip to the bathroom, her water broke. On her way back to the shop she stopped by Yvonne's bookstore and pulled her to the side.

"My water broke."

"Oh, my Lord. Let's call Rick and get you to the hospital."

"I'm not calling Rick. My contractions are eight minutes apart. I think I should go home and grab my bag. I'm going back to my store, and I'll call and let my obstetrician know I'm leaving."

"Okay, okay. I'll meet you at your store. Just stay put." Yvonne nervously ran her hands over her hair.

"Calm down. It'll be hours yet before the baby arrives," Ariene said, and left to try to make it back to her store before another cramp came on.

As soon as Ariene returned to her store, another sharp pain hit her. Recovering, she called her obstetrician, who warned her to get to the hospital when the contractions were five minutes apart.

Ariene grabbed her purse and waited for Yvonne—needing Rick. She had to let Rick go, though, and now was the time to start.

Along with the contractions, came the emotional drain from her day's ordeal. She and Rick had gone to Lamaze classes together. He was supposed to be her coach.

Yvonne would pitch in in a crunch.

* * *

The deep breaths weren't lessening the pain. She breathed in and out, using the Lamaze technique, until the contractions eased. They were three minutes apart, and Yvonne was no help at all. She merely nervously fluttered about in her paper cap, robe, shoes, and mask—Ariene could only see her eyes—resembling a creature from an outer space movie.

"You're making me nervous, Yvonne. Sit down, please." Maybe she should have called Rick, after all. The floral wallpaper kept the birthing room from looking sterile. Her doctor had arrived an hour ago, dressed casually in green slacks and a blouse. This was the first time Ariene had seen her without her usual suit. The young obstetrician used state-of-the-art equipment and techniques, and had no qualms about explaining any minute detail that Ariene asked about. She'd just celebrated her fortieth birthday.

The door opened and another robed figure entered the birthing room. Ariene looked into Rick's eyes, eyes that were stormy with anger.

"How's it going?" His tone belied the daggers flashing from those gorgeous eyes.

"Tough." What right did he have to be angry?

"Thank God you made it. I need a cigarette," Yvonne said.

"You don't smoke," Ariene told her. "I'm the one in pain here."

"She's making no sense," Yvonne said eying the door.

"I'll take over." Rick stooped beside her.

He looked so good, Ariene thought just as another contraction hit her. He held her hand and breathed and talked with her . . . just as they had in the Lamaze class. The anger in his expression had turned to worry. She had some anger of her own hovering in the background.

Right after the contraction let up, the nurse came in to examine her. At that point, Ariene didn't want anybody to touch her. All she wanted was for the baby to get here in a hurry. When the nurse left, another contraction tore into Ariene, and she screamed at Rick.

"How could you marry me when you're engaged to another woman? How could you *lie* to me, and make me believe you'll be there for the baby and me?" she strained out between puffs.

"Just *breathe*. We'll talk about it later."

Ariene breathed because she didn't have a choice. She felt as if an axe had clawed into her. But she wanted to talk *right now*. Finally, the contractions subsided.

"I'm not engaged," Rick started. "I'm married to you. It was over with Veronica before she left for Baluchistan. We agreed to marry to form a business alliance between her uncle and my company, but I couldn't marry for that reason. We didn't love each other."

"You married me, and you didn't love me."

"You're different. I've always had special feelings for you, Ariene. We've always had a special love. I wouldn't have married you if I were engaged to someone else. I don't love her," he pronounced just as another contraction tore into her. "Now *breathe*."

"You . . . sure?" she huffed.

"I'm sure. I'm here aren't I?"

Ariene tightened her hand around his, and with the other she caressed his cheek. She loved him so much, and he was here. She needed him. Their baby needed him. "Stay with me." Ariene forgot to notice that she had made a vulnerable gesture. She wasn't supposed to be vulnerable.

"Always," he whispered and kissed her.

* * *

Mr. and Mrs. Ariene and Rick Cordell were honored
with a precious baby girl they named April, at 2:06 A.M.
The proud papa cut the umbilical cord as the screaming
infant lay on Ariene's stomach.

Yvonne danced around the room, snapping pictures.
She had plenty of blackmail material.

"I'm never having babies. I'll always be an aunt," she
assured everyone.

Ariene's laugh was weak. The nurse handed her her
precious, wrapped bundle of joy, and Rick sat beside her.
They cuddled together while Yvonne continued to snap
pictures and the doctor finished with Ariene.

"Don't you three look wonderful? Both sets of grandparents are in the waiting room."

CHAPTER 10

At six weeks old, April had already started to plump out, and Ella had lessened her visits to no more than once a week. For the first week after Ariene came home, her mom stayed with Rick and her to help out. The second week, Ella moved in, and was more aggravation than comfort. Rick tried to discourage her from staying, but she insisted that they needed help, with Ariene just out of the hospital. She busied herself with fixing meals, doting on her grand-baby, and getting on Ariene's nerves. Ariene kissed her father-in-law for coming to get Ella after four days.

Now, Rick was in California, and her mom had stayed the week to help her. She'd left for home an hour ago.

Today, at her six-week doctor's appointment, Ariene had been given the okay to resume an active sex life. Rick had been his usual caring self with her and the baby. Ariene only wished she knew where things would go from here. For sure, she'd broach the subject tonight after he returned. Since she was breastfeeding the baby, she couldn't take birth control pills, but she needed to use some protection—if she and Rick were to continue.

Sunday was Mother's Day and her life should feel complete with her new baby, but now she needed more.

She wanted her baby's father to stay. Her reaction was totally selfish, and she accepted the blame. That didn't mean she wasn't going to do what she could to keep her baby's father, the man she loved.

Did he love her? She sighed, remembering his words in the birthing room. She really couldn't keep him, if he decided not to stay. Life didn't always work out the way one wanted it to.

Ariene pulled a box containing the nightgowns Yvonne had given her out of her closet. As she opened the cover, the delicate rose sachet Ariene had placed within perfumed the air. The gown she wore her wedding night was neatly folded on top. Could it do its magic again? She hadn't worn it since that night. And his reactions on their wedding night were worth repeating.

Ariene crushed the gown to her chest. She couldn't sex him to death. There had to be more than sex in their relationship for it to be lasting. If not, they were doomed to fail. And he did deserve happiness in his life—the kind of happiness one got when two people truly loved each other.

Ariene dressed April in a beautiful pink romper and tied a pink ribbon around her sparse hair. She spent the afternoon between cooking a dinner to die for and cuddling with April. She was such a good baby.

This was the night. She was determined to tell Rick tonight that she loved him, and . . . what?

Whatever his feelings were, she'd discover them tonight.

Ariene put the finishing touches on dinner and ran

upstairs to finish dressing. She'd washed and tucked April into her crib, and she was fast asleep.

After looking in on April, Ariene donned her sexy garter belt. She smoothed on sheer, skin-toned stockings and three inch slim heels, the perfect complement to her short black, spaghetti-strap dress. She then attached her gold necklace and smoothed it in place. Her hair would be better up tonight, for easy access to her neck.

She intended to trace every heated vein in Rick's body tonight—after he was stuffed with her dinner and revived from the trip in a nice hot tub, if they could stand to wait that long.

Ariene saw the cab pull up in the yard. After only a cursory look, she ran to the nursery. April had wakened, and Ariene plucked her out of the crib before Rick entered the house.

"Ariene!" he called out.

Carrying the baby, she went to the stairs. At the foot stood Rick—and Veronica.

"Yes?" Ariene spoke softly, slowly descending the stairs.

"Hi," he said, looking at the baby. "She looks as if she's grown." He took the baby from Ariene's arms when she reached them.

"Oh, isn't she precious?" Veronica squealed. When the woman lifted a finger to touch her baby's cheek, Ariene wanted to break it. "And she looks just like you, Rick. Ooh."

April gave them a beaming, yawning smile at just that moment.

"And look at that gorgeous smile."

"Honey," he said to Ariene, "we have to go to the office for a few hours. Don't wait up for me." He handed the baby back to Ariene, then went through the kitchen to enter the garage.

The door shutting behind him was like a door shutting on her marriage, and on this happy time in Ariene's life.

So much for the celebration dinner she'd prepared. More important, had she lost Rick? Now that the baby was here, did he think his part of the bargain was over?

Ariene hugged her precious bundle close to her and inhaled the sweet baby smell as April yawned and looked up at her with gorgeous brown eyes.

Ariene ascended the stairs and put April on her bed while she changed clothes and donned jeans and a red shirt. Then she picked up her precious child and went back downstairs. She fixed her plate, and the baby nursed as Ariene ate. Even though she'd lost her appetite, as a nursing mother she had to get the proper nourishment.

When Ariene went to bed at eleven, Rick still hadn't returned. Before she finally succumbed to sleep, she remembered seeing the digital clock flash eight after twelve.

Ariene heard the baby's cry at five Sunday morning. She awakened in Rick's arms. Throwing the covers back, and with her eyes only half open, she went down the hall to get the baby. She changed April's diaper and sat in the rocker to nurse her. Instantly, the baby calmed. When Ariene touched her soft little hand with her finger, she immediately wrapped her little fingers around it.

It was Mother's Day, and she had the precious child she craved so very much—but she didn't have the father. After nine months together she'd expected more of a commitment from Rick. Although he married her for the baby, she'd grown to love him so much more than just as a friend.

So many questions lay unanswered. She dreaded the conversation she knew they must have. Had she driven him away when he was trying to get closer to her? On the trip to California, had he discovered that he loved Veronica, after all? If so, why not tell her?

Where did they go from here?

The baby finished nursing, and Ariene lifted her to her shoulder and patted her back, feeling her reassuring heartbeat. She couldn't resist kissing her sweet cheek where milk had dripped after the burp. Ariene needed her warmth against her, and instead of returning her to the crib, she placed her against her chest and held her as she rocked.

Rick walked in, eyes leaden with too little sleep.

"Hi," he said, yawning.

"Hi," Ariene said quietly. He walked over to them and ran a finger down April's cheek. "I'll put her in the crib for you," he offered, but Ariene shook her head no.

"I want to hold her."

He smiled and ran a finger down her cheek. "I'm sorry I got back so late," he said softly.

"Why were you?"

"We got a new contract while I was away. I needed to do some preliminary work on it for Curt."

"Oh, really?" Ariene said softly, trying not to disturb April.

"What's wrong?" he asked, raising his eyebrow. "You have that look."

"Have you taken up with Veronica again?"

"Veronica?" he pulled back. "Of course not. What kind of man would that make me—living with you, and carrying on with her? Have you ever known me to do that?"

"I know this arra—"

"To hell with the arrangement." The baby stirred in Ariene's arm, and he lowered his voice.

"Then why was she with you?"

"We came back on the same plane. She was on her way to the office to see Curt."

Ariene was only partially mollified.

He blew out a breath, then neared her and pulled her up with the baby. Sitting in the rocker, he pulled her down on him to lean against his chest. The warmth of his chest and rhythmic beat of his heart was all the more comforting than it should have been. He wrapped his arms around her, holding her and the baby close to his heart, and rested his chin on her head.

"We should have talked a long time ago. I missed you. I missed this," he whispered.

She was too vulnerable. "I missed you."

"Ariene," Rick said softly, "I love you."

She turned to face him. "Oh, Rick."

He lifted a finger and moved her chin so she looked directly into his eyes. "You weren't jealous, were you?"

"Hell, yes," she said, and hoped her little precious hadn't heard.

"Why?"

"Because I love you. I couldn't stand for you to love another woman."

"I must have loved you all my life. You spoiled me for anyone else."

And then he kissed her, with April resting on her shoulder—a sweet and comforting kiss that promised all their tomorrows together, and all the happiness she'd experienced with him for the last year.

"Happy Mother's Day, sweetheart." He reached in his pocket and handed her a long, thin package.

Ariene opened it to reveal a diamond bracelet with two rows of diamonds.

"It's beautiful," she said, her eyes misting because he'd thought of her, as busy as he was.

"Not nearly as beautiful as you are. You've made me a very happy man." His arm tightened around her.

Ariene kissed him. "I got my okay from the doctor," she whispered against his lips.

"Then what are we waiting for?"

ALL THE WAY HOME

RAYNETTA MAÑEES

Dedication

This story is dedicated to my grandmother, Annie Mc-Donald Knight. God willing, she will celebrate her 100th birthday the month this story is released. And to my grand-daughter, Zayna Raylon Hurd, for some quotes I never would have thought of on my own!

Acknowledgement

To my good friend, Dr. LaSalles Pinnock. Thank you for being a special godfather to my child.

CHAPTER 1

"Mr. Jamison? Mr. Jamison!" Jolene had to sprint to catch up with the rapidly retreating broad back after a man shouldering a two-by-four had pointed Jamison out to her.

Jamison turned to glance at her briefly. "Yes?" he said in a deep and somewhat irritated voice as he continued on his way.

"Mr. Jamison ..." By then they had reached gravel. One of Jolene's heels caught on a rock, and she stumbled. She threw her arms outward, just barely regaining her balance before falling. Mr. Broad Back stopped, then turned and crouched to pick up the notepad and pen she had dropped.

"Are you all right?" he asked, handing back her things. He seemed grudgingly concerned, despite his full lips being drawn into a severe straight line.

Jolene couldn't help but think how handsome his face

would look had it been cordial. He seemed anything *but* cordial.

"Yes. Yes, I'm fine," Jolene gasped as offhandedly as she could manage. Truth to tell, she had turned her ankle, and had begun to feel a small but very definite throb. But Jolene was hanged if she'd let *him* know that. *Who does he think he is, anyway, turning his back on me and walking away like that?*

Jamison merely grunted in reply. *Jeez, what a charmer,* Jolene mused. *Just a massive—albeit fine—hunk of muscle with no couth, and no class.*

"Mr. Jamison, I'm Jolene Jeffries from Channel Seven, and—"

"I know who you are," he said shortly, starting once again toward the rear of the site. "You were *supposed* to be here two hours ago."

"Yes. I know. I'm sorry." Jolene was losing in her struggle to keep up with him, the ankle aching more and more with each step. "But there was a fire downtown we had to cover, and . . ." *Why am I explaining myself to this . . . this Neanderthal?* Jolene suddenly reflected. She stopped abruptly. Jamison went several paces before he realized she was no longer beside him, and stopped.

"What's the matter?" he queried.

"Nothing. Nothing at all, Mr. Jamison," Jolene replied in her best nice–nasty tone, looking him dead in his charcoal black eyes. "It's just that I'm getting the impression that this is not a particularly expedient time for your interview."

Jamison crossed his arms. "Two hours ago would have been a lot more expedient," he replied pithily.

"Hey, Ronny!" a man yelled from the back of the lot. "You think this cement is gonna wait 'til you *feel* like pouring it? And you know we've only got the mixer until six o'clock!"

"And that's *why* two hours ago would have been more expedient," Jamison continued, sweeping his arm toward the guy. "I'm trying to *construct* something right now, lady. That's what a construction company does. And I ain't got time now for styling and profiling on TV!"

The nerve of him! "I see," Jolene came back frostily. "Perhaps we can set another date for your interview next week—if we can fit it into *our* schedule!" She turned curtly to her cameraman. "Come on, Frank. Let's get out of here, and let Mr. Jamison get on with his *constructing!*"

Jolene's turn was a bit *too* sharp, and the injured ankle suddenly gave. This time she couldn't recover her footing. Frank reached for her, but the camera was in his way. Jolene braced herself for the bruising punishment of the gravel, but instead found herself suddenly lifted up. Jamison had bridged the few feet between them in seconds and effortlessly swept Jolene up into his powerful arms.

Jamison looked down at Jolene, "Maybe *next* week it'll occur to you to not wear high heels to a construction site . . ." He looked down at Jolene, and—wonder of wonders—a smile slowly materialized on his comely features. "Not even ones as cute as these," he continued, looking at Jolene's feet.

Jolene was speechless—and only partially from the suddenness of the situation.

Jamison was staring deeply into her eyes, as if really seeing her for the first time. Jolene found herself momentarily transfixed by his gaze, by the secure strength of his grasp. She noticed for the first time the silver strands liberally distributed through his thick, curly, black hair, and through the thick lushness of his mustache. The deep cleft in his chin became more pronounced in accompaniment to the unexpected smile.

"I'm . . . I'm all right now. Please put me down," Jolene shakily insisted. She was mortified. *He must be so strong to pick me up like that! I bet he's regretting that move right about now.*

"Are you sure?" Jamison asked with a broad smile.

Jolene's thoughts rushed on. *Why, he's laughing at me!* "Yes! Yes, I'm *fine,*" she said forcefully, squirming in his embrace. "Put me down!"

Jamison did, reluctantly. The ankle hurt worse than ever, but bore her weight.

"I'm sorry, but I didn't want you to fall." Jamison's smile grew even wider. "We're operating on a shoestring. The last thing we want is a hefty lawsuit from your station," he teased.

"You needn't have worried," Jolene shot back, not seeing much humor in the situation. She reached up to secure some hairpins that had come loose, causing a large section of her luxuriant, upswept mane to collapse to her shoulders. "I can take care of myself."

"Yeah. I sorta picked up on that already," Jamison remarked with a insightful smile.

"O–Hi–O!" the guy at the rear called out again, apparently still addressing Jamison. "You comin', or what?"

"Your crew needs you," Jolene observed primly. She turned away, the ever faithful Frank close behind.

"Hey! What about next week?" Jamison called after her.

"I'll have my people call your people," Jolene threw over her shoulder as she limped off with as much dignity as she could muster. She didn't want to look back, but like Lot's wife she couldn't resist. He was still standing at the same spot, thoughtfully watching her. The sight of him watching her retreating backside made Jolene strangely self–conscious, but she continued her somewhat unsteady but determined exit.

* * *

Jolene looked down at the Ace bandage swaddling her ankle. *Well, the Bible says pride cometh before a fall,* she thought ruefully. *Much as I hate to admit it, he was right. I should have known better than to go to a construction site in heels. But I had left my flats at the station, and we were already late, as Hulk Hogan Jamison so emphatically pointed out.*

Jolene sighed. *Mercy that man is fine! Just my luck to meet him that way.* She laughed. *As if it would have made a difference if we had met under better circumstances. He probably has an adoring size nine wife and a house full of babies.* No—even in their brief and frenzied encounter, Jolene had noticed he wasn't wearing a wedding band.

Then he probably has a string of willowy females only too ready, willing, and able to satisfy his every whim, she pondered on. Still, somehow she hadn't been able to shake him from her mind.

"Gee–Gee?" a small voice called from in the house, behind her. Jolene smiled as she heard the quick, tiny footsteps, going first into the master bedroom, and then into the bathroom, in search of her. "Gee–Gee?"

"I'm outside, honey!" Jolene called though the patio screen.

The footsteps became a scamper, and Zayna appeared at the patio doors. "What you doing outside, Gee–Gee?"

"Just having my morning coffee, baby. It's such a beautiful morning, I thought I'd have it out here." Jolene knew what was coming next.

Sure enough, the determined little voice maintained, "Well, I wanna come out there, too."

"Okay, dear. You can come out. But you have to go put on some shoes and a sweater, and . . ."

Before she could finish, Zayna was off like a shot, running to her room for the required items that were her passport to the great outdoors.

Jolene had to smile tenderly. *That kid is a pistol. She has so much energy I get tired just watching her.*

In no time flat Zayna was back. Jolene reflected a moment on the items that had no doubt been thrown to the floor of Zayna's closet in her rush to snatch a sweater from a hanger she couldn't yet reach. Zayna came bouncing out the patio doors—to Jolene's surprise, actually stopping to slide the screen door closed behind her.

"Thank you for closing the screen, Zayna," Jolene smiled, hoping her recognition of the feat would further reinforce it in the child's mind. After all, girlfriend usually left the door wide open.

Zayna just flashed her a smile as she ran hell–for–leather for her swing set. Jolene almost laughed at her choice of attire. Over her blue Rugrats nightgown, the child had donned her yellow Tweety Bird raincoat, complete with hood. On her feet were a pair of hot pink boaters. *She's certainly an Equal Opportunity kid,* Jolene concluded with amusement. *She's giving every color in the rainbow a shot with that outfit.*

But having reached the swing, the child stopped short. "Gee–Gee! The birds pee–peed on my swing!"

Jolene was seriously puzzled. "Uh . . . What?"

Zayna pointed accusingly to the swing. "My swing is wet!" She looked around the spacious yard, peering up into its numerous trees at the birds twittering merrily about. "Those birds pee–peed on my swing!"

What is this child talking about? Jolene wondered. Then it dawned on her. She had to laugh. "Oh, honey. That's not pee–pee. That's dew. That's morning dew. It's on the grass, too, see?"

"Doo?" Zayna echoed skeptically. "What is doo?"

Okay, Jolene pondered, *how do I explain the concept of "dew" to a four–year–old, who doesn't have the word "condensation" in her vocabulary?* After reflecting another moment, Jolene replied, "Well, baby, once the sun goes down, the air gets cooler at night, right?"

Zayna nodded. Yes, she knew that part.

"After a while, the ground and things on it are warmer than the air around them. The water in the air likes warm surfaces, so it settles on them."

Zayna thought about that one a moment. "So it's like rain?"

"Yes," Jolene agreed, relieved her explanation had not been too complex for the child to grasp. "Yes, it's similar to the reason it rains."

Zayna nodded again. Rain, she knew about. If this stuff was like rain, it wasn't something gross and disgusting. She looked up, "But my swing is still wet," she pointed out meaningfully.

"We can fix that in a hurry," Jolene replied. She had brought out a roll of paper towels, to wipe off the patio table and chairs. She grabbed it, and limped carefully over to the swing set.

"Your leg still hurt, Gee–Gee?" Zayna asked with troubled eyes.

"It's not my leg, dear. It's my ankle. You know what an ankle is? Show me your ankle," Jolene said as she wiped off the swing set.

Zayna grinned proudly as she triumphantly pointed to her own ankle.

"That's right!" Jolene commended her. "I hurt my ankle yesterday, and I'm staying home from work today, to give it a chance to get better."

Zayna bent over, giving Jolene's ankle close scrutiny. "Did it blood?" she asked earnestly. Lately, for some ungodly reason, Zayna had been fascinated with the process of bleeding.

"That's *bleed*, Zee," Jolene patiently explained. "No, it didn't bleed. It's hurt inside, where you can't see it."

"But I *can* see it," Zayna disputed, jumping into the swing, after checking to make sure its dryness quotient was to her satisfaction. *"See?"* she pointed to Jolene's ankle. "It's big!"

You mean 'bigger', my love, Jolene thought ruefully. *There's not much tiny on your size eighteen 'Gee–Gee', ankles included.*

"That's called 'swollen', Zayna," Jolene continued. "It should be better tomorrow. So today I'm going to stay home with you."

"I'm not going to school?" the child asked, pumping ever higher in the swing. Zayna called her day care center 'school', which Jolene thought was appropriate, since the center had taught Zayna to count to ten in Spanish, and sing the alphabet in Hebrew.

"No, I thought today I'd keep you home with me— unless you *want* me to take you to school."

Zayna pondered this a moment. She loved school. "No," she finally decided, "I'll stay with you."

Jolene bowed deeply from the waist at the honor bestowed upon her, "Well, thank you too much, Your Royal Tiny–ness," she teased.

Zayna just giggled, continuing her soaring reach for the sky, as Jolene painfully made her way back to the patio table, and her coffee. As she reached her chair, Jolene noticed the geraniums in the large stone pots near the rear of the patio. They were so close to the house that rain barely reached them. Jolene had, as usual, been so busy she had forgotten to water them. They looked it. The gorgeous blooms were starting to wilt.

"Oh, no, you don't," Jolene scolded the flowers. "I worked too hard planting you to let you die on me. You get water, stat!" She picked up the plastic pail she kept near the flowers for just that purpose, and set it under the nearby spigot. When the pail was full, Jolene bent to grab the handle, but since she was already favoring the injured ankle, the added weight upset her symmetry even more. She wobbled, sloshing water from the heavy pail onto her slippers.

"Whoa! Better let me get that!"

Hearing an unexpected voice from so close behind her, Jolene dropped the pail entirely. It hit the concrete patio with a loud *blam,* tipping over and spilling the water down the patio and onto the grass. Jolene whirled, grabbing a nearby patio chair for balance.

"I'm sorry. I didn't mean to frighten you. Are you okay?" There stood Mr. Surly Jamison from the day before, hard hat and all. He didn't look surly now—he looked concerned, and more than a little startled himself by Jolene's splashy acknowledgment of his presence.

"What . . . how . . . what are *you* doing here?" Jolene managed to stammer.

"Well . . . and a gracious good morning to you, as well," Jamison replied with an aristocratic nod of his head and a playful twinkle in his eye.

Jolene felt like a fool. "I'm . . . I'm sorry. I didn't mean to be rude." Then her disposition kicked in. "But you *did* creep up on me in my own backyard, unannounced. How did you know where I live, anyway?"

"I called the station."

Jolene eyed him even more suspiciously then. "No way. There's no way anybody at the station would tell a stranger where I lived."

"But I'm not a stranger," Jamison smiled, putting a thumb under the rim of his hard hat, pushing it back on his head. "I'm the subject of your interview yesterday, remember? At least that's what your records at the station show. I told them there was some material for the interview I had forgotten to give you, and they told me you were working at home today, and gave me the address."

Jolene silently thanked her unknown benefactor at the

station, vowing to find out who it was and give him a piece of her mind.

"All right, then." Jolene crossed her arms. "Now that you're here, what do you want?" Crossing her arms was a mistake. When she let go of the chair, she started to wobble again.

"Right now, I think I want to get you a seat," Jamison replied, swiftly pulling out the chair so Jolene could hop to it and sit once again at the table. Jamison casually sat down in the chair next to it, removing his hard hat and placing it on the table.

"Mr. Jamison," Jolene began mustering her composure, "at the risk of repeating myself—*what are you doing here?*"

"Hi!" came a greeting from near Jamison's elbow. Curious about their visitor, Zayna had come over to the table. Starting with her father, Zayna had twisted men around her baby finger with just a smile since birth. She flashed Jamison a particularly brilliant one now. It worked as infallibly as ever.

"Hello, honey!" Jamison replied, instantly taken. "Aren't you a cutie pie! What's your name?"

Zayna, charmer supreme, promptly answered, "Zayna JoAnne Jeffries."

"What a pretty name," Jamison told her.

"Thank you. I'm named after my mommy and daddy. And my middle name is a meditation from my grandmothers' names," Zayna importantly informed him.

"That's 'combination', honey," Jolene couldn't help putting in.

"Com–bin–a–tion," Zayna carefully agreed. Having exhausted that subject, she turned to more immediate matters. "Gee–Gee, can I have some juice?"

"*May* I have some juice," Jolene instructed. "Yes, you may." Jolene started to rise shakily, but it was a tough go. "Mr. Jamison . . ." she said stiffly, "if you'll excuse us, I'm going back in now. I'm sure you can find your way back to the front of—"

"Look, you just sit tight. I'll get the juice for your daughter," Jamison volunteered, rising.

"I'm not her daughter," Zayna said, giggling. "I'm her *granddaughter!*" She leaned toward Jamison. "That means she's my daddy's mommy—not *my* mommy," she patiently explained.

Jamison looked at Jolene in surprise. *"You're* a grandmother?"

Jolene returned his stare head–on. "Yes, I am. And proud of it." She couldn't help but smile at his stupefaction. "A few of us still have our own teeth, you know."

Jamison was taken aback a moment, then threw back his head and laughed. "So I see," he chuckled. He leaned closer, looking into Jolene's eyes. "And a very beautiful smile, too," he finished softly.

Jolene couldn't take her eyes from his. Zayna broke the silence by piping up with, "Can . . . *may* I have my juice now—please?"

Jamison tore his gaze from Jolene. "You sure can, sugar. I'll get it for you." He eyed Jolene's coffee cup. "And it looks like your grandmother could use a refill on her coffee, too." He took the coffee cup and started for the patio doors.

Jolene protested. "Hey, wait a minute! You can't just—"

"Oh, yes, I can," Jamison replied. He stopped, and smiled disarmingly down at Jolene. "But the question is if I *may.*" He gestured toward the door and the kitchen beyond. "May I?"

Is this the same man I met yesterday? Jolene wondered. She ought to send him on his way, she knew, but . . . "Uh . . . well . . . I hate to trouble you . . . I—"

"No trouble at all," Jamison replied, going into the kitchen with her coffee cup.

What am I doing, letting a strange man ramble around in my kitchen? Jolene thought uneasily. *Here I sit in my bathrobe, barely able to walk, with a small child to protect, to boot. I barely know this man at all.*

But that wasn't exactly true. Jolene knew quite a bit about Jamison—his professional life at least—from her preparations for the interview. He and a group of his friends in the construction business had grown tired of working for other people, and started a business of their own.

Their construction company, H.O.M.E., was not your usual construction company. Thus far, they had dealt exclusively with home renovation. Jamison had gotten the idea of buying boarded–up, neglected houses around town, fixing them up, and reselling them. The company made a reasonable profit for themselves, yet maintained prices affordable to most mid to lower income families.

From when she first heard about it, Jolene had wanted to cover this story. She admired the ingenuity and guts of the men tackling the project. It wasn't easy to give up well-paying jobs to strike out on your own. And she also admired the manner in which they gave back to the community, turning eyesore firetraps into respectable homes for people who otherwise would not been able to afford one.

"Gee–Gee? Gee–Gee!" Jolene was brought out of her rumination by Zayna tugging on the sleeve of her robe. "Gee–Gee, who is that?" Zayna wanted to know, pointing to the kitchen, from which issued the sounds of dishes precariously rattling.

"That's Mr. Jamison, Zee."

"So he's not . . ." Zayna lowered her voice to a whisper—"a *stranger?*"

Jolene could almost hear that active little mind of Zayna's working. The child was friendly—too friendly. Lately Jolene had been especially emphatic in cautioning Zayna

ALL THE WAY HOME 145

about strangers. It wouldn't do to admit grandmother had
allowed one into their very midst.

"No, honey. He's not a stranger. I met him yesterday,
for my TV show."

Satisfied, Zayna ran off for the swings again, just as Jamison exited the kitchen with a tray.

"Hey, wait! Don't you want your juice?" Jamison called
balancing the tray with one hand as he held out a cup.

Jolene was astonished. He had actually gotten one of
Zayna's special cups, the plastic ones with spouted tops.
Since they were outdoors, Jolene wasn't concerned about
Zayna spilling her drink. It was just that Zayna wouldn't
use any other kind of cup. These were "her" cups. Jolene
realized then she should have mentioned this to Jamison.
Jolene was surprised at Jamison taking the trouble to find
one of the little yellow cups with the duckies on the side.

He looked somehow incongruous, this powerful, strapping man, as he gracefully sank to sit back on his heels,
and hand Zayna her drink. The small, brightly colored
cup was almost lost in his large, calloused hand.

Then he smiled at the child. Zayna giggled as she smiled
back, reaching for the cup. Jolene was transfixed, her mind
taking a snapshot of the big man handing the cup to the
tiny child on her own level, and with such gentleness. The
golden glow of the early morning sun cast a luminescence
over the two, and Jolene's heart was forever branded by
the imprint of the fleeting, touching tableau.

The moment was broken as Zayna laughed, and happily
skipped off to the swing once again.

Standing, Jamison brought the tray to the table. It bore
not one, but two cups of coffee, and a sugar bowl and
creamer, as well as spoons and napkins.

"I hope you don't mind," Jamison said, gesturing to his
own cup, and taking his seat once again. "I thought maybe
we could talk over a cup of coffee." He smiled at Jolene

as he handed her her cup. "Since you've declared me 'not a stranger.'"

"That was for my granddaughter's sake," Jolene replied, peering closely into Jamison's eyes. "Personally, I think you're one of the strangest men I ever met."

Far from being offended, Jamison actually seemed rather pleased by this assessment. "Oh, really?" He grinned as he leaned back in his chair, and lifted one booted ankle over the opposite, blue-jeaned knee, "How so?"

"You nearly bit my head off yesterday, and then you pop up today trying to charm me to death."

Jamison leaned forward, eyes twinkling, but with a spark of true inquiry in his voice, "How am I doing?"

Jolene caught her breath at the candid captivation in his gaze. *He's . . . he's flirting with me!* Jolene dropped her gaze quickly. *No, he's not,* another internal voice scolded. *The man's just trying to be nice. My goodness, has it been that long since you've been with an attractive man, so that now you're seeing things that aren't there?* Jolene didn't know which voice to believe. She didn't look up. She didn't want Jamison to see the confusion she knew her eyes would reveal.

Jamison reached between his legs with one hand and quickly grabbed the seat of his chair, scooting it forward to be that much closer to Jolene's. "Look, Mrs. Jeffries . . . Jolene . . . I acted like an ass yesterday. I was trying to do about five different things at one time, and I had only had about four hours sleep the night before. That's the reason I acted that way. The reason. Not the excuse. There *is* no excuse for acting that way—especially to a lady, a sister." He leaned even closer. "I'm sorry."

Jolene looked up then, and there could be no mistaking the sincerity of his apology. He was watching her closely, cautiously, as though hoping for the best but expecting the worse.

Her heart melted. His friendly gentleness of the past half hour had succeeded in overcoming the shadow of yesterday. "Well," Jolene said slowly, "anybody can have a bad day." She smiled. "It's been rumored I have one myself every once in a while."

Jamison's gaze never wavered. "I'm really sorry, Jolene. Please . . . forgive me."

"Forgiven. Forgotten . . . Akron" Jolene whispered, offering her hand, suddenly shy.

As they shook hands, Jolene could feel the strength in his fingers, and the roughness of his palm. Her hand in his looked as small and defenseless as did Zayna's. Jolene looked up again, into his eyes. She saw his relief, his thankfulness that she was willing to put the past behind them. And she saw . . . she saw . . .

"That's Ron . . . or Ohio!" he said softly, his hand unwillingly releasing hers.

"Excuse me?"

"Nobody calls me Akron except my father. Mostly it's Ron. My buddies call me Ohio . . . for obvious reasons."

"Were you born there? Akron, I mean," Jolene asked.

"No. Never been to Ohio in my life." Ron chuckled.

"Then how—"

"My dad heard the name when my mother was carrying me. It means 'ninth son' ".

"It does? And are you?"

"Nope." Ron picked up the coffee carafe, and topped off first Jolene's cup, then his own. "Actually, I was their *first* child. Dad used to say he was counting in reverse order." Ron laughed. "And he almost made it, too. There wound up being eight of us." He looked at Jolene playfully. "Although, four were girls."

Jolene had to laugh along with him. "So you were raised with four younger sisters. Is that why you're so good with little girls?" She nodded her head toward Zayna.

"I have a little girl of my own. Though I know she'd go, 'Oh, *Daddy!*' if she heard me call her that. She's fifteen now, going on twenty–five." Jolene didn't understand the shadow that crossed Ron's face.

Ron saw the perplexity in Jolene's eyes. "I lost my wife two years ago," he said softly. "It's . . . it's been . . . tough." Jolene could tell that was a profound understatement. "And for a little girl . . . losing her mother . . ." He clearly didn't know just how to continue.

Jolene reached forward to cover his hand with hers. "I'm sorry," she said softly, not knowing what else to say.

Ron looked up and gave her a fragile smile as his other hand covered hers. "And what about you?" he asked softly. He gently lifted Jolene's left hand. "No wedding ring? Where's the little one's grandpa?"

"I . . . I don't know," Jolene stammered. "We were divorced when my son was a baby. My ex–husband just . . . just sort of disappeared."

"And your son? Where is he?" Ron, discerning that the subject of Jolene's marriage was off limits, deftly changed the subject.

"He and his wife are in Germany. Zane's a career air force man," Jolene said. Her pride in her son was unmistakable. "In fact, he met Marlena in the service. She's career, too. Zayna was born in Germany. As she got closer to school age, they were concerned about her not having exposure to her own culture, her own people." Jolene smiled over at where Zayna had left the swing in favor of the glider. "So she's been with me for the past six months. She's going to stay with me until her parents can get state–side orders."

Neither spoke for a moment, and then Ron suddenly declared, "Hey, have you had breakfast?"

"No," Jolene told him, not comprehending the sudden change in subject.

"Comin' right up." Jamison stood, and headed once again for the kitchen. "After all, since I was indirectly the cause of your . . . ah, somewhat limited mobility, the least I can do is fix breakfast for you."

"But Ron, that's not necessary," Jolene again attempted to rise. "You don't have to—"

"Gee–Gee, I'm hungry." Having heard the word "breakfast", Zayna had come over and felt obliged to put her bid in.

"I am, too," Ron told the child. "Do you like omelets?"

"What's a om–lett?" Zayna wanted to know.

"Eggs," Ron responded.

"Oh. Yes, I like eggs. Especially bald eggs."

"That's *boiled* eggs, dear," Jolene corrected her.

"Eggs it is. In an omelet for us . . ." Ron told Jolene, "and a couple of hairless ones for you." He touched a finger to the tip of Zayna's nose.

"But Ron—"

"Look, I'm hungry. The baby is hungry. Aren't you hungry?"

"Well, yes, I am, but you can't—"

"Considering your delicate condition," he said, pointing to Jolene's ankle, "and the fact that Zayna can't reach the countertop, looks like I'm the only one who can." He smiled and offered Jolene his arm, "That is . . . if I may."

I shouldn't Jolene told herself. *I don't know this man. But I was just barely able to fix myself coffee and hop out here. And it's not as if I know nothing about the man. And he's been so gracious it would actually be rude to refuse.* Then her alter–ego spoke up. *Be honest with yourself, girl. You want to. And, hell, what's wrong with that?* Before she could stop herself, Jolene laughed. She took Ron's arm, leaning on his strong shoulder as he helped her into the kitchen.

Excusing herself, Jolene slowly made her way to the bedrooms, to quickly dress and supervise Zayna, who insisted on dressing herself. That having been accomplished, Zayna ran into the living room to check out Sesame Street while Jolene settled at the kitchen table.

"More coffee?" Ron asked at the sink, washing his hands.

"No, thanks," Jolene replied. "Two cups is my limit. More than that, and I start to vibrate."

Ron laughed. "I should probably lay off the stuff more myself. I drink it all day long. It's hard for me to fall asleep at night sometimes." He had placed eggs, milk, and butter, as well as a tin of Hungry Jack biscuits, on the counter. "Ah! My favorites!" he declared, adroitly tossing the biscuit tin in the air, catching it behind his back. "I see you are a woman of rare taste and refinement." He smiled warmly, at Jolene. "But I guess I already knew that."

Jolene watched in fascination as he expertly moved about the kitchen, starting the biscuits and mixing the omelet with not an iota of wasted motion. "Sausage or bacon?" he asked, peering into the refrigerator.

"Bacon. It's Zayna's favorite."

"Mine, too."

In no time he had the bacon sizzling, and was chopping onion and green pepper for the omelet. "Light on the peppers," Jolene cautioned. "Our friend's not real fond of them."

"Oh. Glad you reminded me—I believe the princess wanted to go the Humpty Dumpty route, anyway." He got a small saucepan and set two eggs to boiling.

"Ron, you're amazing," Jolene marveled. "You really know your way around a kitchen. You must do a lot of cooking."

"Yeah." His happy–go–lucky manner seemed to deflate. "I've been doing most of the cooking at my place . . . for a while now."

Jolene could have kicked herself. "That was thoughtless of me, Ron. I'm sorry."

His face was openly vulnerable as he studied Jolene a moment before answering, "It's okay! Jolene. It's just that it jumps up and catches me by ambush sometimes. You'd think that after two years—"

"I don't think time is a factor," Jolene said softly, looking out the patio door. "I don't think you ever just get used to losing someone you love."

The obvious intensity of Jolene's words made Ron pause, and look at her in contemplation. Just as he was about to speak, the timer went off, and he hurried to remove the biscuits from the oven.

Ron wouldn't even allow Jolene to set the table, following her direction to locate the napkins and silverware.

"Breakfast is ready, little one," he called to Zayna, who didn't have to be told twice. After serving the ladies, Ron took a seat.

"Everything looks wonderful, Ron," Jolene told him, sincerely meaning it.

"Not bad, even if I do say so myself," Ron agreed, rubbing his hands together. "Could you pass the jam?"

"No. Not yet," Zayna advised him in a whisper. "First we have to say prayers."

"Oh. Right. Sorry." Ron accordingly bowed his head, after casting an abashed glance Jolene's way.

Zayna bowed hers as well, and solemnly said, "God is great. God is good. Let us bank Him. Pour the food. Amen."

"That's 'thank Him', honey," Jolene gently reminded, leaving a critique of the rest for another day.

The meal was marvelous, the company making the food taste particularly appetizing. Just as they were finishing, Jolene consenting to share another cup of coffee with Ron, the doorbell rang.

"Who could that be so early in the morning?" Jolene wondered aloud. She excused herself, and limped to the door. There stood a very tall, very handsome, very dusty young man who looked somehow familiar. "Yes? May I help you?"

The young man hastily snatched off the baseball cap that was perched backward on his head. "Yes, ma'am. I hope so. Good morning. I'm glad I found the right house. Ah, you're Mrs. Jeffries, from Channel Seven, right?"

"Yes, I am. Do I know you? Have we met before?"

"No, ma'am, we haven't, although I've watched you on the tube so often it sort of feels like it—to me, at least. I'm LaSalles Jamison. I'm looking for my dad. The guys at the site told me he might be here."

No wonder he looks so familiar, Jolene reflected. *He's a younger, even taller version of Ron. But what would he be doing here?* "Oh, so you work with your father?" Jolene said.

"Yes, during the summer, and school vacations. I go to Ingram State." He paused, and stood a bit taller. "I'll be a senior this fall."

"Good for you," Jolene told him with a smile. "Your father's in the kitchen. Please, come in."

LaSalles stepped tentatively over the threshold. "I'd better not come in too far. Been working around cement this morning. I'm sorta grubby." Though LaSalles was an inch or so taller than Ron, he was not as muscular as his father. Still, he was a robust specimen of young manhood.

"Don't worry about it. You're fine," Jolene said kindly. "Won't you have a seat?"

"No, I'd better not. I'll just wait here," LaSalles told her, staying close to the door.

"Okay. Just a moment. I'll tell your father you're here." Jolene went as quickly as she could back into the kitchen. "Ron, your son's at the door."

Ron was surprised. "He is? But what—" He glanced

quickly at his watch. "Hot damn! I didn't realize the time."
Ron jumped up, and grabbed his hard hat. "I gotta get
back to the site."

Ron followed Jolene into the living room, where Zayna
had already moved in on LaSalles, having asked him to
hold her Cabbage Patch doll while she got her toy stroller
out of the front closet.

"Getting in a little practice, son?" Ron said with a wry
smile as he approached the door.

LaSalles squirmed uncomfortably, clearly embarrassed.
"Aw, Dad, come on. Give me a break."

Zayna stepped forward then, and took the doll back.
"Thank you for holding my baby," she said, looking grate-
fully up at LaSalles.

Despite his chagrin, LaSalles gave her a big smile in
return, "You're welcome, sweetheart." He turned his
attention to Ron. "Dad, Ernie told me you'd come by to
talk to Mrs. Jeffries. He remembered you said she lived on
Village Drive. I saw your truck in the driveway. But we
thought you'd be right back—the building inspector's
coming out this morning to okay the foundation on the
Maple Street house."

"That's right!" Ron exclaimed, smacking his forehead
with the heel of his palm. "I'm sorry, Les. I forgot. Has
he come by yet?"

"No, but he'll be there any minute. You forgot?" LaSalles looked at Ron closely. "That's not like you, Dad. What's
up?"

"Nothing, son, nothing," Ron said hastily. He turned,
"I hate to eat and run. Thank you for breakfast, Jolene."
At this, one of LaSalles' eyebrows shot up.

"No, thank *you*, Ron," Jolene asserted. "After all, you
did all the cooking." LaSalles turned to look at his father
in bewilderment.

"Any time. It was my pleasure," Ron told her, the expression in his eyes betraying the fact that this was no idle compliment.

"I think I'll be out and about again in a day or two. Can we reschedule your interview for later this week?" Jolene asked.

"You bet. I'll be looking forward to it."

So will I, Jolene thought.

"Well," Ron said, lingering at the door, "talk to you soon."

"Okay." She turned. "Nice to have met you, LaSalles."

"Same here," LaSalles replied, looking back and forth between Jolene and his father. "Come on, Dad. We'd better get on the good foot if we're going to beat that inspector to the site."

"Right." Ron settled his hard hat on his head. "See you, Jolene," he said softly.

" 'Bye." Jolene shut the door after them, but just before it closed she heard LaSalles say, "Uh, Dad . . . *breakfast?*"

CHAPTER 2

"So you've been in business a year and a half now?"

"Yes—officially. But we've been doing various projects on a freelance basis for about seven years, while each of us was still working our regular jobs."

"That had to be tough."

"Yes, it was. I was a carpenter, Ernie a plumber, Hakeem an electrician, and Mike a bricklayer. We got to know each other through working various jobs together. Then we started calling each other in on the different private jobs we did in the evenings.

"But it's been even tougher since we went into business for ourselves." Ron flashed Jolene that killer smile. "You never work as hard for anybody else as you do for yourself."

Jolene looked back at the newly poured concrete foundation, and the skeleton of a frame rising from it, "And this project is your first *new* home?"

"Right. Up to now we've just been remodeling and restoring preexisting homes." Ron nodded toward the structure, "This is the first one we've built from scratch." He paused, looking at the framework with pride. "It's my own design."

"It is?" Jolene was surprised. "So you're an architect?"

"Not yet. I've been taking classes at night for years, but I had to stop when we decided to start H.O.M.E. But now that the business is going so well, I plan to start back in the fall. I only need a few more credits before I can get my degree and certification."

"That's wonderful. You are certainly an outstanding role model." Jolene was truly impressed, and as she looked up into Ron's eyes, she momentarily forgot they were on camera. A beat passed before she remembered where she was and hastily asked, "And you named the company H.O.M.E. because you work exclusively on home, rather than commercial, construction?"

"Yes, that, and also it's an acronym for the four of us guys—Hakeem, Ohio—that's what the guys call me . . ."— Jolene already knew this, but Ron knew their audience didn't—"Mike, and Ernie."

"Your story is absolutely fascinating, Mr. Jamison. Thank you for sharing it. And we wish you and your partners only the best in the future."

"Thank you."

Jolene turned to face Frank and the camera, "This is Jolene Jeffries with Channel Seven's weekly feature, "Window on Our World", spotlighting our community's citizens on the move." She waited until the red light on the camera went off. "Okay, Frank, that's a wrap."

"Right, JJ," Frank replied, taking Jolene's microphone and winding up the cord. He turned to Ron. "I need a few minutes to get some lead–in shots. Is that all right, Mr. Jamison?"

"Sure. No problem. Need me to go with you?" Ron asked.

"No, thanks, I'm fine. I'll be right back, Double J."
Frank ambled off with the camera, seeking just the right
scenes for the program's opening and closing shots.

"Well, Ron!" Jolene said, "the interview went wonderfully." She smiled wryly, looking down to her now recuper-
ated ankle. "Since we got off on the right foot this time."

Ron laughed. "Yes . . . and I see you have more suitable
gear on that 'right foot', this time," he teased, checking
out Jolene's sturdy brogans.

Jolene gave him a roguish smile. "I don't make the
same mistakes twice, Mr. Jamison. But seriously, Ron, the
interview was great. Thank you."

"No, thank *you*," Ron insisted. "We don't have much
of a publicity budget. We've mostly been getting by on
word of mouth. The exposure is appreciated."

"You deserve it. This is a tremendous human interest
story. You're doing a true service to the community, fixing
up those old houses. Not to mention all the families you've
helped. Your company could get more for the houses
you've renovated than you've been asking, you know."

"Yeah, I know. But our intention is just to make a respectable profit, not to make a killing, especially at the expense
of those who can least afford it." Ron gave her that smile
again. "We're needy, not greedy. And it's kind of a mutual
thing. We're tapping a market that's mostly of people who
otherwise wouldn't be buying homes at all. So we get their
business, and they get a decent place to live."

"I . . . I think it's wonderful of you." Jolene looked up,
and again got momentarily lost in the depths of Ron's
smoldering black eyes. "Uh . . . of all of you guys," she
finished unsteadily, suddenly looking away. "Well, I'd . . .
better be going. I'll call and let you know when the show
is going to air."

"Aren't you forgetting something?" Ron asked with a
smile, staring at the hard hat Jolene was still wearing.

"Oh. Yes, of course!" Jolene reached up, but Ron beat her to it.

"Allow me," he said softly, gently lifting the protective covering from her head. His hands lingered for a moment. "You know, since we first met I've just been yearning to touch your hair." He moved a step closer. "It *is* just as soft as it looks."

"T . . . thank you," Jolene whispered in reply. She felt agitated under the deep scrutiny of his gaze, but it was a pleasant sort of agitation. She found it difficult to look away.

"Come on." Ron took her elbow. "I'll see you to the van."

They walked along in silence for a short while, until Ron said, "Uh . . . 'Double J?' "

Jolene laughed, "That's what they call me at the station, since I always initial all my memos 'JJ'. In fact, that's why Zayna calls me 'Gee–Gee'," she went on. "Her parents got leave when she was about a year old, and came to visit. She heard some of my friends from the station calling me JJ, and tried to say it, too. But it came out 'Gee–Gee'." Jolene laughed again. "My rascal of a son made it even worse by saying that stood for 'gorgeous grandma'."

"How right he was," Ron put in, smiling down at Jolene.

By this time they had reached the station's van. Ron's smile suddenly faded. He seemed suddenly jittery, unsure of himself. "Jolene . . . I was wondering . . . that is—" he stammered. Ron took a deep breath. "Look, Jolene, what I'm trying to say is, I'd . . . I'd really like to see you again."

Jolene was caught off guard. Another woman might have picked up on Ron's signals, but Jolene had convinced herself it was merely her imagination, her own wishful thinking. Now here it was. It was really happening. She was so unprepared that she blurted out the first thing to cross her mind: "Why?"

"Huh?" Now it was Ron who was caught unawares. "Uh . . . why not? I mean, why *shouldn't* I want to see you again?"

"Ron, I wasn't aware that you felt . . . I mean—"

"Jolene." Ron moved a little closer. "I've rarely seen a lady since . . . in a long time. I guess I'm kinda out of practice. But I've been hitting on you the best I know how since we first met." He took her hand, and looked deeply into her eyes. "Do you mean to tell me my rap is so rusty that you didn't even know?" he finished softly.

Jolene looked down to their joined hands. She didn't know what to say, how to answer him. She couldn't say what *she* had thought—that she was powerfully attracted to him, but had thought it was strictly one way.

When she didn't speak, Ron slowly released her hand. "Jolene, I'm sorry." He was clearly embarrassed. "What would a woman like you want with a guy like me, struggling to hold a new business together—and his family, to boot? I shouldn't have been so presumptuous. But I thought . . . at least, I'd hoped—"

Jolene looked up quickly, then. "Ron, any woman would be flattered by the attention of a man like you," she said softly. She didn't know what to say next. Jolene was seldom in this predicament. She made her living communicating. But that was different. That was TV. This was real life.

"But?" Ron prompted, looking at her with wounded eyes, preparing himself for disappointment.

Jolene was touched by his evident dejection at what he thought was a rebuff. "But you're not the only one out of practice," she said with a gentle smile. "Seems I've forgotten how to accept a gentleman's invitation—at least, so that he *knows* I'm accepting."

A slow grin materialized on Ron's face, "Yeah?"

Jolene grinned shyly back. "Yeah."

They stood contemplating each other for a instant, both

enthralled by the magic of the moment. Then Ron said softly, "In that case, I was wondering if—"

Frank was back. "Okay. Got the stuff I needed. Ready to go, JJ?"

"Ah . . . yes, Frank," Jolene said, quickly switching gears.

"All right, then. Let's roll," Frank said, placing the camera and other equipment in the back of the van. He got behind the wheel. "Nice to meet you, Mr. Jamison," Frank called as he started the engine.

"Same here," Ron called to him. He turned to Jolene. "Look, we're having a barbecue at my place tomorrow evening. No big deal, just a few family and friends. Would you and Zayna like to come?"

Out of the corner of her eye Jolene could see Frank watching them, obviously fascinated by this turn of events, and as deeply into the conversation as she and Ron. But then she looked into Ron's eyes, and suddenly she didn't care who was watching. "Yes. Sounds like fun. We'd love to come."

"Great!" Ron was beaming now. He opened the door of the van for Jolene. "I'll pick you up about six o'clock, okay?"

Jolene smiled back. "Fine."

Ron helped Jolene up the step into the van, and closed the door. "See you tomorrow." He stood waving as the van drove away.

There was silence in the van for several moments, Frank stealing glances at Jolene with a silly grin on his face. Finally Jolene turned to him. *"What?"*

"What? Don't 'what' *me,* Double J. You know 'what'. You and this guy practically come to blows the other day, and now he's asking you for a date? And you accepting? What's wrong with this picture?"

"What's wrong is someone sticking his nose into places

where it doesn't belong." Jolene sniffed, nonchalantly looking out the side window.

"Aw, come on, Jo. This is me, Frank, your devoted friend and coworker for the past six years." Frank prodded Jolene with his elbow. "Spill it."

"Spill what? Ron invited Zee and me over for a family barbecue. That hardly qualifies as being whisked away to the Casbah."

"It does for a woman who hasn't had a date since Hector was a pup. Don't get me wrong, Jo. Jamison seems like a straight up dude. It's about time you got yourself a man."

"Like that buddy of yours you sicced on me last year?" Jolene came back.

"Oh, Jo. The guy was on my bowling team. He seemed okay. How was I to know he was a pervert?"

"Pervert is right. When he brought me home, the wrestling match we had in his car could have made it to Pay Per View. I had to knee him where the sun don't shine just to make him let go."

"Yeah, I know," Frank chuckled. "He was walking bent over for a week. But stop changing the subject. How did you and *'Ron'* get so chummy so fast?"

"Can I help it if the man has exceptional taste in women?" Jolene replied flippantly, but she didn't feel very flippant. Now that she'd had a moment to reflect, she wondered if she were doing the right thing. She was drawn to Ron, and now she knew he felt the same about her. *But we're not kids. We're two mature people with families and careers and responsibilities,* her thoughts rambled on. *With so much else going on in our lives, how can we make a place in them for each other?*

"Ron, I could have driven us over," Jolene said as they cruised down the street in Ron's quad–cab pickup. "Then you wouldn't have had to leave your company to come for us."

Ron just chuckled. "I don't have *'company'*, Jolene. Everybody there is someone I've known for years—or all my life. And I doubt they've even missed me." He grinned over at her, "Jolene, I'm forty–eight years old. I'm in the generation of men who are used to calling for ladies they've invited out for the evening. I'm too old to change now."

"Well, you're only a year older than I am, so don't put yourself in the rocking chair set just yet." Jolene laughed nervously, looking pensively out the side window.

They rode on in silence for a while before Ron asked, "What's the matter?"

"Nothing. Nothing, Ron."

"Jolene, I haven't known you very long, but I know *something's* bothering you. Is it the truck? I guess I should have borrowed my son's car, but—"

"No. No, Ron. Why would I mind the truck?" Jolene smiled over at Ron. "This is fun."

"It sure is!" Zayna enthusiastically agreed, bouncing up and down on the pickup's tiny rear seat. "I like riding up high! I can *see* everything!"

"Just make sure with all that bouncing you 'see' your way into keeping that seatbelt fastened, young lady," Jolene cautioned.

"Is that why you've been so quiet back there, princess?" Ron asked.

"Uh huh. I like this. I can't see *nothing* in grandma's car," Zayna replied, going back to her rapt review of the passing scenery.

"Well, at least I've pleased one of my dates this evening." He looked uncertainly over to Jolene. "I'm not so sure about the other."

"Ron, it's just that . . . well, I'm a bit nervous about meeting your . . . your family."

"Why? I've met *your* family." He smiled, and gestured with his head toward the backseat, where Zayna still had her nose pressed to the window.

Jolene had to laugh. "That's hardly the same. You've completely mesmerized Zayna, and you know it."

"And you'll completely mesmerize my family." He took Jolene's hand. "Just as you've already mesmerized me," he finished softly.

Jolene smiled back. "Well, at least I've already met one member of your family—your son."

"That's right. And this shindig is basically for him—and his fianceé."

"Fianceé? But he seems so young. And he told me he was getting his degree next year."

"He is. He and Shandra are both students at Ingram State. That's where they met. She'll be a senior next year, also. But she may not graduate on time."

Before Jolene could inquire further, Ron was pulling the truck to the curb. "Okay, ladies, we have arrived," he told them, hopping down onto the running board and to the street. Ron went to the passenger side and helped Jolene alight before lifting Zayna from the rear.

But Zayna clung to Ron. "Will you give me a piggyback ride? My daddy always used to before he went away," she finished, a tad wistfully.

"Princess, it would be an honor." Ron swung Zayna around to his back, where she promptly wrapped her arms around his neck. "This way, Jolene," he said, gesturing down the sidewalk to the left.

"Oh," Jolene said, following his lead. "I thought *this* was your house." She pointed to the neat, but rather ordinary ranch house where he had parked in front.

"No. I'm further on down the street." Jolene noted with quiet approval that Ron had taken care to cross behind her, so he was walking on the curbside of the sidewalk.

The man truly did have old–fashioned manners—and the good sense to use them.

"I was parked in the driveway when I left, but I knew somebody would grab my spot before I got back," Ron shook his head in good–natured resignation.

True enough, there were cars, trucks, and vans lining both sides of the street as well as packed into the circular driveway of a large rambling house a few doors down. Ron turned into this driveway a few moments later.

"Ron! What a beautiful house!" Jolene exclaimed.

And it was. An old Victorian manor, it was carefully maintained and perfectly restored. Jolene loved the wide, L–shaped veranda that spanned the front and right side of the house. Graceful cornices and intricate latticework in a cheery green adorned the porch roof ledge and the three gables, each jauntily sporting a dormer window. The trim made the spotlessly white house seem to sparkle that much more.

"Look, Gee–Gee," Zayna cried, pointing over Ron's shoulder with glee. "It's a castle!"

"No, baby." Ron chuckled as he settled Zayna on the ground. "It's not a castle. It's where I live."

"Well, that's what they say a man's home *is*," Jolene said, still staring at the lovely structure before them.

Zayna looked up at Ron with huge eyes, awestruck. "Are you a king?" she whispered.

Ron laughed gently. "No, honey, I'm not." He looked over to Jolene. "But right now I sure feel like one."

The unmistakable smell of barbecue was in the air, along with the sounds of chatter and laughter. The Temptations' "My Girl" was playing in the background. Ron led them to the side of the house, along the porch.

The backyard was a flurry of activity. People were talking in groups, walking around or sitting at tables, and on blankets on the grass. A husky young man was at a table to the side, on which was a CD player and two of the biggest speakers Jolene had ever seen.

A group of people were dancing on the large patio. Jolene had to smile. The ages of the dancers had to span fifty years. There was a white–haired gentleman smoothly guiding a teenage girl in an elegant ballroom move. Next to them were a couple of kids in baggy jeans busting some moves that looked physically impossible.

There was a large gas grill bearing a tantalizing array of ribs and chicken. LaSalles was at the grill, his white bib apron bearing the logo, ALL THE KIND WORDS, ALL THE GOOD WISHES, JUST CAN'T REPLACE HELP WITH THE DISHES. He waved a long fork. "Hey, Mrs. Jeffries! Hi!"

At that, everyone turned. Despite all her experience in the public eye, Jolene felt tremendously self–conscious. "Now, now, none of that," Ron said, seeming to sense her discomfort. He put his arm lightly around her waist to lead her forward. "They don't bite—at least, not until they know you better."

Zayna needed no such prompting. She immediately went up to a group of children playing in a sandbox shaped like a big green turtle, sat down, and started chattering away.

Ron guided Jolene over to the grill. "Uh, Les . . . where's Ernie?" Ron asked, looking down at the grill anxiously.

"Had to make a pit stop, Dad. He'll be back in a minute. Mrs. Jeffries, glad you could come," LaSalles said, blinking at the smoke that was getting in his eyes.

"Thanks for having us. And please call me Jolene." She inhaled deeply. "That food looks absolutely mouth-watering."

"It won't stay that way for long if we leave Sir Burns–A–Lot in charge," a voice said from behind them. A rather short, stocky man stepped up to the grill. "Okay, I'm back now. Better let me take over before this stuff gets carbon-ated."

"No problem there," LaSalles instantly agreed, and started untying the apron.

Jolene recognized the man as the one who called to Ron on her first visit to the site. He offered his hand to Jolene, "Mrs. Jeffries, I'm Ernie Hill, one of Ohio's partners. Sorry I didn't get to meet you before."

"It's Jolene, Ernie. Nice to meet you. And it was a pleasure doing the story on H.O.M.E. It's such a great idea I'm surprised nobody's thought of it before."

"Oh, it's been done before, Jolene," Ernie told her. "Just not the way *we're* doing it. You know that a lot of the old office buildings downtown are being renovated into lofts?"

"Yes. We did a feature on it."

"Did you check out the price tags for those babies?" Ernie shook his head. "Most working folks can't afford fancy digs like that. There's a huge national construction company behind that project. And they're charging all the traffic will bear. And when they get a contract or a grant from the city to clean up old houses, they clean them up, all right. They usually raze them to the ground, or build a parking lot or a party store . . ."—He looked at Jolene closely—"especially in *our* neighborhoods."

Jolene blinked. "You're right. I . . . I just never looked at it that way before."

"We can't stop it from happening, but we can damn sure put a dent in it. Especially after we get that grant from the city."

"Grant? What grant?" Jolene asked.

"I didn't mention it because we just decided to go for it this morning, Jolene," Ron told her. "Those conglomerates have had a virtual monopoly on the city's renovation grants—until now. We've gotten large enough now to put in a competitive bid for a grant."

"Ron, that's wonderful!" Jolene exclaimed. "There're so many wonderful houses, houses like yours, that you could save with that kind of backing."

"That's what we think, too, Jo. So we're going to give it our best shot."

By this time LaSalles had finally wiggled his way out of the apron, and handed it to Ernie.

"Hey, man, you don't have to do that," Ron protested. "You're our guest. I just wanted you to take over for me while I was gone. I've got it."

"No, you don't," Ernie insisted, putting the apron over his own head. "I *know* you're not trying to treat me like *company*, or something. Hell, I got the toilets working in this old dinosaur after you bought it!" Ernie looked over at Jolene. "Besides, if I had a lady this fine on *my* arm, I bet I'd find a better way to keep her entertained!"

Ron laughed and clapped him on the shoulder. "My man, you do have a point. Thanks." He turned to Jolene, "Let me introduce you around, Jo."

They mingled with the group. Jolene met Ron's other partners, and their families. Ron's sister, Habiba, seemed particularly happy to meet Jolene. "It's so wonderful you came! I'm looking forward to the story you did on Ron and the guys. And you're a grandmother!" Habiba babbled on. "I can't believe it. Your little granddaughter is just adorable! She's over at the children's table with my kids."

"Thank you," Jolene managed to squeeze in. "She—"

"Well, I guess we have a lot of young attractive grand-mothers these days." Habiba laughed. "You're even pret-tier in person than you are on TV—*isn't* she, Ron?" she added pointedly.

"Now, Bebe, don't get started," Ron groaned. "You—"

"All he does is work," Habiba went on to Jolene, as

though Ron hadn't spoken. "I've been telling him for the longest, get out and enjoy yourself sometime. Find yourself a nice woman, and—"

"Come on, Lene. Let me introduce you to my dad. Excuse us, Bebe." Ron took Jolene's hand and steered her away, leaving Habiba in mid–sentence.

"Sorry about that," Ron whispered as they approached a cluster of tables. "Bebe has a heart of gold, but she's designated herself the family matchmaker, and . . ."

"And she's looking out for her big brother," Jolene finished for him. "That's what sisters do."

Ron smiled down at Jolene. "Are you always this perceptive and understanding?" He was teasing, but there was some seriousness behind his words.

"Yes," Jolene teased back. "Especially at family barbecues."

By this time they'd reached the tables. The older man Jolene had seen dancing so smoothly stood as they approached. "Jolene, this is my father, Walter Jamison. Dad, this is—"

"Son, I know who this lovely lady is. Pleased to meet you, Mrs. Jeffries."

"Please call me Jolene, Mr. Jamison. The pleasure is mine."

"Then you have to call me Walt. Won't you have a seat?" As Walt held out a chair for Jolene, she couldn't help but reflect, *Now I know how Ron learned such gentlemanly manners.*

"I was watching you on the dance floor, Mr . . . ah, Walt. You're a marvelous dancer."

"Thank you, my dear, but that must have been my brother, William. I just got here." At Jolene's puzzled look, he added, "We're twins."

"Oh," Jolene said. "I'm sorry."

"That's okay, honey. People been mistaking one of us for the other for seventy–two years now. I'm used to it.

Anyway, I'm a better dancer than he is. Before she passed away, Akron's mother and I used to cut a fine figure on the dance floor." He looked at Jolene closely. "Do you dance?"

"Not nearly as well as you . . . ah, your brother, but I took ballroom lessons at the Y last year. It was fun."

The DJ had put on Freddie Jackson's "Jam Tonight". "This is a good ballroom song," Walt said, rising. He extended his hand to Jolene. "May I have the pleasure?"

Jolene was startled. "Walt, I haven't danced in a long time. I don't know if I—"

"Better tell him yes, Lene," Ron advised. "He doesn't take no for an answer." Ron leaned in closer, eyes twinkling. "Like his son."

Jolene laughed, and took Walt's hand. He led her to the dance floor. Before Jolene had a chance to get nervous, Walt put an arm around her and guided her skillfully into the dance. Although she didn't consider herself that good at it, Jolene had always loved to dance. She realized now just how much she had missed it.

Walt escorted Jolene back to the table, where Ron was standing clapping.

"My goodness! I'm out of breath!" Jolene said, taking her seat, looking flushed and happy. "Walt, you even make me look good. Thank you. I hope I didn't step on your feet too many times."

"Not at all, Jolene. Thank *you*. You're a beautiful dancer. You should dance more often," Walt demurred.

The young girl Jolene had seen dancing earlier came up to the table. "Grandpa, what's gotten into you tonight?" She laughed, hugging him around the neck from the rear. "You're burning up the dance floor!"

"Just 'cause there's snow on the roof don't mean the fire's gone out in the basement, young lady!" Walt laughed as he patted her arm. "You young crumb–snatchers didn't invent dancing, you know."

"Jolene, this is my daughter, Kesia," Ron said. "Kiwi, this is Mrs. Jeffries from Channel Seven."

Kesia didn't resemble Ron as much as LaSalles did. *She must look more like her mother,* Jolene mused. *If she does, Ron's wife must have been truly beautiful. She does have Ron's wonderful eyes.*

"Hello, Kesia." Jolene offered her hand. "It's nice to meet you."

"It's nice to meet you, too," Kesia replied. "I've seen you on TV a million times. It's great that you're doing a story on my father. Did you bring your cameraman?" she asked, looking around.

Before Jolene could answer, they were joined by an attractive young woman leading Zayna by the hand. "Here's your grandmother, honey," the woman told the child.

Zayna ran to Jolene. "Gee–Gee, can I go to the playground with the kids?"

"What playground, Zee?" Jolene wanted to know.

"We fed the children first, so they wouldn't get antsy," the woman said. "Now a few of us mothers are taking them to Jackson Park for a while. It's just around the corner." The woman saw Jolene's inquisitive glance. "Oh, excuse me for not introducing myself. I've seen you so many times on TV that . . ." The woman gave a merry laugh. "Well, anyway, I'm Mona Talent, Ron's secretary."

"Actually, Mona is the *entire* office staff," Ron told Jolene with a wry grin.

"Hi, Mona. It's so nice of you to offer to take Zayna along, but—"

"Oh, please, Gee–Gee!" Zayna put in. "Erika and all the other kids are going!"

"Erika is my daughter," Mona explained. "It seems she

and Zayna have already become lifelong friends. Bebe and a lot of the other mothers are going. There'll be plenty of adults to chaperone. We'll take good care of her."

"Please, Gee–Gee?" Zayna entreated.

"Well, if you're sure it won't be any trouble—" Jolene began.

"No trouble at all," Mona assured her. "And this way you can finish your work with Ron on the story while we're gone."

"We've finished the story, Mona," Ron said, putting his arm across the back of Jolene's chair. "Jolene's here tonight as my guest."

Kesia looked up sharply.

"Oh. Oh, I see," Mona said, looking at Jolene in a totally different light.

Habiba stopped by the table with several kids in tow. "Come on, Mona. These hellions are getting restless." She turned to Jolene, "Is Zayna going with us?"

"Yes," Jolene said. "I just was telling Mona how nice it was of you to—"

"Good. I'm sure Zayna will have a ball." Habiba looked at Ron and Jolene knowingly. "And it will give you two a chance to get better acquainted."

A knowing look flashed across Mona's face as she looked from Ron to Jolene and back again. "Well, guess we'd better get going," she said.

Jolene turned to Zayna. "Now you be a good girl, and stay with the other children. Don't you wander off. And mind Erika's mother and the other ladies."

"I will, Gee–Gee!" Zayna promised as another child, presumably Erika, called out, "Zayna! Mama! Come on! They're ready to go!"

Mona gave Ron and Jolene another perceptive look as she turned to follow Zayna, who was already running toward Erika.

"We'll be back in an hour or so," Habiba said as she too turned to leave. "Don't worry about Zayna," she threw over her shoulder as she departed. "You two just concentrate on having a good time! Especially *you,* my workaholic brother!" With this parting shot she was gone.

"Come and get it before I throw it to the hogs!" a loud voice bellowed. It was Ernie, over at the grill.

"Ready to eat, Jolene?" Ron asked.

"Yes, Ron. The smell of those ribs has me salivating!"

Kesia rolled her eyes, and sucked her teeth. "Maybe you'd better have the chicken." She gave Jolene a sweeping glance from head to toe. "Pork has a lot of calories, you know."

Ron drew his breath in sharply. "Kesia Marie Jamison! You—"

Jolene stopped him with a gentle hand to his arm. "You're right, Kesia," Jolene said smoothly. "I probably should have the chicken." Jolene smiled at the teenager. "But I haven't had a good plate of ribs in ages, so tonight I'm going to splurge."

"Jolene, I'm sor—" Ron began again.

"Ummm, smells delicious," Jolene interrupted. "Ron, would you mind getting me some?"

"Well, ah, sure, Lene," Ron said, rising. He gave Kesia a piercing "you'd better—behave—yourself—young—lady" look as he left.

"I should have told Daddy to bring me some, too," Kesia said to nobody in particular as soon as Ron was out of earshot. "Since I don't have a *weight* problem, I can afford to have as much as I want." She tossed a challenging glance in Jolene's direction.

Jolene was at loss for words this time, but felt she had to make some reply. "Weight has a way of creeping up on you, Kesia," she said as calmly as she could. "Believe it or not, I was slimmer than you are when I was your age. It's never too early to start watching what you eat."

Kesia just sniffed. "Not very good at taking your own advice, are you?" she bluntly assessed.

Child or no, Jolene figured this had gone far enough. She looked Kesia dead in the eye. "That may be true, Kesia, but there are worse things than being too heavy." Jolene leaned forward slightly. "Being rude, for instance."

Kesia was clearly taken aback. She started to reply, but then glanced over at her grandfather, who had not said a word throughout the entire exchange. Something about the look on his face made Kesia change her mind. "Excuse me," she said abruptly, pushing away from the table and rapidly stalking off.

Walt looked to Jolene. "You know what's bothering her, don't you?" he asked quietly.

"No, Walt," Jolene said with a shake of her head. "I honestly don't have a clue. She seemed perfectly friendly when she first came over. What did I do wrong?"

Walt chuckled sadly. "Not a durn thing. But Kesia didn't know you were Akron's *date* when she first came over."

"Oh. I see," Jolene said, although she really didn't.

Walt moved his chair a little closer. "You see, Jolene, Kesia took losing her mother very hard. We've had any number of problems with her. Her schoolwork's suffered, and for a while she kept getting into fights. She seems to have outgrown that, but not this thing she has about her father. I think she feels since she's lost one parent, she has to hang on that much tighter to the one she has left. And she can't bear the thought of anyone taking her mother's place."

"Oh," Jolene said softly. This time she really did see.

"Not that any of that excuses her behavior." Walt grinned. "I was about to step in until I saw you were perfectly able to handle the situation yourself."

Jolene grinned back. "You're a wise man, Walt. I see where Ron gets it." She paused a moment. "The poor kid. I remember when my son was a teenager. It's hard enough to go through those years without all this as well."

Just then Ron came back with two food–laden plates. "Where's Kiwi? I got these for the ladies."

"She went off on her own, son," Walt told him.

Ron set a plate before Jolene. "Then you take the other one, Dad. I'll go back for mine."

"No, Akron." Walt stood. "I think I'll go over and see what your Uncle Willie is up to. You take that one. You two young folks go ahead and enjoy yourselves."

As Walt walked away, Jolene smiled. "That's the first time the term 'young folks' has been used to include me in a long, long time."

Ron laughed, then looked solemn. "Lene, I've got to apologize for Kesia. She—"

"No apology needed, Ron. We had a little chat after you left, and we understand each other perfectly."

"Really?" Ron brightened. "You mean she stopped acting so . . . so hateful?"

"No," Jolene said, picking up a tasty looking bone and taking a nibble. "Actually, she started acting even worse. But still, we understand each other. I understand that she doesn't like me, and she understands . . ." Jolene smiled at Ron, "that I'm going to continue to like her in spite of it."

Ron just sat for a minute, looking at Jolene. "Lene, you're one in a million," he whispered.

Jolene gave Ron a flirtatious sidelong glance. "Well, *I've* always thought so," she quipped.

As they were finishing the meal, Marvin Gaye's "Let's Get It On" began to play. "Come on, Lene," Ron said, taking Jolene's hand. "I wanna show you that the older generation of Jamison men aren't the only ones in this family who know how to dance."

Jolene laughed, and let him lead her to the dance floor. She stopped laughing as he embraced her—her carefully cherished memory of the tender strength of his arms didn't come close to the impact of the real thing. She felt her body melting into his. Ron held her even closer, and sighed. "That's better," he whispered. He looked down into her eyes. "You felt so good the first time I held you, I couldn't wait to do it again."

Jolene's heart was beating so fast she felt breathless. For her reply she just put her head down on his shoulder. The crisp freshness of his shirt and his light, spicy cologne were intoxicating.

At the song's end Jolene and Ron slowly stepped apart. "Whew! A couple ought to get engaged after a dance like that," Jolene joked in a whisper, attempting to hide the quivering she felt inside.

Ron didn't smile in return. "That's not a bad idea," he whispered, his eyes never leaving Jolene's. When they finally turned to leave the dance floor they were startled to find everyone had stopped to watch. The crowd burst out in applause and whistles.

"You go, Ron!" hollered one guy. "Owww!" shouted another. LaSalles stood off to one side, and gave his father a big thumbs up. LaSalles had his arm over the shoulder of the pretty young girl standing next to him. The two of them were very obviously not alone—the girl was in the late stages of pregnancy.

"Jolene, let's grab a couple of beers and find a little privacy," Ron said with chagrin.

"I'm with you. Lead the way," Jolene heartily agreed. They stopped by the cooler, Jolene opting for a Pepsi instead of a beer, and headed off into the wooded area behind Ron's house.

   The sun was just starting to go down, casting long shadows from the abundant trees. "Watch your step," Ron cautioned, "the ground's a little uneven in spots." His hands were big enough to hold both cans in one, while he took Jolene's hand with the other.

   "Ron, was that LaSalles' fianceé with him just now?" Jolene asked softly.

   "Yes," Ron said, "and she's just as sweet as they come. That knucklehead son of mine is lucky to have her." Ron looked over at Jolene. "Shandra has been living with us since school let out for the summer. When they found out she was pregnant, her folks wouldn't let her come home. They don't even call to see if she's all right."

   Jolene was scandalized. "What kind of people are they! How could they do that to their own child?"

   "They're good people, Lene. Really. They're just hurt and angry. In time they'll come around. I wish the kids had waited. God knows I talked to Les about being careful. But they're both good kids, and they love each other, and . . ." He paused for a moment. "I don't know how you feel about this sort of thing, Jolene, but—"

   "Ron, I'm no genius, but if living has taught me anything it's not to judge." Jolene's voice dropped to a whisper. "There's not a soul on this earth that hasn't done something that wasn't wise, wasn't . . . right. I just wish them all the happiness in the world, and Godspeed."

   Ron didn't speak. Then he gently squeezed the hand he was holding.

   They walked along in silence until Jolene exclaimed, "Mercy, Ron! Just how big is your property, anyway?" looking out into the expanse of greenery before them.

   "Actually, we just crossed over my property line," Ron chuckled. "This space is public land. It's actually the back end of the park the kids went to. Nobody around here has fenced backyards, to take advantage of it. Hey," he said suddenly, "there's a real live babbling brook nearby. Want to see it?"

"I never met a brook I didn't like." Jolene giggled. "Which way?"

They forged on hand in hand for another five minutes or so. Jolene was just savoring the peace and serenity of the spot. Even the blare of the music was muffled, muted by the crickets' song. She glanced up at Ron's profile as they went along and silently sighed, her fingers unconsciously tightening on his.

"Here we are." They had reached a clearing. There sat a very worn park bench. "Don't tell anybody, but I dragged it over here from the main part of the park," Ron said in a conspiratorial whisper.

"Well, that's a brook, all right," Jolene said with a grin, "but I'd hardly call it 'babbling'. I think gargling might be a better description." The "brook" was all of a foot and a half wide, and about that much deep. There was water flowing through it, though just barely.

Ron laughed. "It's all about quality, Mrs. Jeffries, not quantity." He easily stepped over the narrow ravine, and stood with one foot on each side, hands on his hips. "Bet I'm the only man you know who can span a river in a single bound."

"Uh huh," Jolene replied. "But just a word of advice— don't quit your day job."

Ron came rapidly toward her and lifted her in his arms, as he had the day they met. "Allow me to carry you across the torrent, M'lady." He stepped across the tiny channel to the bench.

"Ron," Jolene murmured, her arms around Ron's neck, "I think I could have managed to get across by myself."

"Think so?" Ron whispered, still cradling Jolene in his arms.

"Yep. And you know what else I think?" Jolene went on, snuggling closer.

Ron sank down to the bench, Jolene perched on his lap. "Pray tell."

"I think you just wanted to take me in your arms again. At least, I hope you did . . ." Jolene's voice could barely be heard now. She looked up into Ron's eyes. "Because I wanted you to."

Ron's lips found hers gently, tenderly. His lips were so soft, so full. She felt his arms tighten about her waist as the kiss intensified. His tongue eagerly sought hers in a delicious caress. Jolene's arms circled Ron's shoulders as she clung to him, letting the incredible feeling course through her. One of Ron's hands left her waist, and began to delicately stroke her thigh. Jolene moaned faintly at the fire his touch ignited in her loins.

Then he abruptly stopped.

"Lene, I . . . I think you'd better get up now, honey," he gasped.

Jolene jumped up, instantly contrite. "Oh, Ron, I'm so sorry. I should have realized I'm too heavy to sit on your lap."

"What?" Ron said, still panting. Then he chuckled and reached for her hand, gently pulling her down to sit next to him. "You're not too heavy, sugar. That's not why I wanted you to get off my lap."

Jolene looked at Ron's abashed face in puzzlement for a beat. Then they both burst out laughing.

"Well, I didn't want to disgrace myself," Ron shrugged. "After all, I'm only a man." He tenderly cupped Jolene's face. "And you're one hell of a woman." Once again he claimed her lips. The fading sun cast an otherworldly light all about them. Jolene felt as though she had stepped into a fantasy. When they finally broke apart, they just sat nestled together, Ron with his arm around her, Jolene with her head on his shoulder.

"Hey," Ron said, patting the abundant mass of hair atop Jolene's head. "Is this all you?"

"Yep. I've never cut it, except for trimming split ends."

"I knew it was real. We men can usually tell, you know."

Jolene gently poked him in the ribs with an elbow. "Right. You guys may *think* you can. If you knew it was real, why did you ask?"

"Just wanted to get it on the record." Ron buried his face in Jolene's hair. "Damn, it's beautiful! Most women don't want to bother with long hair these days."

"Well, my mother used to always say a woman's hair is her 'crowning glory'. I'm not sure, but I think it's in the Bible." Jolene laughed softly. "Anyway, I save a fortune on hairdressers."

"You do it yourself?"

"Sure. What's to do? I wash it when I need to, let it dry, and pin it up."

Ron couldn't seem to keep his hands off the luxuriant strands. "Do you ever take it down?"

"Just to go to bed."

After a long while, Ron said softly, "Hear it? It's not very big, but you *can* actually hear the water flowing. It's a real peaceful sound. I come out here a lot to think. When something's gotten on my last nerve, coming here puts things back in perspective. That's why I pulled this bench over here. This is my special place." He leaned forward, and softly kissed Jolene's forehead. "That's why I wanted to share it with you." Jolene just snuggled closer to him, squeezing the hand that was holding hers.

They sat there in silence, watching the setting sun. They didn't need to speak. Their hearts spoke for them.

When it was almost dark, Jolene stirred. "Ron, much as

I hate to go, we'd better be getting back. Zayna should be back from the park by now."

"Guess you're right," Ron agreed reluctantly, standing and pulling Jolene up with him.

"Thank you for sharing this with me, Ron," Jolene whispered. I can see why you love it. It's a magical spot."

"No. Up 'til now it's just been a glorious spot." He raised Jolene's hand, looking intently into her eyes. "There was no magic here . . . until you came." He lifted her hand to his lips. Ron held Jolene tightly, and kissed her.

"Okay," Ron said. "Much as I hate to, let's go." And he scooped Jolene up into his arms once again.

"Ron, you crazy man." Jolene laughed. "What are you doing?"

"Carrying you back across the moat, my queen," Ron said with great import, stepping over it. "We just inaugurated a tradition. Henceforth, whenever we come here, I will carry you across."

"Oh, Ron," Jolene caressed his cheek. "I told you that you were the strangest man I ever met." She kissed him lightly. "But I like it."

Ron slowly put Jolene down, and leaned across the ravine to pick up the cans that had fallen into it. "We never did get to these, did we, Lene?"

"No, you were too busy," Jolene said, taking his hand again as they started back.

"Well, you helped," Ron told her.

After a few moments Jolene said, "Ron, nobody's ever called me 'Lene' before."

"No?"

"Uh uh. Most people who don't call me JJ just call me 'Jo.'"

"I tried that a couple times today, but it just doesn't fit. Joe is a man's name." His hand left hers as he put his arm around her waist. "And there ain't *nothing* mannish about you." When Jolene didn't reply, Ron asked, "You don't *mind* me calling you Lene, do you?"

"No, it's not so much that I mind, Ron, it's just that . . . that—"

"That . . . what?"

"Well, *look* at me," Jolene finally said. "I mean . . . well, Ron, I'm *not* lean, you know?"

Ron stopped, and faced Jolene. "Are you upset about that smart remark Kiwi made earlier? Honey, she didn't mean—"

"No, Ron. I'm not upset about that. She's just a hurt, confused child. I know she wasn't lashing out at me personally, but at what I represent." Jolene looked down at the ground. "But in case you haven't noticed, Mr. Jamison, I'm what the large size catalogues euphemistically refer to as a 'big girl.'"

"You're not *any* kind of a girl. You're a woman. A real woman. The kind of woman I never thought I'd find again."

"Was . . . was your wife a large woman, too?" Jolene asked softly, almost afraid to hear the answer.

"Size nine from the day I met her 'til the day she died," Ron said bluntly. He turned Jolene to face him, and lifted her chin, forcing her to look into his eyes.

"We might as well have this out here and now, Jolene. I don't care for you because of your size, or in spite of it. I care for *you*—the woman—the person—inside that body. You've knocked me off my feet from the day I met you."

Ron wrapped Jolene up in his arms. "But I sure don't mind that you're also one of the most beautiful, sexiest women I've ever seen." Ron kissed her passionately. "Woman, you have true beauty. And you'd be beautiful whether you weighed a hundred pounds or three hundred. Don't you know that?"

Jolene looked up and saw the devotion and honesty

in his gaze. "I used to know it. I had forgotten," she whispered.

"Okay. So tell you what." Ron was wearing his devilish grin again. "You don't like Lene, and I don't like Jo, so why don't I call you Lena? I've always thought Lena Horne is one of the most beautiful women on the planet . . ."—he leaned forward, and planted a kiss on the tip of Jolene's nose—"and if that doesn't describe *you*, I don't know what does."

Jolene threw her arms around Ron's neck, holding him close. "Mr. Jamison, as of tonight, I give you full permission to call me anything you like!"

CHAPTER 3

"Hi, baby."

"Hello, Ron. Where are you, honey?"

"Just got home."

"So late?"

"Yeah. Even after all the time you've put in helping me get it together, this grant proposal is driving me batty. Those bureaucrats want to know everything, down to what color pantyhose your great–grandmother wore on her wedding night!"

"Uh, I don't think they had pantyhose back then, honey."

Ron had to laugh. "That's my baby. You always know how to reel me back when I get out there in the ozone layer. Did Zee get off all right?"

"Yes. Anna and her husband came by for her this afternoon."

"I'm going to miss that Munchkin."

"Me, too. I miss her already. But she'll be back in a

couple of weeks. It's only fair that her other grandparents have some time with her, too. And Zayna's going to love going to Disney World with them.''

Ron's voice dropped to a whisper. "Look, Lena, I know it's later than we planned ... but are we still on for tonight?"

To her great surprise, Jolene found herself blushing. "Yes, Ron, of course. But you must be tired, having to work so late. Maybe you'd rather wait until tomorrow.''

"Do you want to wait until tomorrow?'' Ron asked straightforwardly.

Jolene took a deep breath. "No.''

Even through the phone, Jolene could hear Ron release the breath he had been holding. "I'll be there in half an hour.''

" 'Kay,'' Jolene said softly. She slowly put the phone back in the holder. Then she stood, and glanced about the living room for the umpteenth time. She rushed over to the sofa, and needlessly fluffed the pillows one more time.

Going into the dining room, Jolene checked the table again. The silverware at Ron's place setting didn't look quite even. She straightened it, carefully aligning the fork and spoon with the knife on the other side. She stood back and contemplated the long candles in their elegant holders. No, that was too much. What had she been thinking of? Jolene hastily removed the candles and put them back into the china cabinet.

She sniffed the air. Oh, no! Was that the roast burning? Had she forgotten to turn down the oven temperature when it turned out Ron would be late? Jolene ran to the oven. No, everything there was just fine. She opened the oven and basted the roast again, although it showed no signs of drying out.

Going back to the dining room, Jolene again contemplated the table. She retrieved the candles and holders and returned them to the table.

Slowly Jolene turned, and entered her bedroom. The twenty–five watt pink bulb she'd placed in her bedside lamp filled the room with a soft, rosy glow. The candle under the potpourri pot wafted the delicate scent through the air. Her brand new Martha Stewart sheets lay in crisp display, enveloping the queen–size bed. *Well, I've certainly got the right bed,* Jolene dryly thought. *I'm queen–size—it is, too.*

She glanced into her bathroom. Yes, she'd remembered to put out extra towels, and a fresh toothbrush. Okay, time for the final check.

Jolene went to her vanity, and studied herself in the mirror. Why had she decided to wear this dress? Red, of all colors! She started for the closet, but stopped herself. *Oh, no you don't, girlfriend. You've changed three times already. You look fabulous in this dress. And red is your best color.*

Jolene sank down on the bed. *Time to get a grip, Jolene. You're a mature woman in her late–forties. You're a grandmother, for heaven's sake, not some schoolgirl waiting for her first date.* It had been so long since her last date—this kind of date— that it might as well have been the first.

And what if this is not what Ron . . . expects? she thought. After all, they hadn't really *said* that tonight would be the night. With children in the house for both of them, it was like having built–in chaperones. And it had been understood that neither felt comfortable with intimacy with the children there. All they'd really *talked* about was Ron coming over for dinner. But with Zayna away, she knew they'd both thought that tonight. . . .

Jolene knew Ron respected her, truly cared for her. But what would he think if they . . . if she allowed him to . . . Zane's father—she had thought *he* cared for her, too.

Woman, wake up, Jolene scolded herself. *This is 1999, not*

1899. You can't even turn on the TV without seeing people twined in every position imaginable—and that's on the network channels! Yes, but that was TV. Since she was a TV personality, no one knew the difference better than Jolene. This was real life. Over the past month her relationship with Ron had become very precious to her. Almost . . . indispensable.

She looked up into the mirror. A lock of her hair had come undone again. She quickly pinned it up, and picked up the brush to smooth it. Just then the doorbell rang. Jolene was coiled so tightly she jumped, and dropped the brush. *Okay, okay, calm down. This isn't some stranger. This is Ron. This is your man.*

Jolene picked up the brush, placed it back on the dresser, and went to the door. The doorbell rang again just as she reached it.

"Hi."

"Hi. I was beginning to think you'd run off with the milkman."

Jolene laughed nervously. "There aren't any milkmen anymore, Ron."

"Oh. Right."

Something was wrong. Normally that would have gotten a laugh out of Ron. Jolene suddenly realized he was still standing there on the porch. "Well . . . ah . . ." Jolene jerkily swept her arm aside, gesturing for him to come in.

"Oh. Excuse me," Ron said quickly, rushing in so fast that he bumped into Jolene. "Oh. Sorry."

"No problem. Ah . . . won't you have a seat?"

"Oh. Thanks." Jolene started to follow Ron into the living room, then he stopped and turned so suddenly he bumped into her again. "Oh. You all right?" Before she could answer he thrust forward the bottle of wine he was carrying, pushing it into her abdomen. "This is for dinner."

"Oh. Thanks." Jolene took the bottle.

"And these are for you." Ron held the bouquet of roses up so high they brushed Jolene's nose.

Jolene sneezed. "Thank you. They're lovely. I'll go put them in water. Why don't you pour the wine?"

When Jolene returned with the roses in a vase, Ron was standing awkwardly in the middle of the living room floor. "Uh . . . can . . . may I have a corkscrew?"

"Oh. Of course.' " Jolene went to the kitchen and returned with the corkscrew and two glasses. "Forgot the glasses," she said.

It took Ron three tries to get the corkscrew inserted. And then he couldn't pull out the cork.

"Maybe running it under warm water?" Jolene suggested.

"No, I've got it. It's coming, it's com—" The cork came out of the bottle with a loud *pop*. Ron was tugging on the corkscrew so hard the neck of the bottle slammed against his chest, spilling wine all over the front of his spotless white shirt.

"Oh. Damn. And this is a new shirt, too." Ron looked down at himself in confusion, as if wondering how he had gotten himself in such a predicament. "Did any get on the carpet?" he asked, looking down at the floor around him.

"No. I don't think so. Don't worry. It's Scotch–Guarded. Let me get you a towel." Jolene went into the kitchen for the third time in almost that many minutes. She came back into the living room so quickly that she stubbed her toe, lost her balance, and came crashing forward into Ron. The two of them fell together on the sofa in a heap.

They looked at each other for a second in total shock, then simultaneously burst out laughing. They laughed until they were both on the floor, with tears running down their cheeks.

"Hoo, boy! What the hell was *that* all about?" Ron said, wiping the tears from his face.

"Well . . ." Jolene could hardly catch her breath. "I don't know about you, friend, but I was acting that way because I was scared spitless."

"Really?" Ron took her hand. "You weren't really afraid of me, were you, Jolene?" he asked with great concern.

"No, Ron. Not afraid of you. Afraid of—well, maybe afraid isn't the right word. Anxious. I guess anxious is the word. Ron, it's just that it's been so long—"

"Yeah. For me, too."

"Really? How long?"

"Since I lost Marie." Ron paused a moment, then asked, "You?"

"You want to know the truth?"

Ron nodded.

"The truth is . . . so long I can't really remember when it was. That long."

Ron didn't speak for such a long while, and Jolene grew anxious all over again. When he finally did speak, she jumped. "Jolene, do *you* want to know the truth?"

Jolene nodded.

"The truth is that I love you with all my heart. I thought I'd never feel this way again. I want you so much I ache. But I want things to be right between us. I want you to feel comfortable with me. I want you to be sure. So I'll wait. I'll wait as long as it takes. Until you're sure you love me, too." Ron took both Jolene's hands in his, his heart in his eyes. "Because I love you that much, my beautiful Lena."

Jolene slowly slid her hands from his grasp, and rose to her knees. She lifted her right hand, and removed the one large clip that held her hair in place. It fell in a rushing black torrent, down her shoulders, down her back, past her hips, past her knees, until the ends lay in a black satin stream upon the carpet. "I love you, Akron Jamison."

Ron stood and took both Jolene's hands once again to help her to her feet. Hand in hand they went into Jolene's bedroom. Ron looked about. "This room looks like you." He turned to Jolene, and took her into his arms. Then he pulled back slightly, and looked into her face with concern. "Baby, you're trembling."

Jolene looked up at him with a shaky smile, "Don't look now, fella, but you are, too."

Ron looked startled, and then a slow grin crossed his face, "Yeah. Guess I am."

"I hope we're vibrating on the same frequency," Jolene teased, unbuttoning his shirt.

"Something tells me we are," Ron replied, unbuttoning Jolene's dress. The dress fell in a puddle at her feet. She was left clad in only the red lace bra and panties she had so carefully selected just for this special evening.

Ron gasped, and stepped back, staring. He slowly sank down to sit on the bed, but didn't move another muscle.

"Ron? Ron, what's wrong?" Jolene breathed.

"Oh my," Ron huskily replied. "Lena. You are so beautiful. You're like a goddess. Come here, baby."

Jolene came forward slowly until she was standing between his open thighs. She reached out and pulled the open shirt down his arms. He wore nothing beneath, and the powerful muscles of his massive chest and arms glistened with the sheen of the sweat now lightly covering them.

Ron reached behind Jolene, and unfastened the slender clasp of her bra. The bra fell away, reveling her lush, full breasts, their light brown nipples plump and crinkled in anticipation. Ron cupped Jolene's right breast, lightly squeezing as he took the swollen nipple into his mouth.

Jolene moaned at the ecstacy of his hot, wet tongue as it flicked back and forth across her nipple.

Ron's hands slipped down to her buttocks, and he pulled her tightly against his body. Jolene could feel the hard throbbing of his manhood against her quivering thighs. Ron slowly stood, and Jolene reached between them, undoing his belt and pants, and unzipped his fly. She sank to her knees as she slowly pulled the trousers down. Standing once again, her hand snaked beneath the fabric of his shorts until it found its target. Ron groaned from deep in his chest. His lips descended on hers, his tongue greedily exploring hers. Then Ron put his arms about her waist, and they rolled onto the bed together, Jolene's hair loosely wound around them both, as they floated off into ecstacy.

Jolene slowly returned to consciousness. Her senses of touch, sound, and smell were immediately activated: the house smelled of roast, the telephone was ringing off the hook, and Ron had his arm across her waist. She decided to deal with them in priority. She leaned over and lightly kissed Ron's lips. He smiled, murmured something intelligible, and snuggled even closer. *This man of mine is one sound sleeper,* Jolene thought, a fragile smile touching her lips. *But then, he has good reason to sleep soundly just now.* The now surely overdone roast could wait. *Who could be calling at this hour of the night?* Marveling that the still ringing telephone hadn't awakened Ron, as well, Jolene picked it up, "Hello?"

"I need to speak to my Dad," came the terse reply.

Still groggy, Jolene shook her head. "What?"

"I *said* I need to speak to my dad." It was Kesia.

"Kesia?"

"Yes?"

"What's the matter, honey? Is there an emergency?"

"Look, Jolene, that's for my father and me to discuss. I didn't call to talk to you. I want to talk to my father. And don't try to pretend he isn't there. I know he is. Where else would he be in the middle of the night?"

Jolene had to struggle to stay calm. "I never said he wasn't here, Kesia."

"Then can I speak to him . . . please?" The way Kesia said it, it was about the nastiest 'please' Jolene had ever heard.

Holding her temper in check, Jolene simply replied, "Hold on." She turned to Ron, who miraculously was still asleep. "Ron?" Jolene lightly shook his shoulder. "Ron? Honey, wake up."

Ron finally stirred and opened his eyes. As he saw Jolene, his face broke out in a sleepy grin, and he stretched his arms and flexed those strapping shoulders. "What is it, insatiable woman? What are you trying to do, girl, cripple me?" He pulled Jolene's face down to his, and kissed her lips.

"Ron, Kesia's on the phone, honey," Jolene finally managed to get out.

Ron became instantly alert. "Kesia? What time is it?"

Jolene checked the bedside clock. "It's four-thirty."

"Oh, no. Something must be wrong." Ron took the telephone from Jolene. "Kesia? This is Dad, honey. What's the matter?" As he listened, the transformation in Ron's appearance and demeanor was frightening to see. First he became flushed, his chocolate complexion initially taking on a ruddy tinge which became so pronounced he actually turned a shade darker. He almost seemed to swell, his lips cramped in an angry scowl.

After listening for a minute or so, he finally said into the phone, "Kesia, I'm only going to say this once. Get off the phone, and go back to bed. We'll talk when I get home."

Ron listened for another moment. "When am I coming home? You'll know when I get there." Ron hung up the phone.

"Ron? Is she all right? What's wrong?" Jolene asked anxiously.

Ron flopped back on the pillow, just looking disgustedly at the ceiling. "What's wrong is that I have a daughter who seems to have forgotten which of us is the child, and which is the parent."

"I don't understand."

Ron rose on one elbow to face Jolene, "She woke up to go to the bathroom, and noticed that I wasn't in my room."

"And?"

"And nothing. That's it. She found out I wasn't home, so she took it upon herself to call over here."

"But . . . why?"

Ron put his arms around Jolene, and pulled her next to him. "That, my love, is the question. Why? Why is she making a career out of getting into trouble at school? Why doesn't she want to go on with her life? Why does she resent you so much? And most importantly, what can I do to help her?"

Jolene paused a moment before she spoke, "Ron, we know the answer to the 'why' questions. She still hasn't recovered from her mother's death. And she's afraid of losing you."

"I know, Lena. When Marie died, it hurt all three of us." His voice dropped to a whisper. "Hell, for a while I thought I was going insane. But the last thing Marie would have wanted was for us to die with her. Les has moved on, and found love." Ron hugged Jolene tighter, and kissed her forehead. "And thank God, now I have, too. But I don't know how to reach Kesia."

Ron's eyes were tortured as he looked at Jolene. "She's my baby, Lena. My little girl. Pain in the butt that she can be sometimes, I love her." A tear slowly slid down his cheek. "And I don't know how to help her."

Jolene leaned over, and kissed the tear away. "We'll find a way, Ron. Somehow, we'll find a way."

"Lena, I know this is hard on you, too, baby. Please hold on. Please don't give up on us. We'll *have* to find a way." Ron kissed Jolene tenderly. "Because now that I've found you, I can't lose you."

Now tears came to Jolene's eyes, as she embraced him. "Lose me? Mister, there's no way you're *ever* getting rid of me."

"Jolene? Jolene, may I see you for a moment?" Keith Mays stood in his office door.

"Keith, Frank and I are on our way to cover the demolition of the Block Building. Can it wait until I get back?"

"No. No, I'm afraid it can't. I'll call the newsroom and have Jennifer go with Frank to cover the story."

Jennifer Paxton was the fluffy blonde Keith had brought with him when he reported as the new station manager six months before. Jolene was already ticked about Keith's repeated attempts to further Jennifer's career at the expense of her own.

"That's *my* story, Keith. I've already done all the background work. Jennifer doesn't know a damn thing about it. You can't send her."

"Jolene, you forget who runs this station. I decide who covers what. Now, please." He turned sideways, and gestured for Jolene to precede him into the office.

Jolene eyed him silently for a moment. "All right, Keith. Maybe it *is* time we had a talk." She went into his office, and took the chair in front of his desk.

Keith closed the door behind him, and sat down at his desk. He picked up the phone and made the call to the newsroom. Then he turned to Jolene. "I just received a call from Vince DeMarco. He's the CEO of DeMarco Construction."

"I know who he is," Jolene replied.

"Then you also know his company is our biggest advertiser."

"Yes, I know that, too. What does that have to do with me?"

"Mr. DeMarco wanted to know why this station is taking a political stand with one of his business rivals."

"Keith, I haven't the faintest idea what you're talking about."

Keith leaned forward. "All right, let me spell it out for you. I'm talking about your affiliation with H.O.M.E. Construction."

Jolene stared him dead in the eye. "I don't *have* an affiliation with H.O.M.E. Construction."

"Jolene, now please." *Every time he calls me 'Jolene' it grates on my nerves. Why does he just refuse to call me JJ, like everybody else here?* "Everybody at the station knows you've been ... ah, seeing Akron Jamison."

Jolene crossed her arms. "Keith, who I'm 'seeing', as you put it, is quite frankly none of your business."

Keith turned red. "It is when it affects the reputation of this station."

Jolene leaned back in her chair and crossed her legs. "Oh, really? How so?"

"Don't play games with me, Jolene. Akron Jamison is one of the owners of H.O.M.E. Construction."

"Yes, he is. And although—as I've already said—it's none of your business, I will tell you openly that I'm in love with Akron Jamison. But my relationship is with *him*, not his company."

"Can you deny that H.O.M.E. Construction has a bid in for the next housing renovation grant?"

"No, I don't deny it. Why should I?"

"You helped prepare that proposal, I believe?"

"Yes, I did. I was a journalism major. I'm good with words, both spoken and written. What of it?"

"And you're scheduled to speak before the city council in support of that proposal?"

"Yes. And your point is?"

"My point is this station's policy is to openly support no political cause unless it is expressly voted on by the board of directors."

Jolene's mouth flew open in shock. "Keith, you can't be serious! I've done nothing to violate that policy. That policy pertains to partisan elections and issues on the ballot, not a matter of this nature. And the actions I took were as Jolene Jeffries, private citizen, not as an agent of the station."

"Really? What about the interview with Jamison a few weeks ago? Didn't *that* involve the station?"

Jolene sat back in her chair. "Keith, Ron Jamison's company didn't even decide to bid for the grant until after the interview was completed. That interview had nothing to do with the grant proposal."

"The board may see the matter differently, Jolene. I plan to put the matter before them."

Jolene stiffly stood. "You go right ahead and do that, Keith. I have nothing to hide. I've been at this station nine years. I'll stand on my reputation. Now, if you'll excuse me." Jolene turned to leave.

"One minute, Jolene. There's another matter we need to discuss."

Jolene turned. "Yes?"

"I've been reviewing some tapes of your past work. You're really quite an excellent reporter."

"Yes. I am."

"But I couldn't help but notice you've changed considerably since you came here." Keith smirked, looking Jolene up and down. "To put it bluntly, you must have gained a good forty pounds since you first started."

Jolene was thunderstruck at his audacity.

"As you know, Jolene," Keith went on, "ours is a visual medium. And I'm concerned that your current appearance may not be of the professional standards we expect."

Jolene's eyes narrowed dangerously. "No, Keith. That's not what you're concerned about. You're concerned about putting that Barbie doll you brought with you in my place. That's what all this foolishness about policy is about, isn't it? And since I'm an excellent reporter, as you accurately pointed out, you know I'd sue the station for every cent it has if you tried to get rid of me because you've decided I'm not cute enough for you."

Keith shot up from his desk. "How dare you!"

"How dare I? Well, I'll tell you how, Keith. I dare like this—if you make one move to in any way unfairly hamper my career, I'll lay a lawsuit on this station, and on you *personally*, such as the world has never seen. How's *that* for a dare?"

Keith slowly sat back down.

"Thought you could dig it," Jolene threw over her shoulder as she turned once again.

"Jolene. One last thing."

Jolene turned once again. "Who do you think you are, Columbo?"

Keith tried to look pained. "Jolene, I was sincerely hoping it wouldn't come to this." He opened a desk drawer, and pulled out a manila folder. "I've been doing some background work of my own, checking out the information in your personnel file. You went to college in Georgia, didn't you?" He browsed through the papers in the file.

"Amazing what a detailed review of college records can reveal."

Jolene slowly sank back down to her seat.

Jolene looked at her watch as she pulled her car into Ron's driveway. She hoped Ron would be there soon. When she'd called him at the site, he said he'd get there as soon as he could.

I should have told him before now, Jolene chided herself. *I love this man. How could I keep this from him?* She knew why. She didn't want to lose Ron—to lose his respect, to lose his love. *But you can't build a life on a lie, girl. You should know that by now. Did you really think no one would ever find out? And now that you've finally found the love of your life, that lie could destroy everything.*

Jolene looked at her watch again. What could be keeping Ron? He knew she'd never call him like this in the middle of the day unless it was urgent. She suddenly remembered Ron showing her the location of a hidden key, under a phony rock in the front yard. Kesia was always losing her house key, and Ron kept one there so she wouldn't be stuck one day with no way to get in. Jolene had been there one evening, working on the grant proposal, when Ron had to replace the hidden key.

Jolene left the car, and retrieved the key from its hiding place. When she got to the front door, she rang the bell. Les was working with Ron, and Kesia was in school, but Shandra, who only worked part–time, might be there. If she were, Jolene didn't want to startle her. Jolene rang the bell several times, but there was no answer. After looking one last time to see if Ron were approaching, Jolene let herself in.

"Hello? Hello?" she called on the off chance someone

was there, and had not heard the doorbell. There was no answer.

The smell hit her a moment later. Marijuana. She'd never used it, but having been a college student in the seventies, could certainly recognize the unmistakable scent.

Ron's not going to like this one bit, she thought. *I know Les is young, but he ought to know his father don't play that, especially in his house.* Les was always running errands to get building materials and such. *He must have come by here on a break,* Jolene's thoughts ran on. *Or maybe it's Shandra. I hope she's not messing with that stuff while she's pregnant.*

Jolene looked around the house. Ron had painstakingly restored all the fine features of the old house—the beautiful hardwood floors, the graceful stairway, the high, beamed ceilings. Much as she loved the house, Jolene had difficulty seeing herself there. *I'd always feel like an intruder here, after all the years Ron spent here with Marie. I don't think I could ever feel that I was the mistress of this house.* Jolene laughed at her own foolishness. *At this moment, it's questionable whether the man will even want to ever see you again, after today. And here you are imagining yourself as his wife?*

Jolene went into the kitchen in the back of the house to wait for Ron. She decided to make a pot of coffee, since Ron drank the stuff all day long.

As she was putting the water in the coffeemaker, the second smell hit her. Smoke. Jolene looked at the stove. All the burners and the oven were off. Anyway, the smell didn't seem to be coming from in there.

Jolene ran frantically though the lower rooms of the house, desperately looking for the source of the smell that was becoming stronger by the second. Upstairs. It must be coming from upstairs. She ran to the foot of the stairway. Yes, the smoke was visible there, drifting down from above.

Just then a piercing screech began. A smoke detector.

Jolene ran quickly up the stairs. Thick, black smoke was pouring from Kesia's room. Even from several feet away Jolene's eyes began to water, and she began to cough.

Putting the scarf she wore around her neck over her mouth and nose, Jolene went into the room, hoping the fire was small enough for her to put out alone. The drapes all along one wall of the room were aflame, and the fire had spread to the walls and the dresser. The smoke was so thick now that it was difficult to see, but just as she was turning to run back out, she faintly made out a form lying motionless across the bed.

"Kesia! Kesia!" Jolene ran to the bed and shook the girl as hard as she could, calling her name over and over. Kesia groaned, but did not move. Too late, Jolene realized she should have called the fire department before she came upstairs. She snatched up the phone on Kesia's bedside table. It was dead. Jolene glanced down. The cord connecting the phone to the wall was melted through. She dashed into Ron's room. This phone was cordless and, thank God, it was working. Jolene quickly called 911 and reported the fire. Then she darted back to Kesia.

The fire had spread even farther, and the smoke was thicker than ever. Jolene was beginning to gasp for breath through the coughing that racked her body. Jolene knew Kesia was too heavy for her to carry. Somehow, she had to wake her. Jolene ran to a window, and flung it open. Instantly the room was clearer as the fresh air poured in. Jolene then bolted into the bathroom. Glancing desperately around her, she snatched up the wastebasket and quickly filled it with water.

She ran back to Kesia. The fresh air had dissipated much of the smoke, but it had also fueled the fire. The flames leaped even higher than before, and were spreading throughout the room. Jolene was beginning to feel woozy, but managed to dash the container of water into Kesia's face. The girl jerked violently and began to cough, but her eyes did not open.

"Kesia! Kesia! You have to wake up! Do you hear me? You have to wake up!" Jolene drew her hand back, and slapped Kesia across the face as hard as she could.

Kesia's eyes flew open and her arms flew out, flailing out at Jolene. "Lemme 'lone. I'm sleepy," she murmured groggily.

Jolene could hear fire sirens in the distance. *I can't leave her here. I won't leave her here. They may not get here in time!*

"No! You have to get up! We have to get out of here!" Jolene screamed. She slapped the girl once again.

"No! Lemme alone!" Kesia said, but this time she sat up.

Jolene crouched, and pulled Kesia's arm around her neck. As the girl's arm raked across her head, Jolene's hair came loose, and fell tumbling down her back. Ignoring it, Jolene grasped Kesia's hand on her shoulder tightly and stood, pulling the girl up with her. Jolene put her other arm around Kesia's waist. "Walk, Kesia! I can't carry you! You have to help me!"

Kesia sluggishly moved one foot forward. "That's it, honey! You can do it!" Jolene encouraged her.

"Jolene! Jolene! Where are you?" It was Ron.

"Oh, thank God!" Jolene breathed. "Ron! Ron, we're up here!" Jolene was trying her best to shout, but her voice only came out in gasps.

Then Ron appeared in the doorway.

"Jolene! Kiwi! Oh, my God!"

"Help me, Ron! We've got to get her out of here!" Jolene screamed.

Ron grabbed Kesia, and threw her over his shoulder as though she was weightless. "I've got her, Lena! Let's go!"

Jolene suddenly felt intense heat at her back. "Ron! I'm

on fire!" Jolene's hair was ablaze. She twirled in terror, only causing the flames to spread.

"Stop, Jolene! Stand still! You're only making it worse, baby!" Ron dumped Kesia back on the bed, and grabbed Jolene's legs in a bear hug. He flung Jolene and himself to the floor, rolling with her, beating the flames with his hands until they were extinguished.

Ron quickly helped Jolene to her feet, "It's out now. Are you all right? Did you get burned, baby?"

"No, hardly at all . . . but, oh, Ron! Look at you!" Ron's hands were charred, and already blisters were beginning to appear, but Ron was already bending to pick up Kesia.

A fireman suddenly appeared at the doorway. "It's all right, folks! This way!" Another fireman grabbed Kesia, and dashed with her out of the room. Ron picked up Jolene and carried her down the stairs and through the door as other firemen rushed in with hoses.

Outside, Kesia was on a gurney, and paramedics were holding an oxygen mask over her face.

"Let me take over here, buddy," a paramedic said to Ron, looking at Jolene, who was coughing and gasping for air. The paramedic had another oxygen mask in his hand for her.

"It's okay, honey. I'm all right," Jolene gasped out. "Go see to Kesia."

"I'll be right back, honey," Ron said, seeing that Jolene was in good hands. Ron rushed forward. A policeman stopped him. "Just hold on, sir. Everything's under control."

"You don't understand! She's my daughter!" Ron cried, pushing the policeman aside.

One of the paramedics stood. "It's all right, sir. She has a bad case of smoke inhalation, but she wasn't burned. She's even conscious now. Come on, you can talk to her."

Ron ran to Kesia's side. "Daddy! Oh, Daddy, I'm so

sorry! I skipped school today. I . . . I had some weed. It made me sleepy, so I laid down, and . . . oh, Daddy!"

"It's okay. It's okay, baby girl. We'll talk about all that later. You're all right. That's all that matters now."

Jolene appeared at Ron's side. "Is she okay?"

"They said she'll be fine, honey. How about you?"

"I'm okay. Just a minor burn on my back."

"We need to get your daughter to the hospital now, sir. It's just precautionary," the paramedic told Ron.

"Then I'm going with her," Ron said.

"I guess you are," the guy replied, looking down at Ron's hands. "Those burns need to be treated."

They wheeled Kesia's gurney to the waiting ambulance, with Ron and Jolene trailing alongside. "Don't worry, honey," Ron told Kesia. "I'm coming with you."

Kesia put out her hand and grabbed Ron's arm. "Daddy, I want Jolene to come, too."

"I'm right here, Kesia." Jolene smiled down at her, taking her hand.

"Oh, Jolene! After I've been so hateful to you, you risked your life for me! Can you ever forgive me?" Kesia looked up at the charred and uneven strands of Jolene's hair. "And your hair! Your beautiful hair!"

Jolene's smile grew even wider. "It'll grow back. I look at it as a pretty good trade—I lost a hairdo, but gained a friend."

"Well, we're quite a pair, Mr. Jamison," Jolene said that evening. "You with your bandaged hands, and me with my bandaged back." They were sitting at Jolene's kitchen table, having dinner.

"And I'd say we were pretty lucky, considering," Ron replied. "We should both be able to go back to work in a few days. And they told me Kesia will be released tomorrow.

They just want to observe her overnight. Even the damage to the house was mostly confined to that one room. Thank God I'm insured to the max. And thank God you were there! When I think what could have happened if you weren't! That reminds me—what was it you wanted to talk to me about this afternoon?"

Jolene's smile faded. "Ron, some things are going to come out soon. Some things you need to know."

Ron placed one of his bandaged hands over hers. "Well, what is it, baby? You know you can tell me anything."

"Ron, this is something I should have told you before. I'm so sorry I didn't."

Ron looked worried now. "What is it, Lena? Are you sick? Are you in some kind of trouble?"

Jolene rose from the table, and walked a few paces away. She abruptly turned to face Ron. "No, I'm not in trouble now. But I was. I *was* in trouble my senior year of college."

"Honey, I'm not following you. What are you trying to tell me?" Ron rose and went to Jolene. "Look, here, girl. You're the woman I love. Whatever troubles you have are my troubles, too. Now, whatever it is, just tell me."

Jolene looked down at her hands, "Ron, I'm Jolene Jeffries, but I'm not *Mrs.* Jeffries. She looked up at Ron, her eyes brimming with tears. "Ron, I've never been married."

Ron blinked quickly. "What?"

"I've never been married. Zane's father was one of my professors. I loved him. I thought he loved me. And he didn't tell me he was married until I told him I was pregnant." Jolene laughed bitterly. "I was the only graduate with a baby under her robe. After Zane was born, I moved to another city, stuck 'Mrs.' in front of my name, and told everybody I was divorced.

"I had to tell you now, because it's going to come out at the grant hearing. My new station manager Keith found out about me. He said he'd use the lie I've been living all these years to discredit me if I testified. DeMarco Construction is afraid of you beating them out for that grant. And Keith is afraid they'll pull their advertizing from the station.

"I should have told you before. It shouldn't have taken this for me to tell you. But I was ashamed. I didn't want you lose respect for me."

Ron didn't speak for a long moment. "You don't have to go to the hearing, Jolene. I'd understand," he finally said.

"No, Ron. What you're doing is too important. And anyway, I'll be damned if I let Keith hold that over my head to control me. The only way to stop a blackmailer is to let the secret he's manipulating go public. I'm going to call Zane tonight to tell him. I don't want him to hear it through the grapevine." Jolene looked down at the floor. "But I had to tell you first."

Ron moved a step closer. "I see. So you've never been married?"

Jolene shook her head sadly.

Ron put a finger under her chin, and lifted her face. His eyes were shining as they gazed lovingly into hers. "Well, would you like to be?"

"You may now kiss the bride!"

LaSalles bent to lift the veil from Shandra's face.

Jolene looked up at Ron, and squeezed his hand. "You're not losing a son. You're gaining a daughter— Gramps." Jolene smiled over at Shandra's mother, who was cradling newborn Akron Jamison the second in her arms.

The guests all applauded as the newlyweds embraced, but instead of starting up the aisle with his bride LaSalles held up his hands for attention.

"What in the world?" Ron wondered.

"Ladies and gentlemen," LaSalles began, "Shandra and I thank you for being here with us on this special day. But we were not the only engaged couple to enter this church this afternoon."

"Huh?" Jolene said.

"As most of you know," Lasalles was continuing, "my dad and his lady are planning to be married in a small ceremony at home in a couple of weeks. We tried to talk them into making this a double wedding, but they insisted this be *our* day.

"But what they didn't know is that we, their children, insist they be married in church, so . . . Mr. Jamison and Miss Jeffries—would you please step forward?"

"But . . . but, son, I don't even have the wedding rings here!" Ron stammered.

Zane stepped forward, "Oh, yes, you do—Dad." He reached into his pocket, and pulled out a black velvet box. "Although we had a devil of a time sneaking them out of your room."

"So *this* is why you and Marlena got leave so early, you rascal!" Jolene scolded her son.

"Who better to give you away, Mama?" Zane grinned at Jolene as Marlena came forward to kiss her mother–in–law's cheek. Zane handed the velvet box to Zayna. "Here you go, baby. Ready to be the ring bearer as well as flower girl this time?"

"Yes, Daddy." Zayna looked up at Jolene, "Come on, Gee–Gee. It's time for you and Papa Ron to get hitched."

"Here's your bouquet, Jolene." Kesia handed Jolene a huge bouquet of red roses. The two just stood looking at each other a moment, then Kesia impulsively threw her arms around Jolene. "Oh, Jolene," Kesia said, drawing away, "I'm sorry! I mussed your hair!" She stroked Jolene's new chin-length bob, brushing the displaced strands back into place.

Jolene just leaned forward and gently kissed Kesia's fore-head. "What's a mussed hairdo," she whispered softly, "between friends?"

"I have your marriage license right here," LaSalles pat-ted his breast pocket.

With tears in her eyes, Jolene looked up at Ron. "Well, looks like we're outnumbered. What do you say, Chief?"

"I've already asked you to marry me, my beautiful Lena." Ron kissed Jolene tenderly. He looked deeply into her eyes, "But, honey, will you marry me—right now?"

Jolene beamed as she nodded, and put her arm through his. "Jolene Jeffries Jamison is the most beautiful name in the world. I don't want to wait another two weeks. Do you?"

Ron lifted her hand to his lips. "No. So, let's go, Triple J."

EPILOGUE

"Papa! Papa, wake up!"

"Huh? What time is it? What is it, princess?" Ron groggily asked.

"It's seven–thirty. And you promised to take me to my dance lesson today," Zayna declared.

"Zayna," Jolene put in, having herself been awakened by her granddaughter's persistence, "your lesson isn't until eleven o'clock. Why are you waking your grandfather and I up at the crack of dawn on a Saturday?"

"I don't want to be late, Gee–Gee," Zayna insisted.

"Be that as it may, young lady," Jolene continued, "your timing leaves a bit to be desired. Now you march . . ."

Suddenly a baby began to cry in the next room. "Now you've done it, girlfriend," Jolene scolded. "You woke your brother!"

"I'll get him, Gee–Gee!" Zayna bustled from the room with all the big–sisterly importance her budding eleven year old body could muster.

Ron rolled over to take Jolene into his arms. "Good morning, Mrs. Jamison." He kissed her tenderly. "Have I told you I love you today?"

"No, I don't believe you have, sir," Jolene murmured, snuggling deeper into his embrace.

"Now, you know my favorite way of saying 'I love you' doesn't need words, don't you, baby?" Ron ran his fingers through Jolene's hair, tenderly winding its copious length around his hand to gently pull her face to his. His lips captured hers once again as they slowly sank back into the still warm, delicious depths of the pillows.

"Gee–Gee! Zayna won't let me play with Zak!" Seven-year–old Akron Jamison the second burst into the room, and with a flying leap, jumped into the bed between Ron and Jolene.

"Ooof!" Ron gasped as his grandson's poorly aimed lunge planted a small foot squarely into his stomach. "Now, look here, A.J.," Ron told the child, "Haven't I told you a hundred times to knock before you come in?"

"I'm sorry, Pops." The boy threw his arms around Jolene, "Good morning, Gee–Gee."

"Good morning, honey," Jolene kissed him. "Now what's all this about Zayna not . . ."

"He's just mad because I said Zak couldn't have that Hershey bar he tried to give him," Zayna said, striding back into the room with ten–month–old Zak on her hip.

"And what were *you* doing with a Hershey bar, young man?" Ron challenged the boy, tussling with him on the bed. "Have you been plundering in the kitchen cabinets without permission again?"

A shamefaced A.J. was spared having to come up with a reply when Zak took a deep breath, and began crying again with a vengeance.

"Uh oh. I think it's time for somebody's bottle," Jolene surmised.

"Yes, I was just going downstairs to get it," Zayna told her.

A.J. put his head on Jolene's shoulder, and looked up at her with beseeching eyes, "Gee–Gee, will you make me some panny–cakes this morning?"

"That's *pancakes,* A.J.—honestly!" Zayna rolled her eyes at her cousin, full of proper pre–teen disdain for such baby talk.

"*You* used to call them panny–cakes, too, when you were his age, honey," Jolene gently chided.

"She did?" A.J. asked with glee. "Panny–cakes, panny–cakes, Zayna Ann likes panny–cakes!" he taunted his cousin.

"My name is Zayna *Jo*Anne, boy. If you're going to say it, get it right."

"Okay, Zayna . . . *Ann,*" the boy came back.

"Look," Ron said, "I can see nobody's getting any more sleep this morning, so why don't we go downstairs. *I'll* cook breakfast this morning."

Breakfast was clearly still the subject topmost on Zak's "to do" list. He stopped crying, looked his sister in the eye, and pronounced in a no nonsense tone, "Bah–Do."

"Okay, big man," Zayna laughed. "I get the message. One 'bah–do' coming right up. Come on, A.J. I'll turn the TV on for you, and you can look at cartoons while I feed the baby."

Ron and Jolene rose to don their robes as the children went downstairs. "You know, honey," Ron said, "I'm overjoyed that our kids have gotten so tight they go out together. But there's only one drawback—we get to baby–sit the grandkids all at one time!"

"Don't even try it, Akron Jamison! You light up like a firefly whenever the kids are here, and you know it."

"Yeah, I guess I do," Ron admitted with a chuckle. "It's

great having Zane and Marlena close by, now that they're stationed here."

"Yes, it is, honey," Jolene agreed, tying her robe, and sitting at the vanity to brush her hair. "And the four of them work so hard, I'm glad they like to get with Les and Shandra for a night on the town every once in a while." She paused with the brush hovering over her head in mid–stroke, gazing dreamily out the window at the beautiful flowers surrounding the yard.

Ron came up behind, and put both hands on her shoulders, "What is it, baby?"

Jolene sighed. "I was just thinking that right out there, on that very spot, was where we first met, when this house was just a shell. I never would have dreamed that I'd be living in this house one day." She reached up to put one hand over Ron's, and looked into the vanity mirror, smiling at him tenderly. "Living here—with you."

"I called this place my dream house. But it never would have been . . ." Ron leaned forward, and kissed Jolene's lips, pulling her up from the vanity bench into his arms, "without you". Just then the door bell rang.

"Gee–Gee? Papa? Somebody's at the door!" Zayna redundantly called up the stairs.

"Be right down, honey!" Ron called. He kissed Jolene one last time. "I love having the kids here, but . . ." he held Jolene a little tighter, patting her behind. "I miss how we *usually* spend our Saturday mornings."

"Behave yourself!" Jolene laughed up at him. "We don't want to scandalize the children, frisky Papa. And anyway . . ." she squeezed Ron's buns with a devilish wink, "there's always Saturday *night!*"

As they made their way downstairs, a baby started to cry. And then another began to cry. And then another. "Uh oh," Ron told Jolene. "You know what that means."

Sure enough, when they entered the kitchen there stood Kesia, with one of her twins in each arm.

"Hello, darling," Jolene said, going to Kesia, and kissing her cheek. Jolene took one of the twins, while Ron took the other.

"What's the matter with Gee–Gee's big girl?" Jolene cooed to the baby, who stopped crying to give her a big toothless grin.

"Hi, Mom. They're upset because I bundled them up and ran out the house when they were still half–asleep." Kesia looked at Jolene pleadingly. "I hate to ask you, but my baby–sitter is sick, and I have an important seminar downtown in half an hour. This *would* have to happen when their father is on a business trip. Would you mind watching them for a couple of hours?"

"Of course not, honey." Jolene sat at the kitchen table, bouncing the baby on her knee. "You go on to your meeting. We'll be just fine."

"Thanks, Mom. You're an angel. Thanks, Daddy." Kesia kissed Ron on the cheek as she made for the door. "I'll be back by one. Oh, and Daddy, don't forget you promised to speak to my tenth–grade class next Wednesday." She flashed Ron a bright smile. "We're studying architecture, and I promised them the world's best architect would come and tell them how it's done!"

"I'll be there, baby," Ron promised. "I have a meeting with the mayor that morning on the grant renewal, but I saved the afternoon for you. My intrepid customer relations manager highlighted it on my calendar." He looked at Jolene, "Right?"

"Yes, sir, Mr. Jamison," Jolene assured him. "I most certainly did."

A somewhat frenzied couple of hours later, the three babies were taking a nap, A.J. was deep into a video game, and Zayna was practicing for her dance class.

Jolene rested her head on Ron's shoulder as they gently rocked on the back porch glider. Ron leaned over to kiss her forehead. "Penny for your thoughts, beautiful Lena," he whispered, putting his arm around her shoulders.

"I was just saying a little prayer. Saying thank you, for my children, for my grandchildren, for my home, and for my heart."

"For your heart? Woman, what are you talking about?"

"I'm talking about you—my love, my heart." She looked up into Ron's eyes. "And you know what they say . . ." Jolene caressed her husband's cheek. "Home is where the heart is."

ABOUT THE AUTHOR

Raynetta Mañees has been an administrator with the federal government for 25 years. She is a graduate of Wayne State University, with a degree in Mass Communication. She has been a solo vocalist since childhood, performing in numerous venues in the Northwest and in the Caribbean. She is also an accomplished actress and former on-air radio personality.

Raynetta welcomes your comments at her E-mail address, *Rmanees@aol.com,* or via "snail mail" at P.O.Box 648, Inkster, MI 48141. Please include a stamped, self-addressed envelope.

And Please enter "Raynetta's World of Romance" at http://www.geocities.com/soho/9823

BRIANNA'S GARDEN

VIVECA CARLYSLE

CHAPTER ONE

Elianna was sure her behavior would lead to being arrested. She couldn't stop peeking through the curtains at her neighbor for the second day in a row. She blamed the real estate agent for mentioning the handsome widower, when all Elianna wanted was some peace and quiet for her daughter Brianna and herself.

Nic Sinclair did not give the impression of a man who was interested in landscape design. The agent said he was a lawyer with a firm in New York. Several rumors floated around the small Cape Cod community that he might be planning to sell his property. All the real estate agents were chomping at the bit to get their hands on it. Elianna understood that. She'd wished more than once since she arrived that she could afford to live in the community.

Elianna had studied him as he dragged his shovel in circles around his property. She'd told herself that she was just curious, since most of his property was tall grass and weeds. She had watched him as he chopped up the overgrown patch of land and put down topsoil. She almost convinced herself that curiosity was her real reason for peeping at her neighbor.

His black hair was a little longer than that of most corporate types, and she would have bet money it was professionally styled in one of those unisex salons that she'd read about.

The day before, she'd watched him move in. He and another man had carried bags with labels from a nearby hardware store, so maybe the rumors were true. She had seen the other man rise early and walk down to the beach. Perhaps the house would be for sale. She'd heard the owner really wants to get rid of it.

Nic had stayed at the house and begun clearing the land. His tan face was all angles, with a solid square jaw, handsome and masculine. He had a lean, athletic body with wide shoulders, a broad chest, and strong, muscular legs. She could tell all this from the way his Ohio State sweatshirt and the tight, black denim jeans hugged his frame. It wasn't as if she'd never seen a handsome, well–built man before. Brianna's father had been cut from that same cloth.

The thought of Brianna's father threw a damper on the fun she'd been having checking her neighbor out. If she'd learned one thing in her life, it was that gorgeous men were not dependable men.

She moved away from the window and went in search of her daughter. She found her arranging her Beanie Babies around the kitchen table. Brianna's mop of auburn curls bounced with her every move. Her daughter did not walk if she could run. Sometimes Elianna wished for that sort of energy.

Brianna had dressed herself in her favorite outfit for this trip. It was a yellow, one–piece sunsuit trimmed in green and yellow plaid. She was barefoot, as usual. Brianna hated shoes, and discarded them as soon as she was in the house, no matter how much Elianna warned her about stepping on tiny objects and hurting herself. Brianna seemed to feel free without shoes.

"They're hungry," she explained, pointing to her toys.

"Umm, does that mean you're a little hungry, too?"

"No. Maybe a little."

"How does French toast sound? Do you think they'll like it?"

A slow grin spread across the four year old's face. "Yes, Mommy. They will like French toast."

Elianna began gathering the equipment and the ingredients.

"Turn on the music, Mommy."

This was a ritual with them—loud rock music. Elianna had played it when she was pregnant. She felt that was why her daughter loved to sing and dance to it. The music had been a way of Elianna forcing herself into an upbeat mode after Brian had walked out on her.

With the thumping beat of Meatloaf's "I'd Lie For You and That's The Truth," Elianna danced around as she mixed the ingredients. Brianna's version was shortened to, "I'd Lie, and That's True."

After a couple of choruses the phone rang, and she had to turn the music down so she could talk. She grinned as she recognized her best friend's voice. "So, was I right about the place?"

"Yes, Caryn. You were right, as usual."

"Good. You needed to wind down after playing Supermom and Super office manager—well, make that acting manager. Then they had the audacity to ask you who should get the job."

"Don't start. We knew the minute Adam came on board they wanted to give the manager job to him."

"That doesn't make it fair."

"No, but the look on their faces when I asked for a three month leave of absence gave me some sort of revenge."

"I just wanted you to have it after—"

"I know."

Caryn had been her staunchest supporter when Brian decided that he didn't want to be a father. Elianna was four months pregnant at the time, and since her parents had moved to Hawaii when her father retired, Caryn was all the family support she had at the time. Despite her parents' pleas for her to move from Compton, California, and come live with them, Elianna didn't want to burden them. They'd raised a child, and this was the time for them to enjoy life. Instead, she'd taken a transfer to the Boston office, and after her maternity leave had become the person everyone turned to when they needed something.

"Did they try to get you to change your mind?"

"Up to the moment I was headed toward the door."

"Have they tried to call you?"

"Yes, but I didn't return the calls."

"Aha!" Caryn shouted. "You're finally learning that you have to take time for yourself. Are you going to the beach all day every day?"

"I uh . . . not all day." She just couldn't lie. She took Brianna to the beach in the morning because it would make her sleep most of the afternoon, and Elianna could work on her project.

"Why don't I like the sound of that?"

"You know me too well." They'd been friends since college. Caryn had been the one to encourage her to move to Boston so they could share an apartment until the baby was born.

"What exactly are you doing?"

"I'm learning about computers and spreadsheets."

"You are hopeless. I'm going to have to come up there every weekend and drag you out to have some fun."

"Don't come too soon. I want to go back to work with some new skills."

"That's just your insecurities talking."

Caryn was so right. Brian had had a way of making her feel as if she wasn't bright enough to travel in his circles. He was an up–and–coming banker, in line for a director's position at one of the largest branches in Compton. That was satisfactory until the bank had sent him to Los Angeles to a training session. The contacts he made there convinced him there were many avenues he could pursue if he weren't tied down. The seductive beat of the city had stolen his heart, and Elianna knew something was wrong when he returned. Instead of planning their wedding, she'd learned that she was going to be a single mother.

She'd gone to Boston and had the baby. Her parents' gift had been enough for her to get an apartment. She'd hired an older woman to live in and care for Brianna. Caryn and her parents tried to talk her out of naming the baby after her father, but Elianna had been using Brianna since she'd learned she was having a girl.

Now she'd come to Cape Cod to regroup, to enjoy her daughter, and have some peace and quiet while she broadened her computer horizon. She loved the area. The house was spectacular—four bedrooms and baths, a view of the beach from each of those bedrooms. The Victorian house with its wraparound porch gave her the feeling of being in a cocoon. She wished she could afford to live there forever. Unfortunately for Elianna, she had only until the end of August.

"What are you doing for yourself, Caryn girl?"

"I'm working on a couple of things." Caryn's voice trailed off.

"You are just as much a workaholic as I am."

"I know, but it's different. I don't have an adorable daughter to play with."

"Don't even go there. You don't have a daughter because you're too wrapped up in that job to have a social life."

"I'm thinking about a vacation."

"Well, why don't you take it? Why don't you come up and spend a couple of weeks with us?"

It was a challenge, one that Caryn couldn't resist. "Just wait till I wrap up this project. I'm gonna surprise you. Did you give anyone from the office your number?"

"Just Julie. I warned her that if any of the partners got it she was dead meat."

"If they call, pretend it's a bad connection and you can't hear anything. Then hang up and put the answering machine on."

"I'm glad this place has one. All the other things are working out. I can actually earn the same salary. I just have to have a lot of little jobs. But the resumés, manuscripts, columns, they're not hard to do, and it all adds up." They had done this all through college—challenged each other until the challenge was answered.

Elianna had convinced herself she had no interest in her handsome neighbor. Maybe he was Caryn's type. The last serious relationship had ended three months, because of Caryn's dedication to her career.

They talked a few more minutes before Brianna tugged at her skirt, begging to talk to Caryn. After a short conversation about the beach and Caryn prodding Bree to insist on going every day, they said good–bye and hung up.

By the time Elianna showered and dressed, Bree was standing at the window peering at the man next door. "Like mother, like daughter," Elianna said.

"Are we going to the beach now?"

"Yes. We're going to build a sand castle." Elianna grabbed an oversized beach bag, and two wide brimmed hats to protect them from the sun.

She took her daughter's hand and led her out of the house and down the path to the front gate. As she lifted the latch and they turned toward the beach, she got another view of the man next door.

He was chopping down another section, and had removed his sweatshirt. She got a real view of the muscles in his back as he swung a machete–like tool to cut the overgrown lawn down to size. She wondered how he kept in shape. Did he plays sports, or did he have one of those fancy personal trainers who put him through a series of exercises to keep that body fluid?

She turned away and walked a little faster until she realized that Bree was running to keep up. She slowed her pace, a little embarrassed that once again she'd behaved like a voyeur.

The beach was crowded by now, but Elianna found a little section of the area unoccupied. She and Bree took turns rubbing sunscreen on each other before beginning their project.

"Don't you think you need a little more water for that?"

Elianna looked up and recognized the man as her neighbor's friend. "Oh, yes. We'll get it in a few minutes."

"I'm Ty Reynolds. I think we're neighbors."

"I think so," she stammered.

"I saw you and your daughter when Nic and I were moving in."

Elianna was even more embarrassed. She'd been so busy spying on her neighbor that she hadn't noticed his friend.

"I'm Elianna Preston and this is my daughter Brianna. We come to the beach every day."

"We're building a sand castle," Bree announced.

"May I help?"

"You have to ask my mommy."

"OK. How about it, Mommy? May I help you build the castle?"

"Sure." Elianna shrugged her shoulders. What else could she say to the man?

They started out with just Elianna, Bree, and Ty working on the castle, but an hour later half the beach had joined in. Ty was patient with Bree. He showed her how to squeeze the sand, so she felt part of the action. People were shouting orders to bring water or more sand or whatever they needed.

"So this is what happens when you promise to help me work on my house?" The deep baritone voice cut though the noise, and Elianna gazed up into the hazel eyes of her neighbor.

"I couldn't help it," Ty said. "They were damsels in distress, and I had to help them."

"Right!"

"Elianna, this is my friend, Nic Sinclair. He owns the house next to yours."

She held out her hand. "I'm just renting for the summer."

"Is your husband commuting?"

"I'm not married." She thought she saw Nic and Ty exchange a look, but it was so brief she assumed it meant nothing.

"Oh. I've seen you at the window. I thought you were looking for someone," Nic said.

Elianna felt the heat under her cheeks. He knew she'd been spying on him. She turned away, pretending to watch Bree, who was now running to the water with a teenage girl. The girl held Bree's hand and stayed with her as she filled the bucket with wet sand, and they hurried back to add another layer to the growing structure. The trip back was slower for Bree than the trip down to the water.

"Your daughter looks as if she's getting tired."

"That's the idea."

"What do you mean?"

"I bring her to the beach and let her play hard, and when I take her home she will take a very long nap."

"Why?" Ty asked.

"So I can get some work done."

"I can understand that," Nic told her, "but aren't you on vacation?"

"I'm teaching myself some new computer techniques."

"Oh? Why don't you ask Nic for help in that department? He's a computer nerd," said Ty.

"I'm not a nerd. I just like computers."

"I think it's better if I learn some basics on my own."

"Well, anytime you need help. I'll be here for a few months."

Elianna nodded, but knew she wouldn't take him up on his offer. Ty nudged her. She turned and saw Bree sitting with the rest of the team as they bragged to each other about the great castle they'd built. Bree wasn't bragging. In fact, Bree's eyes were drooping.

"Uh oh. I usually have her at home by now." Elianna stood and gathered up their beach equipment.

"Guess it's time we headed home," Ty said.

Nic stood up and walked over to Bree. He scooped her up and let her head rest on his shoulder. Ty grabbed the beach bag and they all walked home.

Elianna allowed Nic to deposit the sleeping child on the living room sofa. After the men left, Elianna washed Brianna up and had her change into her nightgown and tucked her in bed.

Then she powered up the computer and began the next lesson in her word processing program manual. Everyone told her that if she learned the basics she would be one step closer to a promotion.

Three hours later she turned the computer off and went to the kitchen to prepare dinner. For a brief moment she entertained the thought of inviting her neighbors, but chickened out at the last moment.

Brianna skipped into the room and climbed into her chair. *Too bad I can't recover that quickly,* Elianna thought.

"Are you going to call Uncle Ty and Uncle Nic to come over?"

"Uncle?"

"Well, Uncle Ty said that's what I should call him."

"Did Nic say you could call him uncle?"

"No. Can I call him Nic?"

"Absolutely not. You may not call adults by their first name." Elianna wasn't overjoyed by the familiarity. While Ty seemed nice, she'd rather he'd asked her before telling Bree to call him uncle.

"Mommy, what should I call him?"

"We'll ask him the next time we see him."

A few hours later she was tucking Brianna in bed. Now it was time for her. The cottage had a Jacuzzi, and Elianna loved to spend fifteen minutes with jets pounding her muscles and relaxing them to the point where she had no problem falling asleep.

She remembered the first time she and Brian had gone to a fancy resort. The first time they used the Jacuzzi they had ignored the warning that it should only be used for fifteen minutes. They'd spent almost forty-five minutes in the whirling waters. By the time they tried to get out, their muscles were so relaxed they couldn't make a normal exit. They ended up crawling out of the tub, and found themselves so weak they could barely dry off. They couldn't even put on nightclothes. Elianna and Brian had just managed to get into bed and pull the covers around them before they fell asleep. They didn't awaken until noon the next day. Elianna never over used the Jacuzzi again.

Now, there were nights like this when she wished she

could share it with someone—someone who wanted a family.

Nic watched Ty as he talked to the woman next door. His friend was a rogue. He could charm women, and he enjoyed doing so, but he never led them on. He was honest about not wanting a commitment. It was too bad that some women didn't believe him when he told them that.

Nic lived for the day his buddy would meet a woman that could take him down a notch or two.

His friend was also a good lawyer. Only a week ago Nic had made a special request. Ty had acted as both friend and lawyer when he counseled him . . .

Ty Reynolds had stared at his friend and client that day. "That kind of rationalization can only lead to trouble, Nic."

"It's been done before. I don't see why you have a problem with it." Nic Sinclair had sat with his elbows on his mahogany desk, his long fingers forming an arch in front of him as he casually made his request.

"Sure it's been done. I just call a few of my associates who specialize in adoption, and tell them you want a son, but not the middleman—or should I say middle *woman?* It's a lot easier for a single woman to adopt than a single man. As your lawyer I'm sure I could find someone who was willing to give you a crack at fatherhood. However, as your friend I'm against the idea."

Nic had stood up and walked to the window. He'd gazed down at the bustling traffic on 57th Street. The lunch hour crowd was in full force. One of New York's best shopping areas was always crowded around this time of the day. Nic wondered if the woman he sought was part of the crowd— a woman who could not care for her child and would be willing to let Nic have that responsibility.

"Ty, it's the best way for me," he'd said.

"No. The best way for you is to let go of the past. You

won't forget Laura or the son you didn't even get to hold,
but you can't die with them.''

"I don't want to die with them, and I don't want to go
through a conventional relationship again. I'm giving you
a direct order as my lawyer. As my friend, I'm asking you
to believe me when I say I know this is the best way.''

Ty Reynolds had shaken his head. He and Nic had been
friends since the first time they'd suited up for their high
school football team. He was the quarterback, and Nic the
fullback. They'd made high school history, been wooed
by the same college, and were later drafted by the same
professional team. College had offered them a chance to
learn more about the world they lived in, and Nic had
given up football for computers. Ty had played a couple
of years as a back up quarterback for three professional
teams, and then decided that he would rather practice law
than be a mediocre football player.

It had been a good move for both of them. After Nic
had opened his own company they were a team again. Ty
had been Nic's best man when he married Laura Zachary.
He'd been there for Nic when Laura died in childbirth
and his son only survived his mother by a few hours. He
knew how much his friend hurt, but he still didn't think
adopting a child was best for him at this time.

"So are you going to help me, or what?''

"Brother man, you know I'm going to help you. I just
have to let you know how I feel.''

"Good enough.''

The men shook hands, and Ty started to leave. "Oh
yeah. I think I'm going to sell the property in Massachusetts.''

"Now that might be something I'd like to take off your
hands.''

The men had laughed. The one thing they'd agreed
about besides football was real estate. Each had prime

property in Massachusetts—Nic in the Cape Cod area called Dennisport, and Ty in the Oak Bluffs section of Martha's Vineyard.

"I'm going to spend the summer up there and get the property ready. I'll do a commuting thing for a while."

Ty turned and grinned. "I'll keep in touch. I hope you won't have to wait too long to become a father."

"Thanks, man. I knew you'd understand."

Nic had returned to his chair and began making notes for his second in command. It would take him a couple of months to get the house ready for sale. He hadn't spent any time there since Laura's death. He'd allowed the service he hired to keep the place clean. Four years was a long time to avoid a place he once wanted. He'd bought it with the intention of having his family use it as a summer home, but Laura's pregnancy was not an easy one, and she'd never gotten a chance to see it. The thing to do would be to sell it, but he loved it so much. . . .

Nic slept late the next morning and then spent time at a nearby nursery before heading home. He drove down the narrow road and turned into the driveway. The pale blue, shingled house with its wraparound porch looked as magnificent as on the first day he'd seen it. He'd wanted to surprise Laura by purchasing something that screamed family instead of the cold chrome and steel of their current apartment. She'd been too ill to travel with him, and he'd told her that he thought they should talk to the doctor because she was still having morning sickness well into her sixth month of pregnancy. She'd ignored him and just said that he'd been reading too many books, and was going overboard as usual. He knew he'd had a tendency since high school to become an expert in whatever held his interest at the moment. He'd asked so many questions the first time they visited the doctor that she'd forbidden him to accompany her again. She was just having a normal pregnancy, she told him. He'd believed her.

She'd lied. Only when she went into labor early had he realized how much she'd hidden from him, and by then it was too late.

Nic shook the memory away and put the pickup truck in the garage. He lifted the tools and a couple of plants from the truck bed and carried them into the mud room that adjoined the garage and house.

He went back through the garage entrance and checked the soil in front of the house. It was too dry to do the kind of plant transfers he wanted. He pulled the hose out. He carefully laid out the sprinkler system and turned it on. The temperature was climbing to ninety, and he felt it was just the time for a shower and a quick snack. He needed the ground to be thoroughly wet before he set out the new plants.

Before taking a shower he turned up the volume on his Bose stereo system and slipped in his Oldies CDs. When he entered the shower Donna Summer was singing about "Bad Girls," and when he emerged it was to the tune of Gloria Gaynor's "I Will Survive." He only had a towel wrapped around his neck as he dried off with another. He began to sing along with the CD.

Somewhere in the distance he heard a voice singing along. Most of the lyrics were mangled, but she got the "I Will Survive" part right.

He looked out of his bedroom window and was shocked by what he saw. The water from the sprinkler splashed over her naked bronzed body. Her auburn hair was plastered against her face as she danced. She didn't have a care in the world, and why not? She was all of five-years-old.

Nic threw on his bathrobe and ran out to pull the little nymph out of the sprinkler system.

"Bree what are you doing?"

After letting out a shriek she mumbled, "I'm Bree, and I'm going to tell my mommy."

"Yeah? Where is your mommy? We'll both tell her."

Nic felt a tinge of remorse as he watched tears blend with the water from the sprinkler. He wrapped her in the towel that had been around his neck and made his way to the front gate. It took him almost a minute to open it and walk to the bungalow next door. This was the high rental season, and he wasn't surprised that the people showed up a day early, but he was really angry that the woman wasn't watching her daughter. She seemed so nice when they were at the beach.

"Ty thinks I can't be a single parent. I wonder what he'd say about your mother."

He rang the bell three long times before lifting his thumb. The woman who opened the door had the same auburn hair as the child in his arms.

"I think this belongs to you." He deposited Brianna in her mother's arms.

"What happened?" she asked Nic. "I told you to stay in the yard," she said to her daughter, whose tears had stopped the minute her mother opened the door. "How did she get wet?"

"She decided to take a shower in my sprinkler system."

The towel fell open, revealing a chubby thigh.

"Where are her clothes?"

"Don't look at me lady. I just happened to have a towel handy."

"I . . . I don't know what to say."

"Don't say anything. Why don't you try to take better care of your daughter? What if she'd walked down by the ocean? What kind of mother are you?"

"I—" The woman turned and put the child down. "Get inside." As the little girl started into the house Elianna grabbed the towel and whirled on Nic. "I'm a very *good* mother, that's what kind I am. Here!" She shoved the towel at Nic. Before he could say anything she'd closed the door, but as he started down the walk he heard the woman shout, "Brianna Marie Preston, you are in big trouble."

CHAPTER TWO

Elianna saw Nic a few days after he'd deposited a wet, naked child in her arms. She wanted to apologize for Bree's behavior. She didn't even understand what had possessed her daughter to do such a thing.

She wasn't too happy about her reaction, but she could tell that the man thought she didn't know how to take care of a child.

She also knew she was spying again. He was drawing circles in the dirt, and she was unable to take her eyes away from his muscular chest and legs. His wide shoulders made her think of a fullback—a man who could crash through the opposition's line and gain the short yardage needed for a first down. She smiled as she made that analogy. It had come from years of watching Monday Night Football with her dad. She was in many ways the son he didn't have. She tended to put her thoughts in terms of sports, despite the ballet and piano lessons her mother had insisted on to "soften" her tomboy daughter.

She watched Nic scraping the ground, and realized he was making a flower bed. His land was already rich with lush, green, grass carpets, and she'd thought it needed a little color.

Elianna turned from the window and walked to the kitchen to prepare breakfast for her daughter. Just as she poured freshly squeezed orange juice into a small glass, she heard rapid footballs. Her daughter seemed to move at the speed of light from dawn to dusk. In seconds the whirling dervish known as Brianna Marie Preston appeared. Dressed in her favorite sweatshirt and jeans, her tiny feet in jogging shoes, she was ready for the day.

"Morning, Mommy," she said as she pulled herself into the chair. "I washed my face and hands already."

"Very good. Now you say grace this morning." Elianna sat down across from her daughter.

They bowed their heads, and Bree said the short prayer she'd learned from her grandmother.

"Can I go outside now?" Bree asked as soon as she'd eaten the last of her cereal.

"Okay. Wash your face and hands. Stay in the yard, and please don't bother our neighbor."

"Yes, Mommy."

She was off again. It took a minute for her to wash up and then let Elianna inspect her.

"I give her five minutes before she bombards the man with questions," Elianna said.

It only took three.

Nic was glad to see Brianna. He'd felt like such a fool when he realized what he'd said. He wanted to apologize. This would be a good time.

"What are you doing?"

"I'm making a garden with pretty flowers."

"I like flowers."

"Well, maybe we'll make *you* a garden."

"OK."

"But first we have to ask your mother."

A minute later he was standing on the doorstep where he'd berated the woman about not taking care of her child.

"I'm sorry about yesterday."

"Me, too."

"Your daughter has asked me to make her a garden. Do you mind?"

"Not at all. I'm not good with plants."

"Well, why don't we go pick up some seeds and get started? Unless you're busy—"

"No. I think it's a great idea. But maybe we should buy plants that have already started?"

"I think seeds are better."

"You're the gardener."

They took Nic's car and drove to the nursery. On the way he explained he was a widower.

"No children."

"Obviously not, or I would have known that kids do some strange things. My wife died in childbirth, and my son died with her."

In saying the words Nic felt the first relief he'd had in months. He could start over.

It became a ritual for them. Nic and Bree tended the garden while Elianna worked, and then they'd go to the beach or shopping.

It was a friendship they both needed.

CHAPTER THREE

The next day had perfect beach weather. For people who had such an inauspicious beginning, Nic and Elianna found they liked each other's company.

Nic became a fixture for lunch. He liked the fact that she set a pretty table all the time. He liked a lot of things about Elianna Preston.

Every day since they'd planted the seeds, Bree ran to check on the gardens and then announced to Nic that hers wasn't working. He tried to explain time, but she still expected to wake up and find flowers blooming all over the little patch of land.

"I hate to see her disappointed every day," he told Elianna.

"She's going to have to learn patience someday. Why not now?"

"You're a tough mom."

"Oh? Wasn't it just a few weeks ago you thought I was unfit?"

"I know. I know. Say, Ty is coming up this weekend. Let's spend the whole day at the beach."

She smiled. "I know you just want to take Bree's mind off her garden. Well, the beach is a good choice. My friend Caryn's coming up, also."

He hesitated for a moment, then plunged right in. "Ty's my best friend and I love him, but I hope you aren't planning to uh try to, uh, set him up with Caryn."

"I'd never do that. Believe me, he couldn't handle her."

"Oh, really?"

"She's my friend, but I'm warning you that if he tries to apply that practiced charm on her, she'll have him for breakfast."

Nic laughed. He'd never seen a woman that didn't fall for Ty. Elianna was different. Ty wouldn't go too far with a woman who had a child. He didn't want to be tied down.

Caryn arrived first. She reminded Nic of Laura. She was tall and model–thin, but her focus wasn't on her looks. She had no problem playing in the sand with Bree, or jumping in the ocean without a swimcap. There was something about her that was uninhibited and yet reserved.

Ty got there minutes later. Nic watched as Elianna made the introductions. His friend was suddenly aware of Caryn. She was cordial, but not too friendly. Nic assumed she'd try to play hard to get. Those were the women Ty went after. He hoped that they wouldn't interfere with his relationship with Elianna. Anyway, he'd warned her about Ty.

Brianna came running in from her garden.

"Hi, Aunt Caryn. Hi, Uncle Ty. I don't have any flowers yet."

Nic groaned.

Elianna giggled and shook her finger at him. She'd told him to go to the nursery, but he'd been adamant about letting Brianna see how seeds turned to flowers.

"Well, why don't you show me where they're going to be?" Caryn suggested.

The two went out to examine the dirt.

"Your friend's quite a lady."

"Yes. She's the office manager of the law firm where I used to work."

"Is she involved with anyone?"

"Not at this time."

"Ty." Nic's voice carried a warning.

"Hey, what's the big deal? So I'm interested."

Nic changed the subject, then remembered it was time to water the garden. He reluctantly left Ty and Elianna alone.

"Nic seems to think that I'm some kind of wolf in sheep's clothing. What do you think?"

"I think you're a wolf in wolf's clothing."

"So tell me more about your friend."

"We've known each other since high school. She got me a job at the law firm. I preferred being self-employed."

"How would you feel if I asked her to go out with me? I respect your opinion."

"How would you feel if she said no?"

Ty laughed. There weren't many women who said no to him, and he didn't think it would happen.

When they got to Elianna's he tried to find a common ground with Caryn, something they could talk about, but he wasn't having much luck.

She liked sports, but talked about volleyball. He didn't think that was much of a sport.

"Don't you realize the condition you have to be in to play?" she asked.

"Yeah, but not like football."

He tried movies. He liked action dramas. She liked foreign films. They had nothing in common. Ty was getting competitive.

Several times Elianna tried to pull them out of this battle of wits, but Nic kept saying they should let it run its course.

"It's a man thing. He wants me to see that he can be charming and get a date with a woman I told him to stay away from."

"Maybe they should just go on a little date, and then they could get back to their lives."

Nic and Ty carried the food down to the beach and found a good spot. Brianna knew most of the people there, and ran from one area to another. She returned a little dejected.

"Linda's father is building her a big sand castle."

"Is that what you want? Another sand castle?"

She nodded. "Yes I want a bigger one."

The next thing Elianna knew, Caryn, Ty, and Nic had formed some kind of assembly line, and the plans for a sand castle got underway. Caryn gave Bree an assignment, and made her part of the project. They managed to eat and work until a large castle stood waiting for the tide.

Elianna ran home and got her camera. She had fun taking pictures of everyone. Caryn took the camera. She motioned to Nic, Elianna, and Bree to get close together. They put Bree in the middle, and Caryn snapped away.

"Don't just sit there. Do something."

Nic called Elianna's name, and as she turned he kissed her. The kiss lasted long enough for Caryn to snap two more.

It was getting late, and Nic and Elianna left to put Bree to bed. That was becoming a ritual they both enjoyed.

* * *

"Maybe we could grab some dinner farther up the coast?" Ty asked Caryn.

"No thanks. I really came to spend some time with Bree and Elianna."

"Well, Bree's in bed, and don't you think that we should give Nic and Elianna some time alone?"

Caryn couldn't argue that point, so she reluctantly agreed to go out with Ty. They made arrangements to change clothes and meet at Elianna's.

When she told her friend, Elianna expressed concern. "You've been so wrapped up in your career that you haven't had a chance to see what's out there."

"Don't be a mother hen. I know perfectly well what he's like. It's only dinner."

She showered and slipped into a casual little dress and waited for Ty.

After they left, Elianna had a hard time keeping her mind on anything but her friend.

"We did everything we could. It's not our fault if they get involved, against our better judgement," he said.

She laughed. "You're right. Caryn and I just spent our lives worrying about each other, and it's hard to stop."

They settled in and watched an old horror movie. After it was over, Nic said he was going home. That's when they heard the screech of tires pulling into the driveway. They looked at each other and ran for the door.

Caryn was the first out of the car. She sauntered up the walk, and as she got to Nic and Elianna she simply shrugged her shoulders and smiled.

Ty called out. "Well, if I'd known you were going to act like that I'd have parked at the curb."

"Uh oh," Elianna said, "I think this may be war."

"What's going on, Ty?"

"Nothing. Just Miss Thang had to show me how many men she knows around here."

Caryn reappeared. "We went to a local place. I've been coming up here for three years. I know some people."

"Yeah. More like you knew the whole band."

"What's that supposed to mean? You were the one telling me that you weren't looking for a commitment."

"Well, I'm used to my dates remembering who's paying for dinner."

Elianna stepped in. "Don't wake Bree."

"Why you—" Caryn reached in her bag and pulled out a handful of bills and threw them at Ty. She stormed into the house while Ty got in the car backed it up and drove into Nic's driveway.

"I think it's true love, Elianna."

"We aren't going to act like that, are we?"

"No way. We're much too reserved." They burst into laughter.

"I would like to have been a fly on the wall for that date."

"I don't think we want to know what happened?"

"I agree. Just remember that I told you she could hold her own."

He kissed her goodnight and went to check on his friend.

"Don't even say it, Nic. I lost it."

"I don't understand why you even tried. You don't have anything in common."

"I know, but she just seemed so smug, and she was looking down her nose at me."

"Now I know you've gone off the deep end. What she did was challenge you. She likes things that you don't. She's different."

"She's snooty, and I wanted to knock her off that pedestal."

"Leave her and her pedestal alone. Chalk it up to incompatibility."

"You're right. I'm going to get some sleep."

Nic could only hope that Elianna was giving Caryn the same lecture. What he really saw was that a woman had gotten under Ty's skin. He'd forgotten all about the practiced charm he normally used, and what they'd seen was a true view of the man. Nic kind of liked it.

CHAPTER FOUR

Bree sat at the table with the seed catalogue. She had the little stick-on neon dots that Nic had given her. His instruction was that she should put a dot on the ones that she liked.

"I think Nic made a mistake," said Caryn. "By the time she finishes that catalogue she'll need more neon dots, and he'll be spending a lot more on shrubs and flowers."

"At least he found something that keeps her quiet for a while," Elianna said. "She didn't even want to go to the beach."

"Maybe she'll discover a career. She can own a nursery, and have lots of exotic flowers."

"I know you said Nic's wife died in childbirth, but was there something else wrong with her?"

"He didn't say. He just said she wasn't strong enough to carry the baby but she desperately wanted a child."

"So he lost both of them. Tragic." Caryn shook her head sadly.

The women continued working on the hors d'oeuvres. They'd just planned to have something to snack on while they watched the movie.

"You don't have to drag Bree away. We're just going to watch a little TV."

"I'm not the one playing matchmaker," Caryn insisted. "I'm just giving the two of you a chance to—talk. You have been—talking."

"Don't play that game with me. I know you have another word you want to use instead of 'talk.' I'm just not going to give you the satisfaction of living vicariously through me."

"Oh, come on. Anyone with eyes can see that you two are hot for each other. So what's going on?"

"If you don't behave, I'm going to set you up with Ty."

Caryn put her hands on her hips and turned to Elianna. " 'Mr. woman–in–every–town? No thank you."

"I think you two like each other. If you didn't, you wouldn't fight so much."

"That's not true. Oh, I admit he is one fine brother, with that black curly hair and those expensive clothes, but there's nothing going on mentally. At least not with a woman."

"Ah, the lady doth protest too much."

"I'm not going to say any more. You are just feeling good because you've found someone, and you want the rest of the world to be in love."

The next time he saw Elianna he knew that what they were feeling was more than infatuation. They'd stopped talking about Bree's garden. He was grateful Caryn was around, because she immediately took Bree off on an excursion so he and Elianna could have some time alone.

They were sitting side by side at a diner. She started to drink her tea, but her hands were shaking and she had to set it down. Nic moved the cup away from her and leaned over. "Just relax. We're still at the get acquainted stage. I'm not going to attack you. Especially in a diner. My reputation would be mud."

"I know it's silly, but we just seem to talk about Bree, and now I know you want to just talk about us."

"What are you afraid of?"

She took a deep breath and plunged right in. "I don't know how a commuter relationship will survive. You love New York, and I'm afraid of it."

"Most people who have never been there or haven't lived there for over a couple of months are afraid. What they don't know is that New York City—and that consists of five boroughs, the Bronx, Brooklyn, Manhattan, Queens, and Staten Island—isn't as intimidating as it looks. Truthfully, it's like a small town. You'd be surprised at the way paths cross."

She laughed. "New York is a small town? Yeah, right!"

"You can laugh all you want. I can tell you stories about my friends. They can be in any borough, and somehow end up at the same bar. You can actually see the six degrees of separation work out."

"Six degrees?"

"You know, the theory that we are only separated by six other people?"

"And you really believe that?"

"It happens. In a city of about nine million people you're as likely to run into the same people as if there were only nine hundred. People who like the same things or want a certain life style will find it."

They went back to Nic's, and he turned on the big screen TV to a sports channel. He found a baseball game with the Boston Red Sox and started watching.

"You are a Red Sox fan?"

"Not really. I try to watch and cheer for the team where

I live. So when I'm here I cheer for the Red Sox, and when I'm in New York it's the Yankees or the Mets."

"That doesn't sound very discriminating."

"You're probably right, but it's fun."

They were sitting on the sofa, and when he pulled her closer she knew he was no longer interested in the baseball game. He kissed her. It was a kiss she'd been waiting for. A kiss they dared not share at her house.

The hot rumblings of excitement coursed through her, and she leaned into him. He couldn't believe her response. She'd told him that she wasn't looking for a man, but there was something so strong between them.

His arms circled her and lifted her so that she was practically on top of him. He ran his hands over her body. With her breasts filling his cupped hands, he rocked back and forth. All this while he branded her with deep, fierce kisses.

"Let's go upstairs."

Upstairs. *The bedroom.* Elianna couldn't. She pulled away, and tried to fix her hair by running her hand through it. "What if some one comes in?"

"The only 'someone' you're worried about is Bree. She's not going to interrupt us here. Does it have something to do with Bree's father?"

"What makes you say that?"

"I don't know. I guess the way you talk about him. You sound as if you'd be afraid if you ran into him."

"I wouldn't be afraid. I would just be cautious."

"Then why won't you sleep with me?"

"It's not that easy."

Elianna had been there before, with other men. They'd promised everything, but she couldn't respond to them. Part of her said that Nic wasn't like that, but part of her said that all men had a little of Brian in them. They had a certain amount of charm that hid their motives. What if she slept with Nic? What if that was all he wanted? How would she explain to Bree that he would no longer be in her life?

"Sure it is. We're two adults with a healthy attraction to each other. What's wrong in taking that next step and satisfying that need?"

Elianna pulled away as much as she could. Nic was still not releasing her. "I can't just let myself go and forget that there can be consequences."

"Everything has consequences. I thought we were beyond that."

"What do you mean?"

"I thought that we were building something special."

She couldn't deny that was what she felt, also. She also knew that she had used Bree to help keep him at arm's length. As long as her daughter was around she knew nothing would happen.

"What we have *is* special."

"Then let's make it perfect."

"I can't just go to bed with you."

"Well, does that mean you can't go to bed with a man who isn't your husband? Will a fiancé do?"

"What's that supposed to mean? Do you think I'm trying to force you into something you don't want?"

"No one forces me into anything," Nic said. "I'm simply trying to find out if I'm going to be taking cold showers until we're married, or just until we're officially engaged."

Elianna scrambled to her feet. He still held her hands. "You think this is a joke. You men always think it's easy. Just because some people don't care, there are still some who do."

"I wasn't trying to be funny. It's been a while since I proposed to anyone, and we were living together at the time."

"Are you asking me to marry you?"

"Yes. What's your answer?"

"Is this supposed to make me fall into bed with you?"

"Yes. Of course, if you insist I'll wait until it's official and you're legally Mrs. Nicolas Sinclair."

He waited for a moment, and when she didn't answer he pulled her back to the sofa and on top of him. "I want you to tell me where I stand. If you're planning to be celibate until we're married I need to know."

"And what will you do about it?"

"First we go get a ring. Then I take the next plane back to New York and I won't see you until our wedding day."

Elianna giggled. "You're crazy."

"No. I think I'm in love."

"Think?"

"Let me stop hedging my bets. I know I'm in love. And I want to marry you."

"Yes," she whispered. "Yes, I'll marry you." She knew so much about him. He'd shared the pain of his wife's death. He'd told her about his football coach, and how he and Ty were indebted to the man. Maybe this time she'd found someone who was truly honest with her, and she needed that.

"So when do we get the ring?"

"I don't want a ring."

"What?"

"I don't want an engagement ring."

"Are you sure? How will people know we're engaged?"

"They don't have to know. They just have to know the wedding date."

"That's a little strange."

"But it's what I want."

"Does that mean you won't sleep with me until after the ceremony?"

"No, but I won't sleep with you on the Cape if we're not married."

"Are you saying you'll come to New York and sleep with me?"

"Yes."

He couldn't believe what she was saying, but then he couldn't believe that he had just proposed and agreed not to buy his fianceé a ring. He found it charming that she wouldn't sleep with him before marriage, with her daughter in the same state.

"What happened with Bree's father?"

"Brian proposed and bought me a fabulous ring. I was so happy I flashed it all around. Then we got married."

"Then you found out you weren't really married, that it was just a technicality."

"I just need to be sure."

"It must have been rough for you."

"It was, but my parents pitched in, and we agreed that I would move away. I couldn't face anyone, except Caryn. She got me the job in Boston. I found my house, sold my engagement ring, and made the down payment on my little piece of the world. My dad gave me enough money to pay the mortgage the first year, and that gave me time to establish myself as a columnist, and then I started my resumé business."

"And you haven't allowed a man near you since."

"That's true. Oh I dated, but men are generally turned off when they realize they will be taking on the added responsibility of a child."

"Except me."

"Yes. I've wondered if you want Bree for a daughter, and will only take me so you can have her."

"Get that out of your mind. I could adopt, as I'd originally planned. I admit that Bree is a terrific little person, but I think any child I would adopt would be just terrific. You know that could still happen. We might decide to adopt."

"So you can have the son you want?"

"I only said I wanted a boy because I didn't think they'd let a single man adopt a little girl. I've found out that isn't true, but at the time I just kept using 'son' rather than kid, boy, you know."

"We still have a lot to work out."

"I think we've cut a few mountains down to size."

"Laura?"

"I still feel guilty about not talking to the doctor about her, but in this day and age you just don't see women dying in childbirth. The signs of trouble were all there, but I was too busy concentrating on our future to pay attention to the present."

"She never told you that she wasn't strong enough to have a child. I guess she wanted it as much as you did."

"I'm putting things in the past, where they belong. I want you to do the same about Brian. I'm going to be the best father Bree will ever know."

CHAPTER FIVE

Brianna danced around her mother's bed. "Come and see them. I have flowers, I have flowers in my garden!"

Elianna showered and dressed quickly, throwing on some faded jeans and a gray and white sweatshirt. There in her daughter's garden were clusters of pink, rose, red, and deep violet flowers known as Sweet William. Elianna wanted to give them another name. She wanted to call them Sweet Nic. He'd let Bree tag along and showed her something else that made a home—a special garden. There would be other flowers that would bloom later in the season, but right now this was the best gift her daughter could ever receive.

The phone was ringing, and Elianna dashed back into the house. It was Nic. It had to be.

"Hello."

"Just thought I'd call and see how things were going."

"Oh Nic. The flowers are beautiful. Will they last? I mean, I know they just didn't spring up overnight."

"Sure. The nursery got them started, and I just gave them a new home. How is Bree handling it?"

"Oh just running through the neighborhood, screaming she has a garden."

"Good. Now she won't be so concerned about the other flowers. Do you think anyone saw me last night?"

"No. We'll just let this be like Santa Claus. We won't tell her until it's absolutely necessary."

"When I get a chance to come back up I'm going to take her to the nursery and buy some more flowers."

"Do you think you'll be back this weekend?"

"No way. We have several offers to look over. A couple of them have a seven day work shift, so that means I'll have to sit down with different groups and watch what they do. Then we can make some recommendations for the computer programs that will help them out."

"I guess it was just wishful thinking that you could come up here every weekend."

"I know. I miss you, too."

"I didn't say—" Who was she kidding? She'd started missing him from the day he left, and she didn't stop until he got back.

Why was life so unfair? She'd finally found a man who didn't mind that she had a child, a man who understood she and Bree were a package deal. Too bad he was geographically undesirable.

"I think I can make it next week. We'll do something special."

"Sounds good. I'll see you then."

She hung up and began to check her appointments. She had to deliver three resumés and stop by the newspaper office to see if Chuck still wanted her to do a weekly series about things to do with kids in the area. She would just have to keep herself busy until Nic returned.

BRIANNA'S GARDEN   253

* * *

Nic frowned as he looked at the contract again. He couldn't concentrate right after talking to Elianna. He had even mentioned her to his parents. That was a sure sign things were getting serious. The only problem was that his work was in New York, and he couldn't move it. Elianna seemed to be afraid of the big city, although she'd promised to come visit him. He was so engrossed in his plans for when she would come to see him that he didn't even hear Ty come in.

"Oh, my brother," Ty said, "I think you have been bitten by that age old creature called the love bug."

"What are you doing here?"

"We're supposed to go over that new contract."

"Oh, right."

Nic tried not to look up, but in the end he had to know if he were right. He *was* on target. Ty had a huge grin across his face.

"You know, one day you're going to meet a woman who wraps you around her little finger, and it will be my turn to laugh."

Ty shook his head. "That day ain't coming no time soon."

"OK. Let's leave the slang to the kids. What do you think of the contract?"

"I think it's too standard for this client." Ty pulled up a chair and got down to business. "I checked around, and he has a reputation of making trouble. He tinkers with the program because he's had some training in programming, and then he blames the company who wrote the program or installed it for the trouble."

"The money looks pretty good. I think we should go for it."

"Nic, I want to add a couple of clauses."

"I know you do. The one we really need is that if we can prove someone tampered with the system the liability clause for us is null and void."

"Sounds good, but how are you going to find out?"

"I'm going to add a couple of traps that will catch anyone who thinks he can fool around and then try to get over on us."

"Planning to go to the Cape this weekend?"

"I wish I could, but looks as if I have too many people on vacation to leave. I wish I could have been there when Bree saw the flowers I set out last night."

"You let her plant seeds, and now she'll think they grew overnight."

"Elianna says she was pretty happy when she saw them. Anyway, the seeds she planted will sprout up by the end of summer, and she'll think she worked another miracle."

Throughout their years together, Ty had only seen Nic this happy a couple of times. Oh, he'd been happy when he won his scholarship, and he'd been happy when he married Laura, but after her death his friend had rarely smiled. Ty was glad to see that was changing.

"So here we are on Monday. How are your plans shaping up for the weekend, Ty?"

"I'm not going to make that Massachusetts trip, either. I have tickets to a couple of Broadway plays. I just have to match the woman with the play with the day."

"If these women ever catch up with you juggling them around, I think you're going to be in big trouble."

"No way. You only get in trouble if you lie to them. I tell them up front that I'm not looking to settle down."

"Get out of here and take care of some of your clients."

"I'll talk to you after I think I've drawn up a contract that we all can live with."

After Ty left, Nic worked on the new system he'd installed for a chain of women's fashion stores. It seemed to be working as they needed it, but if they expanded too fast they'd already talked a contingency plan.

His career was under control. Now, if he could do the same with his personal life he'd be in great shape, once his staff was in full force again. Then he could think about spending every weekend at the Cape.

He left his office for lunch. He'd spent too many days eating at his desk and working. He needed this break. He strolled over to Border's Books on Park Avenue. He meant to look at the computer books, but found himself in the garden section. He saw some books that were geared for children, and decided to buy them. Although they were too advanced for Bree, he thought she'd grow to them. He liked the idea of a whole family. Even though he'd originally planned to adopt a son, Brianna filled that gap in his heart quite well.

Sometimes the week seemed to drag, and other days he didn't have enough time to get all the things done he wanted to do. He and Ty met again on Thursday, and he okayed the contract.

Friday was an endless day of meetings, but by six he'd finished everything. He didn't want to drive up this time. He'd just fly and get a ride from the airport.

Elianna was watching Bree to make sure that she followed Nic's instructions to the letter. From time to time she glanced at her checklist and then told Bree what to do next. She had some more resumés to take care of, and that would mean being up all night.

At eight Bree was asleep, and Elianna turned on the computer and began her work. She heard a car pull up, and she knew Nic must be home. She debated for two seconds about whether she should wait until tomorrow to see him or not. The next thing she knew she was standing in the doorway, watching Nic walk up the path to her house. He only carried a backpack and not a briefcase. Maybe he wasn't planning to work at all this weekend.

He wrapped her in his arms and just held her a few minutes before he stepped back, leaned down, and kissed her. He felt as if he'd been gone for months. Why was it only this woman who could give him a sense of homecoming?

They curled up on the sofa, necking like teenagers. He knew she would not go too far with her daughter in the house.

"So how was your week, Nic?"

"Busy, but the good thing is a couple of people are back from vacation, and that will give me a little relief next week. I wasn't too busy to get this."

He pulled the books from his backpack. Elianna looked them over and began to laugh.

"Hey, cut that out. I know they're too advanced for her, but one day she'll be reading them."

They kissed some more, and then Nic said he needed to get some rest. He and Bree had a busy day planned.

The next morning, true to his word, Nic scooped up Bree right after breakfast and went to the nursery. This would give Elianna time to finish her assignments. Bree and Nic roamed the aisles until they found the perfect shrubs to put around the border of the garden. They decided on forsythia. The yellow blossoms would stand out well against the pinks and purples of the flowers.

After they took the shrubs home and planted them on both his side and her side of the landscape, Bree took a nap.

"I'm glad that gardening tires her out. I'm tired of taking her jogging with me."

"You jog?"

"Yes, I jog. I'm not going to win any races, but it keeps me in shape."

He laughed. "You don't look like a jogger."

"What you really mean is that I don't look as if I've lost any weight."

"That's not what I meant. I like you this size."

She gave him a sidelong look that seemed to say she didn't believe him, so that night when they went to dinner he insisted that she get the triple chocolate cake for dessert and that she eat all of it.

Elianna lay in bed, thinking about how considerate Nic had been. He and Bree had developed a friendship, and now he wanted Elianna in his life. If she hadn't had that conversation with Ty, she'd think he only wanted her because of Bree. But Ty had eliminated those thoughts when he told her Nic had canceled his plans to adopt a child.

CHAPTER SIX

It was odd for the weather to be so warm this late in the year. August was usually a time when the area braced for the winter winds. They always got them earlier than other places that weren't so close to the ocean. The first flowers that bloomed in Brianna's garden were gone now, and Elianna was glad she'd taken so many pictures of them. Now the flowers that bloomed late in the year were decorating the little area.

When Nic had arrived he'd been dressed in jeans and a shirt, because New York was still going through a hot spell. They hadn't had much rain during the summer, and everyone was worried that they might have the kind of drought that had them rationing water, as they had a few years ago. She remembered watching an award show where the Californians had water at their tables, but not the New Yorkers. Elianna felt there was something to global warming, but when she tried to do an article on it, her publisher had nixed it. He'd explained that some people would use any excuse to cancel reservations, so her column couldn't deal with anything but the good things that were going on at the Cape.

They were all set to drive to Boston for a party for Ty and Nic's football coach. Elianna chose a forest green beaded gown that hugged her figure. It made her feel sexy, and she didn't wear it often. As she turned to check herself in the mirror she wished she were a little less *zaftig*. She wasn't fat, but she had curves where women she admired had none. Nic never made her feel she was too fat. Actually, when she'd gained a couple of pounds he mentioned how good she looked. She didn't know why Nic insisted that she get dressed so early. He was going to call his parents, and then they were going to leave. She thought of throwing an old bathrobe over her outfit and wrapping her head in a towel, just to shake him up. She knew however, that if she ruined this hairstyle after the two hours Caryn had put into getting this look, Caryn would kill her.

Elianna was preparing herself for the conversation with Nic's parents. "How much do they know about Brianna and me?"

"They know that you're divorced and you have a daughter. I didn't see any reason to give them your life chapter and verse."

"Do you think we should tell them everything?"

"Yes. When you get to know them better. You'll see that it doesn't matter. But I think you need to feel comfortable before we say anything."

"How do you think they'll react?"

"My mother will want to coddle you, and Dad will suggest we get out the shotgun and hunt him down."

Elianna laughed.

"That's what I want to hear from you. Stop worrying. You're so sensitive about what happened. You're not the first woman who fell in love with someone and he turned out to be wrong. They'll love you just because you got me to think about getting married again.''

"Did they know you wanted to adopt a son?"

"I'd mentioned it to them. They thought I was just going through a grieving period, and didn't mean it.''

What if they'd met after he'd adopted a son? Would that have been all he needed? Would he have still wanted to marry her? She thought of her mother's favorite saying—"Man proposes, God disposes.''

Elianna was shocked when Nic said that it would be a video conference call with his parents. Laura had been a model, a beautiful woman who had worked on the runways of Paris and Milan. How would they handle him marrying someone who leaned toward average size? She would never be glamourous. Even now, all dressed up for the party, she wasn't a standout beauty. She thought about her original plan to wear a bathrobe. She'd never be able to explain to his parents that it was just a joke. Nic would help Caryn kill her.

"I do this a couple of times a year. That way my mother doesn't worry that I'm too thin, or working too hard. You know how mothers can be.''

She did. That's why she tried to speak with her folks at least once a week. Still, the idea of being able to see them was exciting.

She was glad she and Nic were on their way to Boston for the coach's retirement party. Nic would have let her look like an urchin for the call, and not even cared. For a man who had been married to a model, he hadn't learned anything about women.

"Do you want me to set up something like this for your parents?''

"That would be fantastic. They could see how Brianna is growing, and I know she'd love to see them."

"We'll take care of it soon."

Suddenly the big screen television was filled with the living room of Phil and Mary Sinclair. The room was warm and cozy, with a French country look. She'd bet that everything in the room had been selected by his mother. There were a couple of quilts on the sofa, and she remembered Nic saying his mother and her friends belonged to an old–fashioned quilting bee. Both his parents had probably put on a few pounds since their retirement, but that was only natural, he said. Bree would love them.

"Hi, son," his dad called. "Hi Elianna, good to meet and see you."

"Hi, there," his mother said. "I don't care how many times we do this. I'm always amazed that we can be here in Florida, and you in Cape Cod, and we can see and hear each other."

"I know how you feel, Mrs. Sinclair. I didn't even know about this until a few minutes ago. I would have changed Bree's clothes." Elianna looked at her daughter, who was still covered with dirt from the garden.

"Oh, don't worry about that. Be happy she's an active little girl."

"Say hello to your new grandparents, Bree," Nic urged.

"Hi. Can you really see me?"

"Yes, we can. I like those red jeans you're wearing."

"They can see me. They can see me!" Bree danced around. "Can they see my garden?"

"No they can only see what's in this room," Elianna explained.

"Uncle Nic made me a garden," Bree announced.

"We'll be there when Nic and your mother get married, and you can show it to us."

"OK."

At that point Caryn appeared. "I'm Caryn, Elianna's friend. I'm going to take Bree in the other room so you adults can talk."

"Bye, Bree." Phil Sinclair waved.

"See you soon, Brianna." Mary added.

Bree danced out of the room while holding Caryn's hand.

"I can tell you now that at one time Nic hated me dragging him out to the garden. In fact, I used to use that as a way to punish him. He'd want to go off with his friends, and I'd make him work the garden."

"It's good that you taught him. I have the proverbial brown thumb. I think I could kill a cactus."

"Well, don't you worry 'bout that," Phil said. "I'm sure you have other talents that we couldn't shake a stick at."

She liked his parents, and there was something about them that reminded her of her own parents, something solid and earthy that she hoped she would create for Brianna.

"Nic says he's going to set up a video conference call for my parents."

"That's great. You kids can hook us all up, and we can do this a few times a year. When Nic first suggested it I thought it was too expensive, but after the first time I just said to Phil that if he can afford it then let him do it."

"I guess it's going to be a big change for you, son, having a family."

"Laura was—"

"She knows about Laura, Mom."

"Well, I loved her, but it was a foolish thing to try to hide."

Elianna turned to Nic. She saw him flinch, and she knew there was something about Laura he hadn't told her.

His mother continued, "I can see that Elianna isn't

worried about being curvy. These young girls all want to be model thin.''

"No, ma'am. I'm afraid I'll never be any thinner than I am. Curves run in my family.''

"Good for you," Phil boomed. "All that nonsense about sticking her finger down her throat. She never thought about the damage she was doing inside.''

That was it. Laura'd had an eating disorder. She'd forced herself to regurgitate so she wouldn't gain weight. That was why she couldn't carry the baby to term. She'd weakened her body until it was impossible for her to have children.

They talked a few more minutes, and then said good–bye.

"It was good to get a chance to talk to you, Mrs. Sinclair.''

"Please call me Mary.''

"And call me Phil.''

They waved, and then the screen went dark. She liked his parents, and had enjoyed meeting them this way. However, she had some words for their son that they shouldn't hear. How could he have left out Laura's health problems?

Caryn could tell that something was very wrong when she came in to say that she would stay at Elianna's, since she knew the house better than she knew Nic's. She left quietly.

Nic and Elianna were in the car and on the way to Boston before they spoke again.

"I'm sorry I didn't tell you everything about Laura before.''

"No, you chose to put her on this pedestal so that no woman could hope to live up to her.''

"I never said that. I never asked you to be another Laura.''

"You didn't tell me she had an eating disorder." Now she understood why Nic had deliberately complimented her when she gained weight. He was afraid he'd have another woman trying all the wrong things to get thin. That would never happen to Elianna. She'd even joked about it. She'd told Caryn that if she could get control of the fork she'd be fine, but once the food went inside her mouth she gave up the fight.

He didn't say anything for a while. "I should have known that she hadn't recovered. I should have talked to the doctor more. I should have listened to him more. She was trying to please me."

"Don't you think she was also trying to please herself? She wanted that baby because it would mean that she was a healthy, normal woman."

Elianna couldn't let it go. He'd held back something that was important. It told her why he was so good with children. Most single men were uncomfortable with children when they didn't have any of their own. Some men, like Brian, couldn't even handle their own.

She hadn't told Nic about the phone call from Brian. She wasn't sure this was the time, but she'd accused him of keeping secrets, so she couldn't do the same thing.

"I have to tell you something," she began. "I got a phone call from Brian."

"Bree's father! What did he want?"

"He wanted to see his daughter."

"Oh, great. When?"

"He's on assignment in New York, and he hoped he—"

"Absolutely not."

"He's her father."

"So I guess that means what I want doesn't mean anything."

"That's not true. You've seen the papers. We have all these adopted children searching for their birth parents."

"I know. But how do the people who raised them feel?"

"It hurts, but children need to know these things."

"So, is he going to be around for long?"

"No."

"You're sure of that?"

"I know the man. Right now he's probably feeling guilty, but once he knows that Bree and I are doing quite well without him, he'll disappear again."

"But you're going to introduce them."

"Yes."

She didn't know how to convince him that Brian would push until he got to see his daughter, that she'd bet money that once she agreed he would never appear again. He was a man who liked trouble. That's what he'd expected when he admitted he'd never divorced his first wife. He'd been surprised when Elianna had just moved to another city and just made sure he didn't have any real legal claims.

"Suppose I said I needed us to be a family?"

"I know that."

"Are you so accustomed to being independent that you don't need anyone?"

"Everyone needs someone."

"For creature comforts, I guess."

"I didn't agree to marry you because I checked out your bank balance."

"Yeah, but it's a good thing it's healthy, isn't it?"

Elianna couldn't say anything else. She'd thought they'd worked out the perfect agreement. Marriage just seemed the way to go for them.

Maybe they were both wrong.

CHAPTER SEVEN

At the party, Elianna couldn't believe she'd recovered so quickly from the fight with Nic. She found Nic's mentor, Cliff Carson, fascinating. The older man had enjoyed a varied life style, and was now one of the best football coaches in the college world. He'd just announced his retirement, and his former students had prepared this celebration for him. His wife, Lissa, a beautiful former model, was several years younger, but there was no doubt she had to run to keep up with her husband, mentally at least. It took only minutes before Elianna realized that Lissa was not just a pretty face.

"I think it's time this guy found the right woman and settled down," Cliff announced.

"Don't start on that, coach," Nic warned.

"That's right, darling, leave Nic alone," Lissa said. "If you don't, Elianna and I may decide we no longer want your company for the evening."

"Perish the thought, my sweet," Cliff said.

"Do you work?" Lissa asked Elianna.

"Yes. I write resumés."

"Really? That's interesting. How do you get clients?"

"I put out a few flyers around Harvard and Radcliffe, and found out a lot of students don't have resumés and some haven't updated them."

"I guess we see the same thing in our businesses. I'm a recruiter—"

"Headhunter," Cliff interrupted.

She laughed and turned back to Elianna. "Recruiter! I see a lot of young people who don't know how to put together a good resumé."

Elianna was glad to find a kindred spirit. "You're so right. They think that it's just a matter of putting down where they went to school and what degree they received."

"Maybe we can do business." Lissa handed her a business card. "I'm looking to place some people who are slightly out of the norm. I like diverse work experiences."

"Well, I'll certainly give you a call if I find someone interesting. What are some of the big mistakes you see on a resumé?"

"The wrong fonts. They have these fancy computer fonts, and they start experimenting with them. I can hardly read them."

"I know. They just forget about basics when they're trying to impress someone."

"I hope you explain to them—"

"OK., that's enough shop talk for tonight," Cliff interrupted. "This is supposed to be a party." The room had suddenly filled up with people wishing the coach well.

The food was standard, and Elianna found herself drifting around the room, meeting people. For the first time, she understood about mentoring. That might be something she should look into, especially since it appeared that she'd be calling New York home.

There was at least an hour of mingling before Elianna and Nic found themselves alone and able to talk.

"I see you're enjoying yourself," Nic said.

"Yes. I'm glad I came. Lissa's terrific. I hope I find someone for her."

"Does this mean you plan to expand your business?"

"Not really. It just means I won't have to work as hard on resumés."

"Glad you came?"

"Yes."

"I'm sorry we got off to a bad start tonight."

"Me, too. I haven't been in the network area in a long time."

"You now understand how important it can be."

Elianna stared at him. "Was that what this was all about? You want to show me what your life is like, and why it may not be a bed of roses?"

Here she'd thought he was taking her out for a social evening, and it turned out to be a way of Nic teaching her a lesson. She turned away, but he caught her arm and gently pulled her back.

"I'm not the one who learned the art of handing out business cards," he whispered. Then he leaned forward and kissed her.

"Hey, I thought we were here to celebrate with the coach," someone said, "You look as if you have something private going on."

"Ty, I thought you weren't going to make it."

"For the coach, you knew I'd be here."

Ty looked like a riverboat gambler with his long tuxedo jacket and his string tie. The lady with him seemed different from the other women Elianna had seen him with. She was much more reserved, both in her dress and her speech.

They spent another hour or so with the group and then left. As they neared Elianna's hotel, Nic pulled over and parked. He got out, dropped a coin in the meter, and then opened the door for Elianna.

"Why did you park so far away?"

"A New Yorker knows better than to take chances. If you see a spot, get in it."

She shook her head as she got out. "It doesn't pay to have a car when you live here."

"No way. But you do need a car when it's time to make that escape out of the city."

They walked the four blocks to the hotel and Nic rode up in the elevator with her. She wasn't sure she should invite him in. He took the key and opened the door. He turned on the lights, inspected the room, and gave her the key as he walked back to the door.

She followed him. "Nic, I really had a great time tonight."

"Are you ready to admit that New York isn't that tough?"

"Well—"

"Still the skeptic. Well, I'll pick you up tomorrow morning."

He took her in his arms. "I'm probably going to regret saying this in the morning, but goodnight and sleep well." He tipped her chin up so he could see her face. "I might not regret my having to say goodnight if you invite me to stay."

"I think I've had too much to drink to think clearly."

"Don't try to use a little wine as the culprit that's making you want to ask me to stay."

"I don't think it's a good idea tonight."

"Then, till tomorrow." Nic tipped her chin up again and held her face as he kissed her. His mouth was soft against hers, soft and pliant. He took her lower lip between his. At first she felt a gentle, nibbling sort of touch, then he opened his mouth and closed it over hers. This was not a leisurely kiss, despite the slow movement of his mouth.

He didn't stop until he felt complete surrender as she leaned against him for support. His lips traced the line of her throat while his hands slipped up her rib cage until his fingers spread out and covered her breast.

At the base of her spine she felt a tingle of desire, and knew she wanted more of him. In some manner she felt defeated that she couldn't fight him. She felt that she couldn't deny him. It had been that way throughout their brief relationship. He won. He always won.

She felt his body shudder as he put a little distance between them. "Sorry. I meant that to be a casual good-night kiss." he said. "See how easily you control me."

She couldn't breathe. She wasn't the one in control. All he had to do was ask, and she would invite him in for the night.

For a few seconds they remained in that position, not quite touching yet bordering on intimacy. Then he let her go and stepped away.

"I'd better leave while we still have a choice in the matter." He laughed at her pained expression. "I love you," he said softly. He allowed himself one more deep kiss and then turned and stepped out of the doorway. "Goodnight. Lock the door. I'll call you in the morning."

She did as she was told, and threw the dead bolt. He must have been halfway down the hall before she breathed, "Goodnight," knowing that he couldn't hear her.

When Elianna awoke the next morning she realized she must have gone on auto pilot after Nic's kiss. She couldn't remember getting ready for bed, but as she checked herself in the bathroom mirror she knew she'd performed all her nightly rituals. Her face was clear of all makeup, and she could even see the faint traces of her favorite moisturizer. Her clothes were draped across a chair.

How could she not remember anything but the way the man kissed her? He'd told her he loved her, and she hadn't answered back. She felt good. Since she and Nic had begun to grow close she'd worried about their different life styles. That didn't matter now. He loved her. She loved him, and she meant to tell him the next time they were together. It must have taken so much for him to utter those words.

She was now wide awake. It was time for her morning rituals, and she didn't know when he'd call. She showered and dressed in record time. The phone rang, and she forced herself not to run but to walk over to it.

She said hello.

"Hello, Elianna."

Her heart sank.

"Yes, Ty, what's happening?"

"The consultant business is alive and well. One of the systems we installed for a company went haywire. Nic's been over there all morning. He wanted me to take you to breakfast, what about it?"

"Oh, you don't have to do that. I'll be fine."

"He's really sorry, and he would have called you but this client didn't reach him until about two."

"Two in the morning!"

"Yeah. I told you he'd been there all morning."

"I thought you meant a normal kind of morning, like nine or ten."

"We wish. Things usually go wrong at some odd time, and we have to be on call."

"I understand."

"Why don't I give you a tour, and then you'll really understand how a consulting firm works?"

"I'd like that."

Twenty minutes later Ty and Elianna were having breakfast in the hotel restaurant.

"Will this be bad for him? I mean having a system blow up, and he had to go fix it?"

"Maybe. This client has been difficult from the start.

That's why Nic and I put every conceivable clause in the
contract. The guy probably tried to do something on his
own and punched the wrong key. He'd never admit it."

"But can you find out if he did?"

"Sure. Knowing Nic, he'll just pretend they can't pin-
point it to the actual person, but he'll be able to prove it
was human error and nothing Sinclair Consultants did."

While she felt a sense of relief, Elianna knew she
wouldn't be satisfied until she talked to Nic. She needed
him to assure her that everything was fine.

After breakfast, they took a cab to Sinclair Consultants.
She'd only seen the inside of Nic's office, not the whole
company.

Ty led her through the tour as if he owned the company.
He introduced her to the men and women who worked
there and explained their functions.

It was shortly after one in the afternoon that Nic came
into the office. Ty and Elianna were in the lounge area.
She'd just finished telling Brianna she'd be home in a few
hours.

"Hi, honey," Nic said as he dropped a kiss on Elianna's
forehead. "Sorry I couldn't give you the Cook's Tour. I
hope Ty didn't bore you."

"He didn't. What happened?"

Nic sat down across from her. "Exactly what we sus-
pected. Someone was working on the system, and used the
wrong code. Instead of letting the system reject it they
tried to change it, and the database separated from the
host. We had to do a full recover, but I don't think they
lost any data."

"That's good news," Ty said.

"Yeah, but the bad news is that it's almost time for
Elianna to go home."

He smiled, but it didn't reach his eyes. Elianna knew
that Nic had planned to spend time with her and couldn't.

She wondered if this problem would carry over into their married lives. She couldn't see Nic as someone with a nine to five job.

They did manage to have lunch together, and then it was time for her to check out of the hotel.

She packed quickly and left the appropriate tip for the maid. When she looked up, Nic was standing in the doorway.

He came over to her, took the bag from her hand, and set it down. "I really planned to show you what I did for a living."

"I know. It's all right. I'm sure I'll have plenty of chances to see you in action later."

He slipped his arms around her, and just held her for a minute. She wanted to declare her love just as he had, but she was afraid. If she said it now, would they get to the airport in time for her flight, or would she end up staying another day? She might get away with saying she missed the plane to Bree, but Caryn would know the real reason. Somehow, she didn't want even her best friend to know what stage of the relationship they were in.

"Don't," she said when he pulled her close against him.

"Why not?"

"We, uh, we have to go get the car."

"We could always take a cab to the airport."

Despite her words, Elianna didn't move from the embrace. This fact was not lost on Nic. "You smell so good," he said as he lowered his head to kiss her. She couldn't resist his warm lips, and how good his strong, lean body felt pressed against her. The kiss was as long as the one last night. She felt bewildered. She wanted to stay like this forever. At the same time, she wanted to run and hide from the feelings he evoked. He kissed her again.

"I love you," she said. When he didn't move she wondered if she'd said it aloud, or just thought she did.

"I love you, too," he said after a long pause. "I don't think this is the time, so let's get out of here before you have to stay another week."

"A week."

"It would take at least that long for me to let you go."

She felt the heat rise to her face and stepped away. She heard his quiet laugh, but didn't dare turn to face him. If she did, she just might insist on spending that week with him.

There were no more chances for private conversation until they reached the airport. She missed the Cape, and wanted to take care of a million things before her wedding.

They tried to find small talk to pass the time while they waited for her flight to be called. It was impossible. Finally he gave up. "I'll have to spend a few days with my parents before we come up to the Cape."

"I know. They must be anxious to see that you know what you're doing."

"Yeah. I didn't tell them the first time. We just eloped. They seemed pretty happy that this time they would have a real wedding to attend. We'd planned to renew our vows, but . . ."

His voice trailed off. Elianna knew the answer. Laura had gotten pregnant, and then it was too late.

CHAPTER EIGHT

Elianna was continuing her assignment, writing a series about the bed and breakfast inns around the Cape Cod area. It didn't take much effort to pack an overnight bag and take Bree along for a weekend here and there. The bulk of her income still came from writing resumés. The other little items were just icing on the cake.

Elianna left Bree with Nic as she went to interview her next client. The young woman, a recent Harvard grad, had heard about Elianna's success in creating resumés that got interviews. Despite the threat of a thunderstorm, she promised to return no later than dinner time.

She found her client staying at a rented house up the coast with a group of friends. They were celebrating graduation, and giving a final big party before all of them went off to new lives in the corporate world.

Although the sky had been cloudy, the weatherman had said there was only a forty percent chance of rain. While Elianna and her client talked she heard the drops of rain hitting the window. Ten minutes later the group that rented the house charged in to get out of the rain.

The light rainfall became a deluge by three in the afternoon. The radio announced the roads that were closed, and the forecast was not good. She ended up dragging out the emergency suitcase she kept in the car and sharing a room with her client.

"I really thought I'd be home."

"Don't worry," Nic told her. "It gives me a chance to play single father."

Her talk with Bree was less successful. She could tell her daughter, who was usually her traveling companion, missed her.

The good thing about being rained in was that her client's three roommates asked Elianna to do their resumés.

Elianna woke the next morning from a intermittent doze. She thanked her hostess, took a shower, dressed, and climbed into her car.

Three hours later she was home. Nic prepared brunch, and they sat in the living room as she told them about her trip. The wedding was approaching, and Elianna knew that she and Nic were in a denial period about the marriage. It was the commuter part that scared them the most. Each tried to convince the other that it didn't matter. Finally Elianna announced that she would move to New York.

"Are you sure?"

"Yes. It's just not going to work with me living here, and you living there."

"Don't you even want to try it?"

"No. I want to live with you."

"I know I'm being a bit of a baby over this, but I can't let go of this rental just yet. I just need to hold onto it for a little while."

"Does it have some special memory?"

"Not exactly."

What she couldn't put into words was that she couldn't become so dependent. If she gave up her house she would have to depend on Nic for her shelter. That hadn't happened to her for some time. Her parents had flown in the night before and planned to stay at her house and take care of Bree while Elianna was on her honeymoon.

Her mother marveled at the changes Elianna had made to her little house. "I thought you'd lost your mind when you told me you wanted to stay in this place. The way Caryn described it, I thought that you and Brianna would be living in some falling down house while you tried to fix it up."

"I'm sorry, Mrs. Alexander," Caryn said. "It did look pretty bad when I first saw it."

"I wasn't afraid of a little dirt. That's why I got such a good deal on the rental."

"A little dirt? You spent weekends cleaning before you moved in." Caryn added.

"Well, it turned out good for my baby girl and her baby girl," Elianna's father said.

His parents had come from Florida, and would stay a few days to get to know their new granddaughter while they stayed at Nic's place. They were a little reserved at first, but soon Brianna had won them over.

Brianna couldn't wait until she and Nic picked the flowers for the wedding.

"Daddy says I can't pick them until before we go to church," she explained.

Elianna looked up at Nic. Neither of them had suggested Bree move from calling him Uncle Nic to Daddy.

"That's right," he said, his voice husky with emotion. "I'll help you."

Later Ty pulled him to the side. "Isn't this a lot better than your original plan?"

"Yeah, a lot better. I've gotten used to the idea of a

two parent household. I've even gotten used to having a daughter instead of a son."

"Great. You had me worried for a while, man!"

"Now that I'm giving up my bachelor life, what about you?"

"Don't even joke about it. There isn't a woman out there who can convince me to try the house with a picket fence deal."

"You hear him?" John Alexander asked Phil Sinclair.

"Sounds like us some years back," Phil said and laughed. "You'll be caught by the end of next year."

"Wanna bet?"

"Naw. We don't want to take your money," John shook his head. "We all thought we'd be bachelors into the millennium. But believe me, there's a special woman for you."

"Nic got lucky and found two special ladies."

Nic acknowledged his father as he thought of what he'd lost when Laura died. He had the chance to start over. He had one more try at the brass ring, and he was grateful. He just had a hard time telling Elianna how grateful.

They were married in a simple ceremony in a small church on the Cape, where Elianna and Bree usually attended services.

Caryn wore a dark blue, fitted sheath that hugged her figure. Elianna had asked her to wear that color, since she didn't want the ceremony to look too wedding-like. After all, she and Caryn were just into their thirties and not interested in a spectacular wedding. They'd decided that since they were over thirty they didn't want the hoopla that usually surrounded a bride and bridesmaid.

Bree, as the flower girl, wore a pale, pink dress that set off her auburn curls, and Nic had helped her gather some

tiny flowers from the garden that she would throw in lieu
of rose petals.

Eschewing the casual look she preferred, Elianna
selected an ankle–length ivory chiffon dress with tonal
flowers and a bateau neckline and long sleeves. She wore
a veil at her mother's insistence. She carried a tiny bouquet,
made from flowers from Brianna's garden.

That little garden had brought so much happiness to
everyone. Maybe that was why she felt reluctant to sell the
property. The man who had created that garden stood just
a few feet away.

Nic watched the woman who was about to become his
wife as she seemed to glide down the aisle on her father's
arm. He'd selected a dark Armani suit for the informal
ceremony they'd chosen. Ty also wore a dark suit, as the
best man. They'd teased his buddy unmercifully the night
before for not bringing anyone to the wedding. The man,
who was never without female company, explained that he
simply didn't want a woman getting ideas. He had no
intention of getting married.

After their vows, the reception was held at a little inn
nearby. They danced and laughed until Ty whispered to
Nic that the limousine was ready to whisk them away to
the plane.

They arrived back in New York a little after ten at night.
The ride from the airport into Manhattan seemed longer
than the flight from Massachusetts. She couldn't believe
the traffic at that time of night. It was midnight by the
time they reached Nic's penthouse in the East 60's.

Nic gave her the tour. She thought of her parents with
their California life style, and how they would fare with
Brianna while she and Nic spent their honeymoon in his
New York place. He'd offered to take her to Jamaica, Paris,
Rome, and several other places, but Elianna chose New

York. She wanted some time to get to know the place before bringing Bree here.

"Want some more champagne?" Nic held up the bottle that had been waiting for them when they arrived. Besides the champagne, his housekeeper had left a mini feast of caviar, crackers, cheese chunks, and even good old–fashioned chicken noodle soup, and there was an urn of coffee. The way the things were laid out she could tell that Millie had probably left the apartment as they were coming up in the elevator.

"I don't think so. I'm not used to much alcohol, and I think if I take another drink I'm going to fall asleep on you."

"We certainly don't want that to happen." Nic pushed the bottle away.

Elianna walked over to the buffet and picked up a cracker and began to munch on it. She lifted the lid on the soup and the room was filled with the fragrance of what she considered real food. She ladled noodles, broth and meaty chunks of chicken into a large cup. She sat on the massive, brown leather sofa and placed her cup on a trivet on the glass coffee table.

"Aha! So Millie has found her way to your heart, just as she did mine."

"Oh, did you have a contest to see who cooked the best before you hired her?"

"No, I inherited her after a friend's marriage broke up. Both the man and his ex–wife had to move into smaller quarters after the court and lawyers finished with them, and neither had a place for Millie."

"So you hired her."

"Yes. One of my better decisions." He moved behind her and dropped a kiss on her nape. "You of course, fall into the category of the best decision I've made in a long time."

After finishing the soup, Elianna went into the kitchen and deposited the cup in the dishwasher. When she returned to the living room, Nic had discarded his jacket and was checking through his CD collection.

She began to feel tense. It was silly. She'd been with a man before, she told herself—Brianna was proof of that—but it had been a long time. Brianna was proof of that, also. She had not even thought about marriage when she lived at the Cape.

Nic handed her the small overnight bag and led her through the master bedroom to the master bath. "I'll just shower in the guest room bath."

After she closed the door to the bath, Elianna began to shake. Her teeth chattered as if she'd been wandering on the beach in the dead of winter. She drew the water and made it slightly warmer than she normally used. She used a towel to wrap her head, to protect her braids. Then she removed her makeup and cleansed her face before climbing into the tub.

The jets from the Jacuzzi felt good as they pounded the chill out of her body. Fifteen minutes later she was wrapped in a bathsheet. She again, cleansed her face and moisturized it.

From the overnight bag she selected the black satin, slip–like nightgown. She preened in front of the mirror, as she removed the towel and shook her head so that her braid fell around her shoulders.

It was later when he came into the room and slid into bed next to her. She stiffened, and her nerves got the best of her. He frowned and then took her in his arms. She placed her face against his chest, more to avoid looking into his eyes than to create an intimate embrace.

"What's wrong?" he asked. He used two fingers to lift her chin so that she faced him. He kissed her. "Relax," he whispered. "I understand."

He held her tighter, and began to talk about their lives, how the city had a lot of children programs. He told her about story time at the library near them, and how great the windows of Saks Fifth Avenue would look at Christmas time. He shifted from time to time. Each movement brought her closer to him physically.

"Why don't you get some sleep? We do have a whole week of just being the two of us."

"I know. I just need to unwind a little."

It was his gentleness that made her relax. Her sexual experience with Brian had been one of a demanding man and an inexperienced woman. She'd never gotten beyond the belief that this phase of a relationship was for the man, not the woman.

He held her closer and began to stroke her arms, then her legs, and by the time his fingers stroked her breasts she welcomed his touch. He took her hand and let it learn his body just as she had learned his. Elianna found herself stretching, lifting, wanting more than just his fingers to touch her. She felt the taut length of his masculinity and tried to pull back, but he wouldn't let her. He gathered her up and rolled over so she could feel the full measure of his desire.

Suddenly she began to respond. Her mouth sought his, her fingers explored his body as the want became an exciting need.

"Whew!" he said softly. "You're quite a tigress when you unwind."

She giggled. "Can you tame the tigress?"

"Oh yes, lady. I'm fully prepared to do that."

Later, Elianna wondered why she'd been so afraid this wouldn't work. She loved Nic. He loved Brianna. She'd learn to love everything about him, his work, and his life in New York. She *could* make it work.

CHAPTER NINE

Her new office was a writer's dream. The walls were done in a soft cream that set off the cherrywood desk with a hutch. A pentium computer with a seventeen inch screen was hidden behind the doors of the hutch. Just as he promised, Nic had cleaned out one of the guest bedrooms to make this office for Elianna. He'd even put it in the opposite wing from his office.

She loved the layout of their apartment. It was in a building that had been a warehouse. Nic owned the entire eighth and ninth floors. Their real living quarters were on the ninth. The cook frowned when Elianna asked for vegetarian meals for Bree. Before it escalated, Nic appeared and warned all of the staff about complaining when Elianna made a request.

Nic made it very clear that she was in charge, and it was up to her to see that the house continued to run smoothly. Elianna didn't want to be in charge, and was grateful that the housekeeper seemed to he on her side. The woman was good with Bree, also.

The eighth was where Nic did a lot of entertaining. They were mostly catered affairs, and Elianna found herself with nothing to do but meet the guests, smile, and defer to Nic when she was asked a question about anything indigenous to New York that she was expected to know about. She did try to be friendly or civil to those people.

The rudest were friends of Ty. Elianna got the impression that they were women who thought at one time they could have been involved with Nic. They were always talking about clothes and shoes and men. Elianna didn't want to know the details of anyone's sex life. She couldn't believe how willingly these women shared their most intimate secrets.

Furniture shopping turned into another nightmare as they tried to move some of his large, heavy masculine pieces around to make room for something that was comfortable but didn't overwhelm Elianna.

It was obvious at first glance that Nic had left no room in his life for a woman. Just as Ty had mentioned, the man had been determined to be a lifelong bachelor. Even the room he'd reserved for the child he planned to adopt was masculine on a minor scale. The deep shades of blue soon gave way to pink, yellow, and Bree's favorite color of the month—purple.

They redecorated while Nic was at work. Bree met Nic at the door and before he could put his briefcase down she'd pulled him into her bedroom. He made all the right noises, but Elianna got the impression this was the first time he was really seeing what it would be like to live with women.

Their life on the Cape had been so different. Nic's visit had been treated as events. Elianna wrote several columns ahead of time so her calendar would be clear whenever Nic got the chance to come up.

Some people, she knew, would love the myriad things to do in the city. You almost had to be a weightlifter to carry the Sunday entertainment section from the *New York Times*. She was trying so hard to fit in, but this simply wasn't for her.

One of the things she missed most was curling up in bed with Nic and running her ideas by him. With all that was going on in New York, he seemed to be preoccupied. She got to toss out a few story ideas at the breakfast table, but somehow that wasn't the same thing. Now she understood why he'd worked so hard on Bree's garden. He was so used to working hard he just couldn't stop himself.

The houseplants in his apartment were generic green things that practically grew on their own. His mother had mentioned that to Elianna when she and his father came up for the wedding. Mrs. Sinclair was an avid gardener, and Nic had gotten his love for making things grow from her.

Unfortunately, Nic's love was for land, not potted plants. Although he'd listened when Brianna told him she wanted a garden in New York, he'd never found the time to take her to the nursery to find some plants she might like. Elianna didn't even try. She'd never been able to make anything grow, and that's why she was surprised at Brianna's love of plants and flowers.

When he gave her a credit card on his account she thought of it as an emergency gesture until he told her to buy something fancy for an evening out. She called Caryn, who thought it was great to have the means to buy something fancy. She suggested a couple of stores and colors for Elianna. After the conversation, Elianna was more depressed. She knew how to shop. She just didn't want to be forced into it. There were several events at the Cape that required formal dress, and Elianna didn't mind them. Unlike New York parties, they were few and far between. Lately all they had done was attend Friends of the Opera and Friends of the Library, kind of fundraisers.

Since Nic and his business contacts supplied computer training and sold computers to several organizations, and it was imperative that he attend these gala affairs. He and Ty worked the crowd and made the right contacts, while Elianna just tried to find someone she could talk to at each of these functions.

She worried that they were leaving Bree home too often. Nic admonished her, "You spend the whole day with her. By the time we go out, she's in bed."

"Yes. I do. You're the one she doesn't see."

"I know, but by the winter these things will wind down, and I promise to set aside some time for her."

Elianna had asked him to try to make it soon and he'd nodded, but she knew that by winter there would be a new set of soirees and Bree would be forgotten again. She didn't want to push—after all, he wasn't her real father—but he was the one who had pushed his way into their lives, and now he was a workaholic that Elianna didn't recognize any more. They'd had more quality time when he was commuting between the Cape and New York.

Elianna was happiest with the times she and Nic had a quiet dinner at home and put Bree to bed together. Nic was so good with Bree when he found the time for her. Then Nic and Elianna curled up in their bed and talked about the day. They still had both the houses on the Cape, and just couldn't seem to decide which one to sell and which one to keep.

They spent Christmas at the Cape, and stayed in his house. Nic and Bree bought poinsettias at the nursery and took hours to find the perfect setting for them. Elianna decided that the tree would be different. She purchased one hundred plaid bows from a store in Boston. The green and red plaid bows were tied on the branches instead of lights. There was only one ornament, a star atop the ten foot tree.

They attended a Christmas Eve service at the church where they'd been married. Elianna wondered if it had really been only six months since she'd met Nicolas Sinclair. Her life was changing so fast she couldn't imagine what would happen next.

While Bree was asleep, Ty and his girlfriend arrived. Every time she saw him it was with a different woman. Elianna worried that the gifts she wrapped would appear shabby next to the gilt–wrapped ones Ty and his girlfriend brought from New York.

They'd sipped potent eggnog and stayed up until the wee hours just talking until the conversation turned to business. Ty and Nic were about to launch one of their marathon sessions about where to take the computer firm next. The women had decided this was a good time to get some sleep. Elianna knew it wouldn't be much—Bree was always an early riser, and Christmas morning was too special to sleep late.

It was a beautiful time of renewal for Elianna. She bundled up and walked along the deserted beach. The brisk winds brought a sense of peace to her. She didn't realize how long she'd been away from the house until she saw Nic jogging toward her. She glanced at her watch. She'd spent two hours wandering in the cold, and feeling warmer and more complete than she had in months.

"Are you all right?"

"Fine. Sorry I seemed to have lost track of time."

They walked back, hand in hand. The last time they'd done this was just before they made the decision to make New York the home base rather than continuing their commuter marriage.

Brianna seemed reluctant to return to the city—she too,

had missed the community of the Cape area—but Elianna was determined to make it better for her daughter, somehow. She didn't realize how quickly she could become soft.

Elianna was still reluctant to move in with him and let the agency have the house back. This became the source of several arguments between Nic and Elianna. He offered to sell his house or buy the one she was renting but still Elianna was reluctant. He accused her of not wanting to give up her freedom because he might turn out like Brian and run away from his responsibilities.

It was Ty's turn to have the New Year's Eve party, and he pulled out all the stops. It was strictly black tie. Elianna didn't mind getting dressed up for this one, since none of the hostess duties fell on her. She could just enjoy herself and her husband. A glittering crystal ball was set to drop at the same time as the one in Times Square. He lived in an apartment that had a terrific view of the area where thousands gathered to ring in the New Year.

One of Ty's girlfriends acted as his hostess. She wore an elegant black and white evening gown. Just before the ball dropped they all gathered at the window and watched as a new year came into being.

Elianna and Nic had left Bree with the housekeeper. They danced for another hour and then went home to bring in the new year in their own way—by making love.

The entertaining didn't let up until late February. They'd given a Valentine's dinner, and Elianna was grateful that March was close so she could use the weather to avoid some of these parties. She hated the type of parties and dinners that came across like command performances.

Another thing she hated about New York was that she couldn't drive. She was so accustomed to hopping into her little car and zooming all over the Cape. In New York there never seemed to be a time when she felt comfortable in traffic, nor did she ever feel comfortable about finding a parking space, and the garages were quite expensive. Most people relied on mass transit. The buses and subways did seem to run on schedule, but she hated the crush of people. Nic thrived on the fast–paced beat of the city, but Elianna longed for the Cape's way of life.

Nic was seething by the time they got home from Ty's party. He seemed much calmer. He spent some time with Bree, as he usually did before she went to bed. Then he came into the bedroom, where Elianna waited.

"So, did you two just happen to run into each other?"

"No. I called him. He'd spoken with Caryn, and said he wanted to meet his daughter."

"And I guess you jumped at the chance? I thought we would talk about it before it happened."

"I started to tell him to come here—"

Nic slammed his fist against the pillow. "You'd invite him to *my house*?"

Elianna cringed when he said, "my house," but Nic didn't notice. "No. I remembered that this is the staff's day off, and I didn't want to be alone with him. So we decided to meet in front of Tiffany's."

"Why didn't you tell me before sneaking off to meet him?"

"I wasn't sneaking. He *is* her father, and he has a right to know her."

"Really. I thought I was the only father she needed."

"I need a cup of coffee," Elianna announced.

"I need something a lot stronger."

By the time she'd poured the water into the coffeemaker, Nic joined her. He sat at the table with a glass of bourbon and waited until Elianna had fixed her coffee and was seated across from him.

"So how did the meeting go?"

"I was going to tell you about it. I even picked Tiffany's

because you said you'd been in the area, and I thought we might run into you."

"He didn't seem that anxious to meet me."

"He was afraid you wouldn't understand. I guess he was right."

"I don't understand why you didn't call me and just tell me."

"Why would I? Look at how you're behaving."

"The man hasn't been much of a father—"

"I know that better than anyone. I still don't want my daughter growing up and saying I deprived her of a chance to meet her father. Who knows? It may be the last time she'll see him."

"So what did he have to say for himself?"

"We talked a few minutes, and Bree seemed to understand about natural fathers and stepfathers. She wasn't impressed."

"What about you?"

"I beg your pardon?"

"Were you impressed with him?"

"He seems to have turned his life around. He's getting married, and she has a little boy. I guess that made him want to meet his daughter."

"If there are going to be any more 'meetings'," Nic said, "I don't want them here."

"I'm well aware that you don't want him in 'your house.' If there is another meeting, I'll make sure it's in a public place." She watched Nic toss his drink down.

Elianna drained her coffee cup and sauntered off to bed.

After Nic left for work, Elianna went into the office Nic had had decorated for her. The new computer, with all of its upgrades, couldn't match her little computer back at the Cape. She felt comfortable there—her thoughts flowed freely, and she didn't have to worry as much about what she wrote. She forced herself to finish the article about the different events going on at the Cape.

Her mind drifted back to the night before, to how Nic had been exceptionally nice to Bree. They'd built a little log cabin, and he'd made up a little story about the people who might have lived in those cabins. Elianna knew he was talking to Bree because he didn't want to talk to her. She decided that Nic had wanted to be a father without being a husband, after all, and she had to let go of her little fantasy that he might love *her*.

She lay in bed waiting for him. She was going to talk to him about how she fit into his life—they would fight, and she'd know where she stood—but Nic never came to bed. Elianna swore as she snuggled under the covers. She'd fallen asleep waiting.

The next morning she went to the kitchen and found him fully dressed and putting his breakfast dishes in the sink. He muttered good morning, and something she thought was "see you later." He was gone off to work before she could even suggest they talk first. This made her angrier than she'd been the night before. How could he treat her this way?

Elianna finished the article and faxed it in. She went into the media room, turned on the TV and grabbed the remote. She flipped through the channels, but her mind wouldn't let her concentrate and she turned the TV off after fifteen minutes.

Bree wandered into the room and Elianna noticed she wasn't the usual bouncy little girl she was accustomed to seeing.

"What's the matter, honey?"

"Daddy didn't wait for me."

"Oh honey, he had to go to work early."

"OK. Maybe next yesterday."

Elianna couldn't help laughing at her daughter's concept of time. As she thought about it, she realized that Nic was now ignoring or forgetting about Bree, and she knew it stemmed from her meeting with Brian. Nic hadn't even given her a chance once he found out who she was talking with. He'd just behaved as if she was sneaking around with the man. She didn't like it.

Lately there were a lot of things she didn't like. She didn't like the way everyone seemed to be in a rush. She didn't like putting on fancy clothes and hanging on Nic's arm as he entertained business associates. She felt these people were always trying to lead her into discussions about things she didn't know, so they could feel superior. She missed her old way of life. She missed putting on casual clothes and walking down a street where she knew everyone and was greeted with nods and calls of *good morning*.

She knew with clear understanding that she didn't fit into Nic's life style, nor did she want to. Her earlier feelings of wanting to learn the city had faded. Elianna decided that there was only one place she could be happy. It was a place she could make Bree happy.

"Bree, honey, we're going home."

Nic couldn't believe the note Elianna left him. She'd written that she couldn't stand New York any longer, and was going back to the Cape for a while. He knew something was wrong when Bree didn't meet him at the door. When he checked Elianna's office, he found the area neat and clean. All her ideas were gone from the bulletin board. Her note said she was leaving for a while.

That was such a lie. She had no intention of returning to New York. She had no intention of returning to him.

CHAPTER TEN

Elianna walked to the window of her living room and held the negative up to the light. The last of the summer pictures had been developed. This one showed Brianna sitting on Nic's shoulders. They were behind the huge sand castle they had built, and she felt drained and triumphant at the same time. She'd enjoyed her time with Nic.

It was almost perfect, just as she had pictured it in her mind, even better than she'd remembered. She held up another, this one with the three of them. Here, they'd been a family. In New York she had failed as a wife.

She went back to her desk and carefully packed the pictures in a box and addressed it to Nic. Bree had come into the room, and she'd let her pick one of the pictures to put in the package.

He had not contacted her since she and Brianna had left on that snowy March day. She had wondered at first what she would say when he demanded an explanation, but he never had. She had expected him daily on the first days, as she and Brianna picked up their old lives. She'd tried to pacify her daughter at first, saying that Nic would come to the Cape to see her. The puzzled look told her that her daughter knew something was wrong, and soon Bree stopped asking about Nic. Elianna had dreaded— and yet in a way looked forward to—a confrontation. At least on her home ground she felt more confident, less likely to allow him to bamboozle her into trying again.

After a while, she concluded that he had been relieved to find her gone, that he, too, had realized that they had made a mistake, and decided to call it quits. The ache in her heart was like a tearing pain, and she wondered if she was such an awful wife that he wouldn't even care to hear her side. She worked long hours at her computer. A few more businesses opened. She made flyers for them and continued to write her monthly column about the activities around the Cape. Her life with Nic never entirely left her, and often at night she lay awake, fighting tears and remembering when she and Nic spent the nights wrapped in each other's arms.

The day before Mother's Day, she was polishing another article when a familiar engine sound made her stiffen and raise her head. She went to the window in time to see Nic emerge from his car, his mouth in a grim line across his face.

She met him at the door. They stood for a moment staring at each other, then she silently stepped aside to let him in.

"Brianna?" he asked abruptly.

"She's with Caryn at the theater."

He didn't go into the living room, but instead strode into her office, and she followed him.

He picked up the article she was working on, read it, and then turned to face her.

"How is she?" he asked.

"Fine, and happy to be back." She wouldn't tell him the truth—that they were picking up their lives but she and Bree missed him terribly.

"Is that why you left?"

Elianna hesitated. A mother couldn't be blamed for thinking of her child, but she wouldn't use that as an excuse. "Not really," she admitted, "I wasn't happy, either."

"Obviously. You didn't think it worth explaining it to me?"

"I couldn't. It was difficult to put into words. You love New York. I just felt lost there. You wouldn't understand."

"How do you know? You just told me you were leaving. You didn't give me any explanation."

"You've taken a long time to ask for one."

For the first time Nic showed anger. "What was I supposed to do? Come running after you, begging to be told why you were leaving me?"

"No."

"No? Why did you send me the pictures? Did you want to torment me some more? Did you want to show me what I'd lost?"

"I wanted you to know you could still see Bree," she said.

"It was a message, too, wasn't it? No card, no note, just the most exquisite examples of what a happy family looked like. Especially the one of us kissing—"

"What are you talking about? I never sent you that one."

"Yeah, right!" He reached in his coat pocket and pulled out the picture. "Was this to really rub my face in the fact that I couldn't keep you happy?"

"Nic, I mean it. I didn't send that one to you."

"Then who did?"

She remembered she'd left Bree alone with the pictures.

"I think it was Brianna. I told her she could put her favorite one in the box."

"I see. So was this one of your *favorite* pictures, too?"

"I wasn't certain, then," she said huskily. "I thought— maybe it was something I'd just lost for good."

"How about now?"

Elianna turned away from him. "I don't know. I just remembered when I told you I was still going to do my column, you laughed."

"I laughed because I thought that meant you were ready to give it up," he said. abruptly. "I'd been thinking you regretted having married me, that you didn't love me, after all. I was right, but at the time, when you said it was your work that was worrying you, I thought that you understood you could live with me and still hold on to a piece of your past life."

"A *piece* of my life?"

"I'm not trying to suggest it's unimportant. I know it's important to you—more important than I am."

"That's not true," she said swiftly.

His face hard, he said, "It's the one thing in life you can't do without. Nothing else can satisfy you, fulfill you. Marriage to me certainly couldn't. Look how you ran back and picked it up again. I'm trying to understand. You can't help the way you are. I'm sorry if marrying me killed your talent. Still, it seems that leaving me had the desired effect of bringing it to life again. This article has all your old spark."

He couldn't keep the bitterness from his voice. Distressed, she begged, "Nic, please stop! It wasn't your fault. I mean, you tried to make me feel good. You married me and took me to New York thinking that I'd love it as much as you did. But I'm not used to that pace. It wasn't being married to you that affected me, not that in itself. I can't live anywhere away from the coast. I can't be myself there. I can't—"

"Find anything to really interest you," he finished for her.

"Yes," she said, "I suppose that's what it is. I wanted it to work. Please believe me."

"Trying to soothe my ego, Elianna?"

"No, I am not! I'm trying to explain. This place is a part of me. I have its heartbeat, just as you have New York's."

"Why didn't you give me the chance to do something about that? I never asked you to give up your work."

"I know! I know you didn't! You asked me to be your wife. And I wanted to be. But it can't work, because I don't fit into your world, Nic."

"I never said that," he objected. "I never even thought it. I know you were angry when I said I didn't want Brian around our house."

"You didn't say 'our.' You said 'my house', and you were right. It *was* your house. I never felt at home in it. Your house, your life, not mine. I have to live my own life, Nic. I'm sorry. Maybe I've been single too long to be someone's wife."

"I've not expected you to be *just* my wife," he said.

"That's how it felt."

"In your mind! Not in mine."

"In fact," she said, "it's just the way things are. I should never have accepted you, never imagined that I could settle into being your wife. We knew how different our backgrounds, or life styles, were. I'm not cut out to be Mrs. Nic Sinclair."

"You were not a failure," he said, "at anything."

"I was. I hated dressing up and playing hostess. Your friends found me—inadequate."

"My friends, the real ones, thought you were a talented writer. Who cares what the others thought?"

"They did?"

"That's right," he said to her astonishment. "Especially the women. They were afraid of boring you because things that bored you ended up in your column."

"That's crazy!"

"Maybe. It's the truth."

Elianna shook her head disbelievingly.

Impatiently, Nic said, "All right, don't believe me. It isn't important."

He moved closer to her, his eyes intent. He took her face in his hands and said, "The problems really started when you saw Brianna's father. We're you angry that he seemed at home in New York?"

"Yes. He moved in the same circles as you did. I was afraid he'd find out that I didn't belong. It wasn't like that. It was the first time Brianna had seen him—the first time I'd spoken to him since she was born. I tried to tell you that."

"Was that true?"

"Of course it was. In a way, what you kept telling me was right. You said that New York City was like a small town, and you never knew who you'd run into. Brianna and I met him by Tiffany's. He was a little put out when Bree told him she already had a daddy. That's when you and Ty arrived."

Nic's hands moved to her shoulders, but he still stared directly into her eyes. "So she wasn't impressed?"

"No. That frightened me. I was afraid he'd come around trying to bribe her until she saw him as a good guy, instead of the creep he turned out to be."

"Do you still want to see him again? Did you find you still felt something for him that you couldn't feel for me?"

"Oh, no!" Elianna took an involuntary step closer to him. "No! I was civil for Bree's sake. I had no feelings for him."

"Is that how you feel about me, now?"

"I love you," she said simply. " I can't live with you, but I still love you."

"And I love you," he said soberly. "I can't just leave the business. But I might be able to sell it and find something here."

"Would you really sell the business?"

"To be with you, yes."

"I never thought you would," she said. "Don't do it for me."

He laughed and took his hands from her shoulders. He said, "You never considered that there might be an alternative, did you? You just cut and run."

"You love your life. It makes you happy."

"You didn't even ask me to discuss the problem! We're married, Elianna. Don't you think you owed me something in the way of explaining how you felt?"

"I'm sorry. I didn't know how. I thought I could come back here and work it out for myself, and then contact you, or that you'd contact me. But the longer we didn't communicate, the less chance I thought I had."

"If you really loved me, how could you feel that way?" Nic lowered his hands and walked to the window. "I want to stay married to you, even if we can't always be together. I thought you'd stopped loving me, but when the pictures arrived I got different message."

"I couldn't put it into words," she said. "I guess we can thank Bree for putting in the right picture, to bring us together so we could talk."

He came back to her, put his hands on her waist, and looked at her face, his mouth grim, his eyes searching hers. "I think I'm beginning to understand," he said. "Don't send me away."

"I won't do that, Nic. I want you to stay forever. But I know you can't."

He kissed her, gently at first and then deeply, with growing passion. Elianna kissed him back until she felt him shudder with desire.

"When will Brianna be home?" he whispered.

"We have a couple of hours," Elianna murmured.

"Good."

He picked her up and carried her through to the bedroom. "You fought me last time I suggested we make up like this."

"I'm not fighting now." She slid her arms about him, and met his kiss with parted lips.

"I don't know why you thought I wanted you to be a little wife," he said. "I fell in love with the woman you are, not some image."

A slow warmth was growing inside her. She felt her breath quicken, she said, "Nic, can we really work it out? You in New York, and me here? It won't be a conventional marriage."

"I don't want a conventional marriage. It was the unconventional about you that attracted me, I think, in the first place."

"What about additions to the family?"

They hadn't used any contraceptives once they married, and she hadn't gotten pregnant.

"If it doesn't happen, we still have Bree. But if it happens—would you mind having my baby?"

"I wouldn't mind," she said. "I wouldn't mind at all."

He smiled down at her. "Is it possible?"

"Very possible."

"Barefoot and pregnant sounds rather suitable for you."

"Didn't I call you a chauvinist once?"

"Didn't you say once that you loved me?"

"I do."

"Then nothing else matters. Stop talking, woman, and kiss me."

She stopped talking. For quite a long time.

"Brianna will be home soon." She lay against his bare chest, listening to the steady beating of his heart.

His fingers trailed down her spine. "Will she be pleased to see me?"

"Yes. She's missed you, but she's happier on the Cape, too."

"Do you know, I think I was even more upset about Brianna preferring her natural father than I was about you having him in the house," he confessed.

Elianna sat up. "You love Brianna, don't you?"

"Yes. I missed her, too."

"She may want to see her father again when she's older. I wouldn't stop her, Nic," Elianna warned.

He said, "You're right, of course. I'll have to try to accept that. By then I hope we'll have established a relationship, become a family."

"So do I." She smoothed the faint frown between his brows, and kissed him lightly. "Don't look like that. Brianna loves you."

"It wasn't Brianna I was thinking of."

She hesitated, starting to draw away, but he caught her wrist in a hard grip. "It won't be just Brianna seeing him, will it?"

"Probably not. You have nothing to worry about, Nic, I promise."

His eyes searched hers, then he relaxed. "I'm sorry. You know, when I first saw him—when Brianna told me who he was—I just thought he wanted a second chance, and you were going to give it to him—"

"You're the only one I'd give a second chance."

"Thank you. I'll make it all up to you."

"No. Let's just stop living with regrets, and concentrate on how today can make happier tomorrows."

"I need to get to know you all over again."

Elianna held herself away from him a little. "I want to know you, too. But it won't be easy, with a part—time marriage."

"It's a full—time marriage. We just may happen to be in different cities most of the time."

"I agree."

"Tomorrow's Mother's Day. I never thought I'd be celebrating that. I didn't buy a gift."

"You're the best gift I could ever have."

"Will you spend the other holidays with me in New York?"

"Yes, I will. Satisfied?"

"Very." Nic pulled her down to kiss her. "I plan to spend most of my weekends here."

"I'll be waiting."

"Always?"

"Always," she promised.

Nic gave a long, satisfied sigh, and pulled her into his arms until she lay beneath him.

"Brianna," she murmured as he lowered his mouth again to hers.

"Mm, I know. She's coming home." Reluctantly he released her, and lay watching as she slipped on her gown. Then she tidied up the room before she came back and sat on the bed beside Nic.

"You look satisfied," she told him.

"I didn't get this way by myself. How do you feel?"

She answered soberly, "Wonderful. It's been so—oh, Nic, I know I left without really talking to you. I just didn't want to look in your eyes and see that you didn't want me any more."

"Why didn't you call me?"

"For the same cowardly reason. I just knew the next time you talked to me you'd be asking for a divorce. I thought I'd call you and work something out so you could see Brianna. She thinks of you as her father."

"What about Brian?"

"She thinks she has two fathers. Most of the children she played with in New York have stepfathers and step-mothers. She thinks it's natural to have more than one parent."

"I've been so miserable without you," he burst out.

"I thought you'd be relieved, since I was a terrible wife."

He pulled her down on the bed, shaking her. "That's ridiculous. Don't ever say that—don't even think it. You're all I could ask for. Sure, I wanted to be a father, but you made me love being a husband. Other couples have successful commuter marriages, and so can we. Physically we may have to be apart, but I'll be here so much you won't even notice it. I'm going to be as much a part of you as this beach you love so much. You might as well know that."

"You already are. All the time we were apart, I wanted to be with you. But New York is just too fast for me. I mean, I'll come there occasionally—"

"And I'll make it as painless as possible."

"It won't be painful any longer. You're still part of me, and I don't have to fight that any more."

"Never fight it again, Elianna."

She smiled and reached up to let her hand trail over his face. "I'm not going to fight you any more," she promised. Her voice still held a husky undertone, as always after lovemaking. "Anyway, you always win."

Now he looked down at her flushed face and grinned as he said, "Yes, I do."

Early the next morning Nic and Brianna spent some time gathering flowers from Nic's garden. He was careful

not to take too many or damage the plants as he gently cut
them from the stalk and put them in Christmas wrapping
paper. It was all he could find.

"Is it really OK for us to take some of them?"

"Sure. We won't take too many, so the garden will still
look pretty."

"Can I take some from my garden?"

"Mm, I don't think that would be a good idea. You live
here. You can't take anything from there now. Some one
else is going to live there. Your garden will be their gift."

"Then I need a new garden," Bree announced.

"Yes you do, honey. We're going to have three gardens.
A marigold garden for you, a vegetable garden for me,
and a rose garden for your mother."

Nic wrapped the flowers securely in the paper. He took
Brianna's hand, and as the walked back to the house he
saw Elianna waiting for them. His heart skipped a beat.

The flowers were for the day he once thought he'd never
celebrate—as a husband, Mother's Day.